Greed

Happy Reading!

Tim Beeden

Remember: Be more Ralph. Unless you can be Eve. Always be Eve.

3P
PUBLISHING

First published in 2020 in the UK
3P Publishing
C E C, London Road
Corby
NN17 5EU

A catalogue number for this book is available
from the British Library

ISBN: 978-1-9163940-1-8

Cover design: Marie-Louise O'Neill

For Tara,
who let me borrow her study guide.

Contents

Chapter 1
We Plough the Land and Suffer...

As the morning light danced gently across the tops of the surrounding trees, a faint orange-yellow glow settled upon the tips of the recently ploughed land. It was on these wondrous September mornings, full of promise for the year to come, that Gregory Hoffenbach felt the most alive. He was a farmer, doing what all farmers do: turning his land in preparation for the new seed and the promise it held.

Never mind the poor year before, when he, his new wife and his brother had nearly lost everything due to a meagre crop and high taxes. This was a new year and it was full of all the endless possibilities that being a farmer held. Who could think of a more noble profession? Certainly not Gregory Hoffenbach.

Without farmers like him, the Kingdom would fall to its knees.

Greg took a deep breath, filled his lungs with the rich autumn air and pushed his plough onwards. Clara, his long suffering and past useful ox, shunted forwards in her harness and the plough began to move. These days, Gregory only really used her as a token

1

gesture, a throwback to the days when his dad had tilled the land with a team of oxen.

Even though she was useless and quite slow, he couldn't bring himself to get rid of her, no matter how much his brother Ralph moaned. Which he did, quite a lot.

'Just take her round the back of the shed and give her a whack with a shovel,' was Ralph's advice.

'I can't do that, Ralph. She's the last thing we've got that used to belong to Dad.'

'I'm sure Dad would be really proud that Clara's happy whilst we starve to death.' Sometimes there was no arguing with Ralph.

Things had gotten pretty rough this last year. The King had put taxes up, most of their crops had failed and whilst Greg had finally married the love of his life, Mollie, Ralph's wife Mae had left him for a pig farmer. She'd said she deserved more in life and that she couldn't stay married to an arable farmer.

'She's always been a social climber, that one,' Ralph had confided in Greg one night after a few beers. 'I'll always love her, you know. Even if she did leave me on our wedding anniversary. With everything we owned.'

Things had been rough, but life was for the living, as Greg's dad used to say, and on days like today, Greg could see what he meant.

The light was good, the land was soft and even Clara seemed spritelier as she trudged forwards.

Greg started to whistle as he pushed onwards.

The whistle died on his lips as the plough crunched into something incredibly hard. With a sound like a sheet of rusty metal being hit by a cannonball, the plough split clean in half, sending Greg face first into the dirt. His fall was broken when he landed, head first, onto a potato-sized object; the same object, in fact, which had broken Greg's only plough.

Greg rolled over on to his back and looked up at the stunning morning sky as it slowly turned black at the edge of his vision.

As he began to pass out, he had enough time to contemplate what a terrible life-choice farming was.

***

'If you're dead, can I have the farmhouse?'

'Nrughm, grumpf...'

'If that's meant to be some form of protest, then it won't stand up in a court of law.'

Greg tried to sit up but the moment he moved his head someone tilted the horizon first one way, then the other. 'Oohgh. Blarg,' he said, or tried to say, through the fog that had enveloped his head.

Ralph looked down at his younger brother. He had mud plastered down the left side of his face and a lump the size of a goose egg above his right eye.

'Listen. If you're going to carry on like that, then I'm going to have to give you a slap. You're making no sense whatsoever. It's quite annoying.'

Greg closed his eyes. The clanging behind them quietened down a bit.

'Help me to sit up,' he managed.

'You know, you really must be more careful,' Ralph said as he bent over, put his arms under Greg's armpits and heaved him into a sitting position. The clanging returned behind Greg's eyes as a wave of nausea swirled through his stomach. He leant over and vomited.

Ralph danced back as his brother's breakfast splattered over his left boot.

'Oh, that's just bloody marvellous!' Ralph shouted, shaking his leg.

'That's not the worst of it,' Greg managed.

'You've not crapped yourself too, have you?'

'No. At least I don't think so.'

'Thank heaven for small mercies,' Ralph said, brushing his boot with a rag.

'The worst of it is that I think the plough's broken.'

Ralph stepped in front of Greg, bent down and inspected their plough.

Greg allowed himself a tentative touch of the bump on his head. He immediately wished he hadn't.

'Is the plough broken?' Greg asked.

'Unless we're going to start ploughing in very small circles, then yes, I'd say it was buggered.'

'Sorry, Ralph,' Greg said. 'I hit a stone. Size of a potato.' He started to scrabble through the soil. 'Here it is! Look at that, who'd have thought something so small could do so much damage?'

Greg turned the stone over in his hand. It looked like a normal stone, but it was hard to tell all covered in soil.

Ralph leant in for a closer look. 'How in the blue hell did something that size split our plough in half?'

'Dunno,' Greg replied, still turning the stone over in his hand. 'Erm... Ralph... think you could give me a hand inside? Only there's four of you and my head feels like someone's trying to break out of it through my eyes.'

Ralph shook his head and helped his brother to his feet. He put Greg's arm around his neck and started walking him back to the farmhouse.

'Suppose we could look on the bright side,' Ralph said.

'What do you mean, bright side? You never look on the bright side.'

'Sometimes you've got to, oh brother of mine. And the bright side here is that we're having beef for tea. Clara's dead.'

Greg looked back over his shoulder to see Clara lying on her side in the as yet un-ploughed field.

'Talk about a bad morning,' Greg said, shaking his head. As he did so he dropped the stone into the front pocket of his jerkin, totally unaware he'd just become the richest man in the Kingdom.

Chapter 2
An Interlude – Welcome to Town

Hello there. You must be new around these parts. Pull up a chair next to the fire and I'll fill you in on a few details.

My name? Oh, that's not important right now. There's plenty of time for names, just not right now. More pressing matters to discuss, you see.

Throw another log on the fire, pour me a drink and I'll tell you all about this Kingdom of ours.

Well now, the Kingdom – which now contains one very wealthy Hoffenbach – is an interesting and varied one.

Imagine, if you will, a pond. Drop a stone in that pond and everything ripples out from it. That's how it is in the Kingdom. You start with the city of Calver, smack-bang in the middle and everything else sort of spreads outwards.

The lands spreading out from Calver contain many settlements. Some of these settlements – predominantly those closer to the Great Hill – contain enough buildings to be classed as a town whilst others, further out, could best be described as little more than a collection of one or two homesteads.

The towns and their smaller counterparts are often places where buildings gather around a main road and offer the townsfolk a place to trade, buy essentials and visit their local inn. Everyone needs a good inn.

Calver is an immense city which clings to the side of a great hill, and is split into three levels by three vast, stone walls each encircling the Great Hill. Thus, the city of Calver is split into its Upper, Middle and Lower parts.

For the most part, certainly in recent history, the people of the Kingdom go about their daily lives without needing to venture further than their own town.

It hasn't always been this way.

You see, up until the present King's great-grandfather – King Paeter the Bold – won the right to rule the entire Kingdom and had his castle built atop the Great Hill, the Kingdom was a divided place. Tribes roamed the land. Some were nothing more than a collection of families looking for good land and a spot of shelter whilst others, the larger ones, contained hundreds of like-minded individuals. For the most part, those minds liked the idea of killing and taking whatever they could get their hands on.

As you can see, this made settling down a hard thing to achieve. No sooner had a tribe established a settlement than they were raided by a much larger, mobile tribe.

I suppose you can see what's coming.

As each tribe grew larger and swallowed up the smaller tribes, the Kingdom was left with a collection of about ten nomadic tribes (it's hard to get an exact number as to how many tribes there were; not much was written down back then).

These tribes each found themselves a spot of land, spread out across the Kingdom, upon which they all settled down and lived happily ever after. The end.

Which, of course, is exactly what *didn't* happen. Man's desire to have much, but want more, coupled with the long-held fallacy that the grass is always greener, led to a series of bitter and bloody battles culminating in the Battle of the Blood Wastes. Skipping through all the gory details brings us to King Paeter's tribe winning the Battle of the Blood Wastes and banishing whatever was left of the remaining tribes (which wasn't much) to the four corners of the Kingdom.

Jump through time to today and the Kingdom is a very different place. In a little over one hundred and fifty years, the Kingdom has become the place you recognise now.

For most of the inhabitants in the outlying settlements, the only time they might choose to leave their settlement would be for the market held once a month in Lower Calver.

For it is between the first and second wall encircling the Great Hill that the vast majority of the people of Calver live, trade and generally go about their day-to-day lives. A rabbit-warren of cobbled streets and over-hanging buildings, Lower Calver is – to some – the heart of the

Kingdom. It is a place where you can buy just about anything with a fairly even chance you'll return home with it the next day.

If you are street smart and have a good head on your shoulders, Lower Calver is a Pandora's Box of opportunity. If not, then there's a very good chance you'll get robbed blind.

Right, I think that's enough for now. You've got enough to be getting on with and I need another drink. All this talking makes me thirsty.

You be on your way now. And before you go, throw another log on the fire, would you? Old bones feel the cold.

Chapter 3
And So it Begins...

It was times like these when Greg missed his dad. He would've known just the right thing to say, would've sat him down, tended to the throbbing lump on his head and generally done whatever he could to make his boy feel better.

Which was about a world away from the level of care he was getting from his older brother. Halfway to the house, Greg passed out again so Ralph had to carry him. As he crossed the stone entry way — like a husband carrying his new bride across the threshold — he'd smacked Greg's head on the limestone door arch.

'Oh, horsecrap! Sorry, Greg!' Ralph said, stumbling backwards, whereupon he promptly lost his grip and dropped Greg onto the stone doorstep.

Mollie opened the door and stepped out, a basket of washing in her hands, ready to be hung on the line. She took one look at Greg lying unmoving on the floor, then looked at Ralph.

'If he's dead and you think I'm marrying you, then you need to think again.'

'Oh, that's real concern for you, that is,' Ralph said. 'Her newly-wed husband lies prone on the floor and all she can think about is digging the knife in.'

'Nrughm, grumpf...' Greg said.

'Trust me, Ralph, it wouldn't be a knife I'd use. It'd be something much blunter.'

'You really are a piece of work, sister-in-law, you know that? You really know how to hurt a person's feelings.'

'Oohgh. Blarg,' Greg said.

'Brother-in-law, you and feelings are two words never before uttered in the same sentence.'

'You know, it's negativity like that, makes a person wonder how I remain so full of sunshine each and every day. It really does.'

'Ralph, you're an arse. You really are.'

Greg slowly sat up and promptly threw up over his brother's other boot. Mollie laughed so hard she thought her sides would split.

***

Between them, they got Greg indoors and laid him on the bed. By then he was starting to talk sense and could see clearly if he closed one eye.

Ralph went out back to the pump to get some cold water for Greg and to clean his boots. Mollie busied herself sorting out some wet cloths to put on Greg's three lumps.

'So the plough's broken?' she asked.

"Fraid so.'

'And Clara's dead?'

'Yes.'

'I've got to be honest with you Greg, we've had better starts to the day.'

'That's an understatement. I don't know what we're going to do without the plough,' Greg said, sitting up.

'Nice to have a bit of beef, though,' Mollie said.

'Well yes, but...'

'I know,' Mollie said walking into the bedroom. 'She was the last thing of your dad's but I'm sure he'd rather us well fed.'

She sat down on the bed next to Greg and started to inspect his lumps.

Greg clenched his teeth as Mollie prodded and poked, sending explosions of pain crashing around the inside of his head. Just as Greg was about to introduce his wife to a few new words of the colourful variety, Ralph walked in carrying a bucket of water.

'Took me ages to clean my boots,' he said, slopping the bucket on the floor at Mollie's feet. 'It's very hard to get bits of carrot out of the stitching, you know.'

'Sorry, Ralph. Didn't mean to... well, you know... Ralph on you.'

Mollie coughed. Or at least, it sounded like a cough. Ralph looked at his brother and the three lumps on his head, two of which were technically his fault.

'No harm done, I suppose,' he said. 'Which is more than can be said for our plough.'

Mollie dipped a cloth into the bucket and pressed it to Greg's largest lump.

12

'Mother Funker!' Greg shouted.

'Don't be such a baby,' Mollie said. 'It's not like anything's hanging off. Anyone would think your arm needed stitching back on. And if that's the best curse word you can come up with, then you're a bitter disappointment, Gregory Hoffenbach.'

'I was trying not to be offensive,' Greg said, blushing.

'I reckon your wife's heard far worse than that,' Ralph said. 'Some of it to her face too.'

They both ignored him.

'I'll leave you the bucket and cloth. You lie down for a bit. Me and your brother have got Clara to deal with before the flies get at her.'

With that, Mollie got up and ushered Ralph out of the bedroom.

As Greg lay back he could hear them talking in hushed tones as they made their way into the kitchen. He was sure his wife and brother secretly got along. Or at least, that was what he told himself. It was just easier that way. He heard the front door shut and shuffled his weight so he could reach the bucket. As he did so he felt something dig into his side, the sharp jab of which was a welcome relief from the booming in his head. He dug his hand into his pocket and pulled out the dirt-covered stone that had ruined his morning.

His first reaction was to toss it across the room but he quickly changed his mind when he realised there was a fair chance he'd hit one of Mollie's trinkets; a ridiculous word used to describe anything Mollie decided should be displayed anywhere in their house. Instead, he turned the stone over in his hands. It didn't feel particularly heavy and he marvelled once again at how something the size of a potato could shear his plough clean in half.

As he turned the stone over in his hands, some of the dirt flaked away onto the bed.

Carefully, as if his head was made of fine china, Greg sat up. He reached down whilst trying to keep his head relatively level. Eventually, after much groping about and the uttering of words he now knew his wife probably *did* know, he grasped the bucket and hauled it up on to the bed.

Once there, he placed the stone into the water and started to scrub away the layers of muck. As the water in the bucket started to first turn cloudy, and then an earthy brown colour, Greg caught a glimpse of the stone. What he saw confused him.

As a farmer, he'd seen his fair share of stones; they were somewhat of an occupational hazard. They tended to get in the way quite a lot and interfered with the places you wanted to put seeds. Most stones were dull, grey and as interesting as... well... a stone. What he thought he'd seen through the water in the bucket was completely the wrong colour and shape, and looked far more interesting than a stone. He rubbed harder and as layer after layer of dirt washed away, the stone started to feel sharper.

Slowly, Greg lifted the stone out of the water. As it broke through the surface to reveal itself, Greg felt his breath catch. The stone that had broken his plough this morning wasn't like any stone he'd ever seen before. It was still the size of a potato, but that was where the potato-related similarities ended.

It was very jagged, very red and very peculiar. Greg rubbed the stone on his tunic. It glistened in the light. He held it up to the window. As he did, the morning sun moved from behind a cloud and shone directly into the room and onto the red stone. The room lit up in a blinding array of colours, each one more beautiful and glass sharp than the other.

Greg saw none of this. As the first ray of light exploded from the red stone, it hit him squarely in the eyes, magnifying his headache so much so that it felt as if he was being stabbed in the eyes with a very, very sharp knife.

With a whimper, he collapsed onto the bed and for the third time in as many hours, passed out, his arm held aloft, the red stone still clutched in his hand.

***

When Mollie and Ralph arrived back at the farmhouse some four hours later, they found Greg lying flat on his back, arm back over his head, with something red in his hand. The sun had moved around to the back of the house so the stone no longer gleamed in the light.

Both Ralph and Mollie were tired to their very bones; dragging a dead ox across recently ploughed land was no easy task. It then had to be butchered, salted and stored in the cellar underneath the barn so the rats couldn't get it. Normally such a task was a job for at least four people, but it needed doing and neither of the two would admit to being tired so as to not lose face.

'What is he doing?' Ralph asked as they stepped into the bedroom.

'He's been hit on the head three times, Ralph,' Mollie said, as if that would explain away most things.

At the sound of their voices, Greg sat bolt upright. 'Ooh, the pretty lights!' he said and swung his feet off the bed.

Mollie turned to Ralph and shot him a look that said *two out of three of those lumps are your fault.*

Mollie and Ralph slowly walked towards Greg as if approaching someone who was sleepwalking.

'Hey, buddy,' Ralph said. 'What you got there? Wanna give Ralphy a little look?'

'Ralph, he's slightly concussed, not three years old.'

Greg looked up, and seemed to notice his wife and brother for the first time. He had a silly, lopsided grin plastered across his face and the swelling on the largest of his lumps had started to migrate over his right eye.

'You two!' Greg said. 'Come and sit beside me, I've got something to show you!' He patted the bed by his side.

Mollie and Ralph exchanged a quick glance and then sat on the bed either side of Greg.

'I've cleaned up the stone that broke the plough. Want to see?'

'Not really, as far as stones go I think...' Ralph started to say and then Mollie shot him a *two out of three lumps* look. 'You know what? I think I would love to see your stone, Greg.'

Slowly, as if holding a newborn in his hands, Greg opened his palms to reveal the red stone. Both Ralph and Mollie stared at it.

'That's actually pretty nice,' Ralph said.

'Yeah, it's kind of pretty,' Mollie added. 'It'd make a nice trinket.'

'That's not all,' Greg said, getting off the bed. He wobbled slightly as he stood up but managed to get his boots on without falling over.

Without another word he headed out of the bedroom. Realising they were supposed to follow him, Mollie and Ralph got up, walked out of the bedroom and then to the wide-open front door in time to see Greg disappear around the back of the farmhouse.

'Have a look at this, you two!' Greg shouted. 'It's magnificent!'

'If I walk round this corner and he's got his tally-whacker out...'

'Shut up, Ralph.'

Mollie and Ralph came around the corner to see Greg holding his stone aloft towards the sun, with one hand shielding his eyes. Beautiful, iridescent light streaked from the stone and danced across the ground towards them. When it hit the back of the house it seemed to shimmer there, the colours of the rainbow flitting in and out, up and down. The red stone itself looked as if it were lit not by the sun but from within, a pulsing blood-red light source full of energy.

'That's much better than his tally-whacker,' Ralph said.

'I'll say,' Mollie replied.

'Told you it was magnificent!' Greg said, still covering his eyes. Then he moved the red stone out of the sunlight and held it out to them. 'I think this should cover the cost of a broken plough.'

***

Later that night, the three of them sat around the table after finishing their dinner of beef stew. They'd said little to each other for the rest of that afternoon, each lost in their own thoughts. Right after Greg had finished with the red stone and his light show, Ralph had headed back out into the field to see if he could fix the plough. They all knew he couldn't and they all knew he had no intention of even trying; it was what Ralph did when he needed time to think. For a whole month after Mae had left him, Ralph tried to fix just about everything on the farm, culminating in him nearly burning down the barn when he tried to fix the long-defunct potato distiller. In the end, Greg banished him to the far fields, for his own safety.

Mollie spent the rest of the day preparing the stew for dinner, also lost in her thoughts. Twice she'd nearly sheared off the end of her finger, staring out of the kitchen window whilst chopping carrots.

Greg didn't spend much time thinking at all. He knew what he wanted to do: take the stone into Calver on the first of the month and trade it for a new plough. The stone had broken the plough, but now he could use it to replace the plough. With that sorted in his mind, he went back to sleep and only woke when Mollie called him for dinner.

After their wooden bowls were cleared away, all that remained on the table was a lit candle and the red stone, which Greg had placed there after finishing his stew.

'Right then,' Greg said.

'Right then,' Mollie and Ralph repeated.

'I'll start then, shall I?' Greg said. 'The most obvious thing to do is for me and Ralph to take the stone to the market and use it to buy a new plough. It'll fetch at least that much.' He pushed himself back from the table and started to stand.

'That's certainly one option,' Ralph said.

'As far as I can see, it's the only one,' Greg said.

'Allow me to help you see a little further, brother.'

'Here it comes,' Mollie said, leaning back, arms folded.

'Now just hear me out, that's all I ask. I agree we should take the stone to the market, I'll give you that. But what if it's worth more than a plough?'

Greg sat back down. 'But we need a plough,' he said.

'That we do, that we do,' Ralph said. 'But if this stone is worth more than a plough, we could get lots of other things, you know, according to market forces and all that.'

Greg turned to Mollie. She shrugged. 'As much as I hate to say it, Ralph's got a point,' she said. 'We could see if the stone's worth more than the value of a plough, that much I agree with. However, when it comes to your brother, there's always more and it's usually something I disagree with.'

Greg turned to Ralph, starting to feel like he wasn't ever really a part of the decision-making process at all.

'All I'm saying is,' Ralph said. 'We're all agreed we should take it to the market, okay? Now in order to get the best price possible, I know a guy...'

'Bingo!' Mollie said, 'and there it is. You were doing so well, Ralph. Let me save you the trouble. There's no way on the god's green earth you're taking this stone to "*a guy*". I'll tell you why; because some how, some way, we'll end up getting ripped off. You aren't even the best businessperson sat at this table, let alone in Lower Calver. No way, no how. Not going to happen.'

For the rest of the evening as the candle burnt further and further down, Greg watched his wife and brother argue over what should be done with the stone. He tried to be the voice of reason, interjecting with calming words but he was either ignored or told to be quiet.

In the end he got up and went to bed, leaving Mollie, Ralph and the stone still at the table. No one seemed to notice he wasn't there.

***

He wasn't sure when Mollie came to bed. He awoke in darkness to find her lying next to him, staring at the ceiling.

'Hello,' he said.

Mollie turned to face him, leaning her head on her hand. 'I think I may have gone too far,' she said.

Greg said nothing. Sometimes it was best to say nothing and let nature take its course. And besides, no one ever fell out with his wife by saying nothing.

'It's just that, sometimes, he makes me so mad. I know deep down he's a decent person, it's just that you have to dig so bloody deep!'

'He's my brother.'

21

'I know, I know. But honest to goodness, you two couldn't be less alike.'

Greg laid back, his fingers laced behind his head. 'Whatever you said, it'll be fine. Ralph's got thick skin. We'll sort it in the morning.' Greg turned, kissed his wife on the cheek and went back to sleep in his own bed for the last time in a very long while.

Chapter 4
A Matter of Time

Greg burst through the bedroom door, sending it slamming into the wall. Mollie sat bolt upright.

'What did you do?' he said.

'Nothing. I... er... well, it's just that he got me so mad.'

Greg had got up early, his head was hurting him and he found it near impossible to sleep. After carefully sliding out of bed, he tiptoed out of the bedroom and closed the door softly behind him. Then he put on his boots and headed into the kitchen. All that remained from last night was the stub of the candle and three wooden bowls on the kitchen bench by a bucket, ready to be washed.

No stone. No Ralph. Greg searched the kitchen for the stone, and then Ralph's room for the stone and Ralph. As their farmhouse only had three rooms, it didn't take long. Greg stood, arms folded and stared at his wife.

'Both the stone and Ralph are gone.'

'I did try to tell you last night that I might have gone too far. If you'd've listened to me instead of going back to sleep...'

Greg resisted the urge to get drawn into an argument. Mollie was very good at drawing him in to an argument and normally he struggled to come back out the other side.

'What did you say to him?'

Mollie sat up, tucked her knees under her chin and stared out the window. 'I tried to be reasonable, honest I did, but he said I didn't get it, that he was made for this kind of action, that he was thinking of leaving farming anyway, getting into the import/export business — whatever the hell that means...'

'What did you say to him?' Greg repeated.

'You've got to remember, he'd been on at me all night about a guy he knew and how he could hit the streets of Lower Calver and fix us up a good deal. You and I both know he's never been in Lower Calver for more than an hour; there's definitely no guy and as for fixing us up a good deal...'

'Mollie. *What did you say to him?*'

'After he called me short-sighted and a simple farm girl, I may, or may not, have mentioned that he couldn't sell beer to an alcoholic...'

'And?'

'That if he tried to sell the stone in Lower Calver, he'd probably end up getting ripped off...'

'And?'

'He wouldn't last five minutes in the city as he doesn't have the smarts to survive...'

'And?'

'It's no surprise that Mae left him.'

24

Mollie turned away from Greg and wrapped herself up in the covers. 'I'm sorry, Greg. You know I didn't mean it. He just pushed me too far.'

Once again, Greg chose not to speak; only this time it was because he didn't trust the words that might come out of his mouth.

Ralph had taken Mae's leaving him hard. To him, she was perfect; he devoted himself to her. He couldn't see what others could; she was playing him for a fool, just waiting to move on. After she'd left him there were plenty of '*I told you so*'s' from 'helpful' friends which did nothing to help Ralph. To this date, neither Greg nor Mollie had said a single word about Mae leaving him. Until last night.

Greg grabbed the remainder of his clothes, stuffed them into his cloth bag and strode out the door. He turned north and headed across the fields towards the only road that lead to the nearest town. Even though everything Mollie had said to Ralph last night was true, Greg knew where Ralph was headed. He just hoped he could get there in time.

***

As Greg walked the single track that wound its way across the rolling hills surrounding his farm, for the first time since he'd inadvertently found the red stone, he wished he hadn't.

For such a little thing, it had already caused so much trouble. His brother was goodness knows where after a blazing row with his wife

— a wife who would no doubt want to 'talk' when he got back home again.

All of this for a potato-sized red stone that lit up in the sunlight. His only hope was that his brother hadn't got too much of a lead on him and that he could catch him before he did something he'd regret.

The last thing Greg needed right now was another four months of Ralph sulking. That would be unbearable. And besides, they'd not long finished rebuilding the barn.

Greg decided to pick up the pace. As he lengthened his stride, he crested a small hill which afforded a view of the patchwork landscape before him. The Great Hill loomed far in the distance, its three walls encircling it like the segments of a fat worm. There was no way Ralph could've made it into Lower Calver yet, but the thought of his brother wandering the streets, trying to fix up a 'good deal' caused Greg to shudder.

Once again, he quickened his pace.

It was just starting to get dark when Greg heard the unmistakable rumble of a heavy cart approaching behind him. By now his legs felt heavy and he had dirt in his boots. He turned to face the oncoming cart and prepared to flag it down, to see if it would take him further on his way.

As the rumbling grew louder and louder, Greg stepped from the edge of the track to the middle, so the driver could see him better. He knew that almost all the carts that passed along this section of track belonged to farmers which meant they were built to carry heavy loads and not for speed. Sure enough, as the cart lumbered around the bend, Greg could see it was moving only slightly faster than a slow jog. He waved his arms and waited for the driver to reign in the giant shire horses pulling a cart laden with hay.

He waved and he waited. And waited. And waved. The cart wasn't slowing. So he waved and shouted. Still the cart didn't slow.

Then he shouted and jumped as the cart very nearly hit him.

'Whoa there!' came a shout from the cart as Greg landed in a heap in the tufts of grass by the side of the track. 'Is somebody there?'

Greg stood up, brushing the bits of grass off his clothes.

'There very nearly wasn't!' Greg said. 'You nearly ran me down!'

The cart and horses had come to a stop a short distance down the road. 'Sorry about that,' came a shout from the cart. 'Are you looking for a ride?'

'I'm looking for a clean pair of underwear at the moment,' Greg said, walking towards the cart.

As Greg got closer, the driver jumped down to greet him.

'The name's Smart. Keith Smart,' the driver said and stuck out his hand. He was roughly half as tall as Greg and had a small, round face and on it were the thickest pair of spectacles Greg had ever seen, affording him the appearance of a mole. He was also about to shake hands with the rear end of one of his horses.

'I'm over here,' Greg said.

'Of course you are!' Keith Smart said and shook Greg's trouser pocket. 'Now, do you want a lift or not?'

'That'd be great, thanks Mr Smart. How about if I drove the cart and you sat back and rested up for a while? How does that sound?'

'Sounds like a plan, young man,' Keith Smart said, clambering back onto his cart. 'These bloody horses keep bumping into things anyway. See if you can do any better.'

***

By the time darkness had completely fallen, accompanied by a flicker of stars, Greg had covered a lot of ground. The horses were good and the cart rode well.

During the journey, Greg learned from Keith that he was headed into Lower Calver to sell his hay at the market. When Greg had remarked that the market wasn't for another three days, Keith had told him that if the early bird catches the worm, then he was going to catch the early bird and would therefore have both the bird and the worm.

He'd also let Greg in on a little secret; he had a catchphrase guaranteed to bring in the customers. He said his plan was to set up a stall near the entrance and hit the unsuspecting public as they entered, before they had a chance to peruse any other market stalls.

When Greg asked to hear his catchphrase, Keith looked first left, then right, then leant over to Greg and shouted, 'Hey! Buy my hay! It's great for a good night's sleep and it soaks up wee too!' He then sat back, tapped the side of his nose with his finger and nodded.

'That's... brilliant,' Greg said.

'You see, you got your greeting spelt H.E.Y., and your product spelt H.A.Y. Put the two together and wham, the product sells itself. I don't know how these ideas come to me, they just do. I guess it's a gift.'

Before Greg was forced to devise an appropriate response, the cart rounded a bend and they reached the town of Bothurn, home of the famous Hairy Apple Pub and Inn.

The Hairy Apple was more than just a place to stop for a drink on the way to Calver.

Not much more, but it had been around for as long as anyone could remember and that meant it automatically qualified for the golden goose's egg: it was a part of *tradition*. Anytime a farmer passed on the way to or from Calver, it was *tradition* to stop in The Hairy Apple for a jar or two. Just like it was *tradition* to eat one of their nearly famous thick-crust pies.

Shortly after the new landlord took ownership of The Hairy Apple, he added 'Inn' to the name thus making it *tradition* to stop over for the night.

The main building housed the pub and behind this the rooms were gathered in a horse-shoe shape. Greg pulled Keith's cart into the yard and they both went in through the back door.

Well, Greg did. Keith walked straight into the kitchen, sat at the sink and ordered a pint.

Although he would've liked to press on, Greg had a feeling that Ralph might have stopped off at The Hairy Apple for the night (it was tradition, after all).

Entering the bar, Greg scanned the crowd for his brother. His gaze was met by a variety of eyes. Some hard, some trying to be, others jovial and some slightly crossed. None of the eyes belonged to Ralph.

Greg approached the bar and elbowed himself some room. As his hands touched the thick oak of the bar, a slim, dark-haired man with a tiny pencil-thin moustache appeared as if he had been hiding under the floor behind the bar.

'Good evening, sir!' said the man. 'My name's Trevor. I'm the new owner of this fine establishment. How may I be of service to you?'

Greg wasn't quite sure what to do. Every time he'd been in The Hairy Apple, the most he'd got in the way of a welcome was a grunt and then a mug of ale slapped down in front of him. He looked to his left at the man next to him who, by the look of him, had been sat at the bar for most of the day.

'Don't worry, son,' the man said through fog-like breath, thick with alcohol. 'He's from the city.' That said, he turned back to his drink.

'I have many fine beverages available this evening!' Trevor said.

To Greg, he seemed like the kind of person who spoke with an exclamation mark at the end of every sentence. 'Would Sir care to see the wine list? Failing that, I have a fine collection of cocktails, which can be prepared fresh to order!'

'Actually, I'd like to ask you a few questions,' Greg said.

Trevor's face lit up. 'Ooh, excellent! They told us about this on the Publican course. Witty banter, back and forth; that's the cornerstone of a successful landlord's thriving business!'

'Yes, I'm sure it is,' Greg said, 'but all I need to know...'

'Problem with the missus?' Trevor said. 'Or maybe it's the weather you'd prefer?'

'No, I just need to know if you've seen someone, that's all.'

'Really? That's it?' Trevor said, looking dejected. 'I do a great line about the local sports team and how they couldn't find a way to score within the confines of a brothel.'

'I'm looking for my brothel – I mean, brother,' Greg said, pressing on. 'He looks like me, only he has dark hair and he's a bit shorter. Goes by the name Ralph.'

'Ah, yes!' Trevor said. 'He's out in room seven. A most interesting character. Came in a couple of hours ago. Hired a room, set up a tab, bought everyone a drink, then another, then one more and then next thing you know, he's heading out the back to his room. Said something about a quick nap before carrying on the party. Left not five minutes ago. Now, about that drink...'

Greg was already on his way out the door. He crossed the small courtyard and headed for room seven which was the last room on the left. Greg knocked twice and waited. He didn't know what he was going to say to Ralph; for the moment he was just glad he'd found him.

No answer. 'Ralph, it's me, Greg,' he said as he knocked again.

Again, no answer.

Just as he was about to try and peer in through the window, Greg heard a rusty creak and then a thud coming from the back of the room. He ran around the back, just in time to see Ralph following his knapsack out the rear window.

'Ralph?'

Ralph turned as he leant back out of the window. His jerkin caught on the ledge, he lost his balance and fell backwards onto the gravel.

'Ralph, what are you doing?'

Ralph stood up, brushed himself down and turned to face Greg.

'Quite clearly, I'm doing a runner. Now, are you going to help me or not?'

32

'Ralph, I don't understand. Why are you doing a runner?'

'Because, Greg, I owe the landlord three rounds worth of drinks, there's four blokes sat at a table near the back of the pub who want to break my legs and oh yeah, I lost the stone. Enough about me. How are you?'

Chapter 5
If in Doubt, Hit It

'You're going to have to run that by me one more time.'

'Okay. I'll tell you again but you've got to promise not to try and hit me this time. And please temper your language, there are women about.'

Greg and Ralph were crouched behind a baker's across the street from the Hairy Apple. Ralph had insisted on putting distance between them and the place before he would say anymore.

They'd been there for about five minutes, first whilst Ralph explained what had happened, and then whilst Greg tried to calm down. 'Right, here goes,' Ralph said and turned to face Greg. 'After your wife viciously assaulted me with words that cut to my very soul, I decided to take matters into my own hands. I decided I would take the red stone, make my way into Lower Calver, speak to a few people in the know, do a little bit of business wheeler-dealer style, and return home to you with more money than you could ever imagine. I'd even planned to forgive Mollie, as I feel that I could indeed be the bigger person. How's that sound?'

'That much I get. Highly unlikely that it'd ever happen, but I get it,' Greg said. 'It's the part which ends with you falling arse-first out a window with no red stone. Help me understand how you failed to last a day with the stone in your possession.'

'That's the easy part, and you'll laugh at this, you really will.'

Greg looked at Ralph. 'Somehow I doubt that,' he said.

'Maybe not now, but years later, this'll be...'

'Ralph. The stone. What happened?'

'Well, I decided to spend the night at The Hairy Apple, now it's got rooms. Tradition and all that. Rest up, get myself fresh for the morning. As I was going to need a few contacts, I decided the smart thing to do would be to make a few friends. You know what they say: you've got to spend money to make money. Anyway, I ordered a few drinks for people, then a few more and before you know it, my plan worked. This great big bear of a man asked me to join him and his associates at their table.'

Greg could see where this was going.

'So I sat with them for a while and we talked about this and that, then the big fella asked me if I was looking to do a spot of business. Obviously, he could tell I was another businessman just like him from the way I handled myself. So we did a bit of business and hey presto, here I am! Right, let's head off home!'

Ralph stood up to leave.

Greg grabbed him by the shoulder and yanked him back down. 'You did a bit of business?'

'Yeah, a bit of business. You know.'

'No, I don't know. Why don't you enlighten me?'

'When I say a bit of business, what I mean is... he took the red stone from me. Then he said I had to go home and find some more and if I didn't bring him more within two days, he'd burn down the farm. That kind of business.'

'Ralph,' Greg said very slowly. 'How does he know where the farm is?'

'Before he took the stone, I may or may not have told him where the farm is. I thought it would earn his trust.'

Greg slapped his brother. It was a quick backhand but it caught Ralph completely by surprise and knocked him over. Ralph lay on his back, eyes wide, rubbing his jaw. Then Greg started to feel bad as he saw tears welling in Ralph's eyes.

'Ralph, I'm sorry,' Greg said. 'But it needed to be done. What Mollie said to you about Mae was wrong, but that in no way excuses what a monumental tit you've been.'

Ralph sat up. 'You've never hit me before. That was a first for sibling violence. You know, I could've blocked it and then snapped your arm like a twig. It's just that I chose not to.'

Greg shook his head and helped his brother to his feet.

'I suppose we should head off home then,' Ralph said. 'I guess Mollie will have a few things to say to me with a month's worth of gloating thrown in for good measure.'

'There's no way we're going home without that stone,' Greg said. 'It's our stone and we're going to get it back.'

'Of course we are, Greg. Course we are. I did tell you the part about the four extremely large gentlemen taking the stone off me, didn't I?'

'Don't worry, I have a plan,' Greg said, which was almost true.

***

As the new landlord of The Hairy Apple sat huddled in a ball on a shelf under his own bar, he started to re-evaluate his career choice.

At Publican College, they'd told him he'd be mixing exotic cocktails, waiting on cultured guests who tipped big money and how he'd generally provide a much valued and respected service to the public. Yet here he was, dodging flying glasses, minus his front teeth and scared witless. It had all started when the one that everyone seemed so interested in, Ralph was his name, had marched back into the main bar. Although he strode confidently, his face was as white as a sheet and he looked as if he was trying to stop himself bursting into tears. He walked right up to the table in the corner, almost all of which was taken up with the bulk of four very large gentlemen.

'Right then!' Ralph said, his voice only quivering once. 'You numpties have got my stone. You took it from me unlawfully, which means I could report you to the appropriate authorities. However, because scum like you disgust me — preying on an innocent businessman — I'll settle for giving you all a quick slap. Outside, now!' With that, he turned on his heel and walked very quickly back past the bar and out the back door.

The four large gentlemen stood as one and without a word headed towards the back door as if this was a regular occurrence for them. As they reached the corner of the bar a voice from behind them shouted, 'Oi, lumpy-nuts! I'm here collecting the ugly tax which means you four owe big time!'

Once again the four men moved in practised synchronicity, swivelling on the spot to face their insulter.

'Over here, ass-clowns,' came a shout from another corner. 'Jeez, do you four share a brain or just loan one from the village cow?'

This time the four weren't quite as together. The front two turned to the second voice, whilst the back two tried to move towards their original destination, the back door. The effect was similar to four irritated and confused bears stumbling into each other as they tried unsuccessfully to get out of each other's way.

'Good Lord above!' said the first voice.

'Indeed!' shouted the second.

'It's like square dancing for the recently lobotomised,' said the first.

'For crying out loud!' roared the largest of the four men, his face beetroot red. 'Stand still, you blithering idiots!'

At which the other three stopped banging into each other.

'If anyone says another word,' the leader said pointing to the rest of the pub, 'I'll—' but he was cut off as a tankard arced through the air, spinning end over end and struck him flush on the forehead. He staggered backwards and clutched onto one of his large friends as his legs buckled. In situations such as these all it takes is one wrong move, one poorly thought-out decision before all hell breaks loose.

'Excuse me,' said the newly appointed landlord of The Hairy Apple as he tapped one of the large men on the shoulder, 'but if you need it, I am trained in first aid.'

The large man turned around and punched the Landlord in the mouth.

All hell broke loose.

Glasses flew across the room as did people. Amongst the chaos, Greg and Ralph crawled along the floor, both coming from separate ends of the room.

'Nice plan, Greg!' Ralph said. 'Now if we can just find the stone and manage to get out of here alive, I think we can call it a success.'

Greg was about to respond when what sounded like a tree crashed into the sawdust between them kicking up a cloud of dust. As the dust settled they both recognised the leader of the large men. He had a huge lump on his forehead and he was wearing his nose across one side of his face. As he landed, the red stone had fallen out of his pocket and rolled to a stop by Greg's hand. Greg quickly pocketed the red stone in his jerkin and looked up at where the large man had fallen from.

'Even I couldn't miss a big fecker like that,' said Keith, clutching the remnants of a chair.

'Ralph, meet Keith. He's a businessman, just like you,' Greg said scrambling to his feet.

'Mind if we save the introductions for later?' Ralph said. 'Only, I think we should leave and do it quickly.'

The three of them crouched down and made steady progress first towards, and then out of, the back door. They left the sounds of a Friday night at The Hairy Apple behind them and jumped into Keith's cart and the relative safety of the road to Calver.

***

For the remainder of the night, the three of them took it in turns to drive the cart onwards, although Ralph and Greg made sure they took more of the turns. They'd decided to put as much distance between them and The Hairy Apple as possible, so they rode on until the sun came up. Once dawn had broken they headed off the main road, down a smaller track and pulled over to sleep. None of them had any trouble sleeping as the exertions of the night took their toll and Keith's hay lived up to its marketing promise.

It was mid-afternoon before Greg woke up. He stretched, leant back against the tree he'd slept under and yawned. He actually felt pretty good. Keith's hay had been incredibly comfortable and he felt completely rested.

'Well hello there, twinkle-dreams,' Ralph said. He sat opposite Greg, with his back also against a tree.

'How long have you been awake?' Greg asked.

'Only about two minutes longer than you. Which is long enough.'

Ralph certainly didn't look like he'd had a good night's sleep. His face was drawn, his eyes sagged and he looked in need of a good wash.

'Ralph, you look like hell. Didn't you sleep well?'

'I slept fine, thank you very much. In fact, I awoke feeling refreshed and full of the joys of the harvest. Till I saw this, that is.' Ralph held out a hand-written note.

'It was pinned to the tree above where you were sleeping,' he said.

Greg took the note, rubbed the sleep out of his eyes and read it.

Dear Gregory and Ralph Hoffenbach,

I, Keith Smart, being of sound mind and noble spirit, have taken, as payment, the lovely shiny red stone that fell out of Mr G. Hoffenbach's pocket when he rolled over in his sleep. As the morning light hit said stone it produced a glorious light show and I was able to determine it would cover the cost of, and recompense me against, the following:

> *1)   Cost of transport (cart ride to, and continuing from, The Hairy Apple)*
>
> *2)   Personal protection duties (bashing an individual in the chops with a chair)*
>
> *3)   Lodging facilities (sleeping on my hay)*

As I am sure you will agree, I have certainly earned the payment of said red stone, however, if you feel aggrieved with my decision, you have three working days to dispute my claim, after which you can both get knotted.

Yours Faithfully,
Mr Keith Smart Esq.
P.S. Please keep the hay you've slept on as a gesture of goodwill.

'What's the matter?' Ralph asked. 'You look like hell.'

Greg wanted to shout and scream. He wanted to get up and kick the tree he was leaning against. He wanted to run after Keith and bash his head in with his bare hands.

42

I just want a new plough.

But it was more than that. What was it about people that they thought they could take something, something that clearly belonged to someone else? First Ralph, then the four large men and now Keith the-bloody-hay-salesman Smart.

He'd found the stone. He'd dug it up. He'd taken it from the earth and therefore it was his. What right did anyone else have to take it from him? Admittedly, anyone could've dug up the stone and it could've belonged to someone else before it somehow ended up buried in his field, but those were minor details as far as Greg was concerned.

'I think it's despicable,' Ralph said. 'Stealing from someone who's fast asleep. What right has he got to take the stone and make off with it? Bloody cheek, that's what it is.'

'You mean just like you did?'

'Well... no... I mean... what I did was different. We're family aren't we? That should count for something, shouldn't it?'

Greg chose to say nothing. *I just want my stone back. And a new plough.*

'So what are we going to do, Greg?' Ralph said.

'I'll let you decide, Ralph,' Greg said, standing up. 'We could either head into Lower Calver, find Keith and get our stone back, or we could go home and tell Mollie we got robbed by a short-sighted hay salesman.'

43

Ralph got up, picked up his bag and headed down the track and onto the road to Lower Calver.

Chapter 6
All Across the Blood Wastes

Greg and Ralph spent the next two days walking to Calver. They marched ever onwards with grim determination, the Great Hill a constant presence, looming on the horizon. By day they walked through the many towns and settlements, some bigger than theirs, some smaller, and by night they'd find an inn, usually located by the roadside in one of the larger towns. These towns often only had one inn to choose from, but they were usually clean and often served a warm meal.

Whilst they walked, they spoke little and rested only once night began to fall. Soon, the rolling hills, patchwork fields and clusters of buildings which constituted the towns gradually disappeared as they got closer to the Great Hill.

The land eventually flattened out as they came ever nearer to the edge of the Blood Wastes.

Although once the site of one of the greatest battles in the history of the Kingdom, the Blood Wastes had lain mainly empty for decades and now consisted of little more than a ten-mile-wide expanse of mainly flat grassland with the occasional stream, hill or clump of trees.

It was early morning as Greg and Ralph crested the last hill and descended down onto The Blood Wastes. The Great Hill stood ten miles away, its three segmented sections a morning's walk away.

The Blood Wastes were empty, aside from a collection of mercenary tents clumped together, just over a bridge that crossed the river before the Blood Wastes began in earnest.

Greg and Ralph set off across the bridge, determined to cross The Blood Wastes as quickly as possible and get into Lower Calver before night fell.

They passed the collection of tents, each one a different size and shape to its neighbour, the bigger and more expensive looking ones obviously belonging to the better-paid mercenaries.

'You know, Greg,' Ralph said, 'I always fancied myself as a mercenary.'

Greg shook his head.

'Now don't you shake your head like that,' Ralph said. 'I reckon I would've been a good mercenary. Maybe not all that killing stuff, but I could get used to the money side of things, I mean, look at some of these tents. They're bigger than our farm house!'

It was true. A few of the tents towards the middle of the encampment were the size of small homes, draped in the finest material with more than enough room for a family.

'Having said all that, though,' Ralph continued, 'I don't reckon I could put my high moral standards to one side. Hurting people, possibly even killing them and all for the highest bidder? No thank you. What kind of an individual does that and aligns their moral compass so it points directly at money? I mean, they basically pimp themselves out like some third-rate citizen? Again, who does that?'

'Me.'

Greg and Ralph spun around and came face to face with the end of an extremely large sword.

'Although, if I'm annoyed, I'll kill for free,' said the owner of the sword.

He was about Greg's height and of a similar build but that was where the similarities ended. His face was covered with scars, some small nicks, others ran the length of his entire face. Most had healed and now criss-crossed in a series of white flashes, but some were still fresh.

'Ah,' Ralph said.

'Ah, indeed, Mr High Moral Standards,' said the owner of the scars.

Sometimes Greg was glad he was Ralph's brother, he really was. Countless times, Ralph had used his quick wits and even quicker tongue to talk them both out of one predicament or another over the years.

'You know,' Ralph said, 'it's considered rude to eavesdrop on a private conversation.'

Unfortunately, this wasn't one of those times.

'Is that so? Well, excuse me,' the man said, lowering his sword slightly. 'You see, I'm a third-rate citizen and therefore unaware of what is considered rude in polite society.'

'Not to worry,' Ralph said, stepping back slightly. 'No harm done, Mr...?'

'Oh I do apologise!' the man said. 'See, there's another act of rudeness for you. Here's me pointing a sword at your throat and I haven't even introduced myself. My name's Charlie McGowerty, although my pimped-out-to-the-highest-bidder name is Death-Knoll.'

'Death-Knoll? What an inter—'

'Shut it!' Death-Knoll said, snarling.

'Erm, excuse me, Mr Death-Knoll,' Greg said, desperately trying to hide the fear in his voice.

Charlie 'Death-Knoll' McGowerty turned to face Greg, his sword still pointing at Ralph. 'Yes, what is it?' he said.

'As you may have guessed, my brother's a bit of an idiot. Sometimes, his brain isn't aware of the things coming out of his mouth. I'd tell you he meant no harm with what he said but I'm not even sure he knows what he said. We think he must have been dropped on the head as a child. A lot.'

'Listen pal,' Death-Knoll said. 'I understand your concern, he is your brother after all, but my hands are tied on this. He's insulted my bloodline and called into question my moral standing. Can't have that. Nowadays, us mercenaries have a tough enough lot as it is without half-wits like your brother thinking they can say what they like about us and get away with it. Not like it used to be. Times are hard. We trade on reputation, you see. The more we're feared, the higher price we can command. So with that said, I'm going to have to cut his innards out.'

Ralph made a noise in the back of his throat, halfway between a squeal and a gurgle, as Death-Knoll turned back to face him.

'Everything all right here, fellas?' came a female voice from behind Death-Knoll, who immediately lowered his sword, turned to the side and attempted to hide his sword behind his back. The voice belonged to a small woman with short, cropped black hair. She wore an outfit which seemed to mainly consist of animal furs.

'Oh, everything's just hunky-dory, Eve,' Death-Knoll said, shifting his weight nervously. 'I was just talking to these gentlemen about morals and how we mercenaries thrive on the concept of fear. Isn't that right, boys?'

Greg and Ralph nodded rapidly up and down.

'Is that so?' the woman called Eve said.

'That is exactly so,' Death-Knoll said. 'And if you two gentlemen don't mind, I must be off now. Things to do and all that.'

Death-Knoll nodded to Eve, nodded to Ralph and Greg – who continued nodding rapidly – and hustled off back towards the tents.

Eve stepped closer to Ralph and Greg. 'You can stop nodding now, boys. Death-Knoll's all right really, just gets a bit touchy when he thinks folks are looking down their noses at him. Hence why he has a collection of noses on a long piece of string back in his tent.'

'Thank goodness you came along when you did,' Greg said. 'He was just about to cut out my brother's innards.'

'Yes, he has a nasty habit of doing that. Although he doesn't collect those.'

'My name's Greg and this is my idiot brother, Ralph.'

Eve stepped closer and shook Greg's extended hand.

'Well,' Ralph said, turning to shake Eve's hand too. 'I don't know what kind of a hold you have over that savage, but I'm glad you turned up when you did.'

'Is that so?' Eve asked.

'That is exactly so. These bloody mercenaries with their over-inflated sense of self-worth. We've moved on since the time when they were actually relevant. Left-over from a bygone era, is what I say. I don't know, you make one comment about their low moral standards – which, by the way, is true – and they fly off the handle, threatening you with physical abuse.'

'That's the difference between me and Death-Knoll,' Eve said as she turned to face Ralph.

'What's that?' Ralph asked.

'I don't threaten. I act.' And she promptly kicked Ralph in the testicles.

***

'Sorry about that,' Eve said to Greg as Ralph lay on the ground in a foetal heap.

'No need to apologise,' Greg replied. 'He had it coming.'

Ralph whimpered.

'I take it that you too are a mercenary?'

Eve took a step back and bowed low, which for a woman of her diminished stature was very low indeed. 'Eve Manslayer at your service. For a price, of course.'

'Well it's nice to meet you, Eve, and thanks for helping out with Mr Death-Knoll there.'

'Not a problem. Where you boys headed?'

'We're off to the market in Lower Calver.'

'Something to sell?'

'Sort of,' Greg said.

'Don't think you'll make much money selling *sort of* something. I'm known more for my fighting prowess than my business brain, but where I come from, sort-ofs don't sell too well.'

'It's a long story, which gets a bit embarrassing in places. Me and Ralph don't really come off too well in the telling of it, to be honest.'

Eve looked down at Ralph, who had his hands down his jerkin and was trying to massage the feeling back into his extremities. 'And here's me with such a high opinion of you already,' she said.

So Greg told Eve the story about the red stone. He wasn't quite sure why he did, and the look on Ralph's face told him to keep his mouth shut, but what was the point? If they'd had the red stone with them, then maybe telling a paid killer such a story would've been a bad idea, but they didn't. The red stone could be anywhere at this moment so telling someone how they'd managed to lose it twice in as many days didn't seem to matter so much.

To her credit, Eve didn't laugh too much and when Greg finished; she simply stood shaking her head.

'You realise that you two won't last two minutes in Lower Calver?'

Greg stiffened. 'We've been to the market before. We should be all right. Granted we're not mercenaries, but...'

'That's my point,' Eve said. 'You've been to the market, sold a few turnips and gone straight home like good farmer boys. Who in their right mind would waste their energy on a couple of farmers and their root vegetables?'

'We also sold some cucumbers.'

'My point, Greg and Ralph Hoffenbach, is that this time you're going to Lower Calver to find something that's been taken from you.

'Which means leaving the market and asking around. Maybe even venturing into the backstreets. Where the people of Lower Calver actually live.

'The difference between most people and those who live in the backstreets is; you get in a scuffle with someone where you're from and they'll bite, scratch and claw till they can't fight anymore. You get into a scrap with anyone from the backstreets and they'll cry off the minute you get serious then rip your kidneys out the minute you turn to walk away. If, however, you do manage to somehow get your red stone back, then you'll want to sell it and let me tell you, it's probably going to create more interest than a sack of turnips.'

'And cucumbers.'

Eve looked up at Greg. Even though she was almost half his size, Greg still felt the weight of her gaze.

'Will you help us?' he said.

'Now wait just a minute,' Ralph said several octaves higher than his normal voice. 'This person just assaulted me.'

Eve whirled around to face Ralph who instinctively crossed his legs and clamped his eyes shut. She then turned back to Greg.

'Ralph,' Greg said. 'We could use her help. It's not like we've been all that successful on our own, now is it?'

Ralph opened one eye and peered at his brother.

'But she kicked me in the dangle-berries.'

'I know, Ralph, I know. You did have it coming, though. Look on the bright side: ten minutes ago, you nearly had your innards cut out. A kick in the dangle-berries is nothing compared to that.'

'Easy for you to say,' Ralph said.

'Let me make life easier for you,' Eve said. 'I'll come with you into Lower Calver. I was heading into town anyway. Once we're there, I'll go off, make a few enquiries then get back to you. If my enquiries lead to you getting your stone back, then when you sell it, you give me twenty-five percent. If not, then we go our separate ways.'

'At the risk of another violent and unprovoked attack, this is why you can never trust a mercenary, Greg. It's all about the money. It's why they never settle in one place for very long. Take the money and run.'

'It's hardly like we're swamped with other options,' Greg said. 'Besides, twenty-five percent of nothing is still nothing. Which is exactly what we've got right now.'

'Okay, five percent,' Ralph said.

'Twenty,' Eve said.

'Ten.'

Eve nodded. 'Fifteen percent and I promise not to kick you in the stones ever again.'

'Deal!' Greg said and shook Eve's hand.

'I still think this is a bad idea,' Ralph said, gingerly getting to his feet. Together, the three of them turned and started the walk across The

Blood Wastes and into Lower Calver, although for the first few miles Ralph limped more than walked.

Chapter 7
For Whom the Gate Opens

By the time Greg, Ralph and Eve reached the Great Hill, it was getting close to midday. They'd made it across The Blood Wastes without further incident and after a couple of hours, Ralph had even started talking to Eve.

As they neared the end of the Blood Wastes, the road narrowed until it funnelled into a pathway only just wide enough for two carts to pass by each other. The pathway led up to, and then through, the huge wooden gates which stood sentry in the immense wall that marked the boundary of Lower Calver.

The wall itself ran completely around the circumference of the Great Hill, even though only its north face was inhabited. Along the top of the wall, stationed every hundred yards or so, stood members of the Royal Guard. It was the job of the Royal Guard to protect the Great Hill at all times. Mostly, the protection wasn't against invading nations (the Kingdom hadn't been invaded in over 300 years; it was an island at the bottom end of an ocean which nobody really thought much about), but more a show of force from the King towards those in the Kingdom who had short memories. They might consider the fanciful idea of trying to bring back to power some of the clans long-since disbanded, but if any of them got any strange notions about testing their king, then the Royal Guard soon put a stop to that.

The Royal Guard were originally the remnants of those who fought in the last battle on the Blood Wastes but, over time, it had been strengthened to the point where they now represented a formidable army. The best of whom stood guard on the north face of the walls. In these positions, each of the three walls contained men who would die for their king but were much better at making others do so first.

Around the south side, where the Great Hill was completely uninhabited, those soldiers who were either new recruits or had committed something that required punishment stood guard. It was considered an insult to be sent to guard the south side. Nothing grew there, it was twice as steep as the north side and covered in loose rocks. Often the wind and poor weather lashed the south side of the Great Hill, making guard duty there a tortuous affair.

Positioning his Royal Guard on each of the three walls meant that King Siguld was incredibly safe inside the third wall, in Upper Calver.

At this point in time, Upper Calver couldn't have been further from Greg's mind. As they neared the gates, Greg strained his neck to look up and glance at those members of the Royal Guard who had pulled gate duty. The top of the wall was so far above him, he could only just make out a glimmer of armour. Greg followed Eve through the open gates and up to the gatehouse.

Each wall contained a gatehouse built into the thick mortar, where anyone wishing to gain entry had to present themselves. These places were often crowded, especially at the time of a market. The gatehouse was split into four separate sections, one for traders, one for residents of Lower Calver, one for residents of Middle Calver and a final one for those fortunate enough to live in Upper Calver. Each section got progressively better, or worse, depending on where you lived.

Those who lived in Upper Calver were greeted by a member of the Royal Guard who politely waved them forwards, offered them a drink whilst their papers were checked and even provided them with a small room in which to refresh themselves had their journey been a long and tiring one.

'Oi, you three!' shouted a guard in front of the trader's entrance. 'Get a bleedin' move on!'

Greg, Eve and Ralph were summoned over to the furthest entrance on the left. It was the smallest of the four and was little more than a turnstile made of wood in a gap in the stone.

'What you doin' here?' the guard asked. His body was constrained by armour which probably fit him when it was first issued twenty years ago.

'We've come to trade at the market, my good man,' Ralph said, offering a winning smile.

'That so?' The guard looked the three of them up and down. 'Who's the little minx with you, your bodyguard?' he chuckled.

'Her?' Ralph said, chuckling too. 'Yeah, right. Look at her. First sign of trouble and this one would be hiding under a table!'

The guard looked them up and down again, his eyes taking their time when they reached Eve.

'Yeah, well, you three be careful in there. Stick to the main streets, do your buying and selling and don't go wandering off. Hate to see you country folk getting in to any trouble.'

'Will do, sir!' Ralph said.

The guard waved them through.

Once they'd cleared the gatehouse, Eve smacked Ralph on the back of the head.

'What was that for?' Ralph said, rubbing his head.

'Because I can't kick you in the balls.'

'I was just playing a part, Eve. Look, it got us past the gatehouse without any trouble, didn't it? What did you want me to say, this is my brother Greg and my name is Ralph, we're farmers. This is our friend Eve, she kills people. May we come in?'

59

Greg left Eve and Ralph to argue. Each time he came to Lower Calver it took him a while to get used to being there. It was a place which was a complete contrast to home. He was used to wide open spaces, quiet, and the feel of grass under foot whereas Lower Calver felt more like stepping into a living thing. It had its own pulse, the buildings crowded in on each other, the cobbled streets seemed to hum as people moved about. It was easy to become overwhelmed by such a sight.

In front of him was a large open space. In a day's time, it was where the market would be, but for now it was empty, save for those few people who funnelled through the gatehouse and then went on to different parts of Calver.

Beyond the open space, the streets began. Most people headed for the King's Pass, the main street which ran directly up the Great Hill, through the other two walls and up to the main entrance of the King's palace.

It was along the King's Pass that most of the places of business clung, vying for the trade of those who passed by. It was said throughout the Kingdom that it was possible to buy anything you could imagine at some point along the King's Pass. It was also widely known that anyone visiting Calver could wander along the King's Pass, take in the sights and sounds, purchase the occasional item and then leave for home nothing more than a few coins lighter.

However, should a visitor stray from the King's Pass onto any of its side streets, then being able to leave for home was considered a good result. For it was on these streets that Lower Calver became interesting. Whereas the King's Pass ran true and straight, the backstreets of Lower Calver resembled a spider's web of interlocking narrow passages, sometimes leading to rows of houses wedged on top of each other like a child's set of building blocks; other times they led to dark culverts where anything could, and probably did, happen. Others still led to streets that simply appeared to stop. Anyone who lived in Lower Calver knew these backstreets intimately as they had in fact been forced to learn them from an early age.

Greg shuddered at the thought of Ralph heading down one of those narrow streets, looking for 'a good deal'.

'Gregory,' Ralph began, still rubbing the back of his head. 'I feel I cannot work under these circumstances. This *individual* you have chosen to enter into business with keeps physically abusing me.'

'That's because you're a turd,' Eve said.

'You can be a bit of a turd,' Greg said, nodding. 'What we need is a plan.'

'How does this sound,' Ralph said. 'Madam Slap-Happy buggers off and leaves us to find Mr Smart and our red stone?'

'Actually,' Eve said. 'That sounds quite good. I've got some things to attend to anyway. Whilst I'm out and about, I'll do some digging,

61

see if I can find out where your stone is. How's that sound?'

'Fine by me,' Ralph said.

'Okay then,' Eve said. 'I'll meet you back here, by that statue – tomorrow morning – just as the market's getting set up. See you later, Greg. Ralph, try not to get killed.'

Eve walked away up the King's Pass and then slipped off to the left and disappeared from view.

'That's better,' Ralph said.

'You know, you could make more of an effort, Ralph.'

'She's just lucky I don't hit women.'

***

Greg and Ralph wandered a short distance up the King's Pass, until they came to an inn. It looked like somewhere a tourist might choose to stay with its nicely swept front cobbles, two wooden pillars marking the entrance and even a doorman waiting to open the door for guests.

'Good morning, gentlemen, and welcome to The First Inn,' the doorman said, nodding in their direction. 'Will you be staying with us this evening?'

Greg and Ralph looked at each other. 'How much does a room cost?' Ralph asked.

'Ah, I can see you are men who cut to the chase. Why bother enquiring about our facilities, standard of food or selection of cask ales, when a simple *how much* will do?'

'Listen, pal,' Ralph said, striding over to the doorman. 'It's been a long few days. Don't push it with your city sarcasm.'

Greg followed his brother over. 'We need to find a room for the night and we haven't got much money,' he said. 'We didn't mean to be blunt, but—'

The doorman waved them even closer. He took a look in both directions, then over his left shoulder towards the doors of the inn.

'Sorry, fellas,' he said in a whisper. 'I have to give it the whole spiel, the bosses think it's important to sound stuck up your own arse. Me personally, well, I think it's having airs and graces where they don't belong.' He looked around again and waved Greg and Ralph even closer. So close in fact that the three of them were huddled together, their faces inches apart. 'Listen. I could see my way to sorting you boys a nice little room in this inn tonight, all for a minimal cost. Of course, it couldn't go through the books or anything like that, but if you don't mind, I don't mind, know what I mean?'

'When you say minimal cost...' Greg said.

'I like it! Straight to the point, this one!' the doorman said, slapping Greg on the back. He waved them back down into the huddle. 'When I say minimal cost, what I actually mean is free of charge. How does that sound?'

'Too good to be true. Or legal,' said Greg.

The doorman stood upright and put his gloved hand on his chest.

'Sir, you've insulted me. To think that Ronald Freepepper would break the law whilst trying to help out a couple of boys such as yourselves... I'm offended. Besides, there is a little thing I'd need you to do for me; a favour, as such.'

'And what might that be?' Ralph asked.

'Don't worry yourselves about that now. I'll explain all later. I'll meet you round the back at seven tonight. Don't be late or I'll have to find someone else and I can assure you that there's plenty of folk who'd snap my arm off for a free night's accommodation. Now clear off, someone's coming. Remember, seven o'clock.'

Ronald Freepepper stepped back to open the door just as a man and a woman stepped out onto the gleaming cobblestones. They too looked as if they'd been polished to within an inch of their lives, both so immaculately presented that Greg couldn't help but wonder if they'd come free with the hotel.

'Good morning, Mr Geoffrey. Good morning, Mrs Geoffrey. Pleasant day isn't it?'

Mr and Mrs Geoffrey paused momentarily as they drew level with Ronald but neither turned to look at him as if turning their heads would invite creases.

'Mr Freepepper, we pay you to comment on the pleasantness of the day for the benefit of our customers, not us. Social responses between employees are a waste of time and counter-productive. It breeds familiarity and ultimately lack of effort. Kindly refrain from such behaviour. We will dock your wages for the time you've wasted talking with us.' The Geoffreys promptly turned right and walked off in tandem in the direction of the middle gatehouse.

'There you have it, ladies and gentlemen,' Greg and Ralph heard Ronald mutter under his breath as they walked off. 'The caring face of corporate hospitality.'

***

'I suppose we could do with a plan,' Greg said as they made their way up the King's Pass.

'Thought you'd never ask,' Ralph said. 'Let's go in here for a sit down and so we can strategise.'

They walked into a large bakery with a sign over the door which read:

F. Chesterton & Daughters. Lower Calver Bakery: You Knead Us

As they entered they were hit by a smell that, throughout the history of time, was clearly designed to end more diets, sell more houses and generally make you feel hungry even straight after a huge meal than any other: the smell of freshly baked bread.

On their left ran a series of trestle tables, each covered with a red polka-dot cloth and a mountain of pastries. Behind each table stood a slightly different version of the same girl;

65

thick auburn hair tied back, red cheeks, flour covered aprons. On their right, an older man with the same thick auburn hair (his thinning), served the long line of customers from a fourth table, this one covered in pies.

Further back, a collection of tables, most occupied, were attended to by another copy of the three girls who navigated through them with surprising grace as she made her way in and out the kitchen.

'Here we go,' Ralph said, sitting down, just as an elderly lady was about to do the same.

'Well I never!' she huffed.

'Oh, I'm sure you do, madam,' Ralph said. 'Just only when the cod-liver oil kicks in.'

Greg sat down next to his brother and they both ordered from the girl.

'Okay,' Ralph said after the food had arrived and he'd taken a huge bite from his pastry. 'Actually, these are really good,' he said, inspecting his pastry. 'Anyway, the way I see it, we've got eight hours until we need to meet our new friend Mr Freepepper back at the inn.'

'That's saying we're going to take him up on his offer,' Greg said, munching on his own pastry.

'Look, Greg. If it sounds like we'll end up in bother, we'll say thank you very much and walk away. Trust me, the last thing I need is more hassle. This trip hasn't exactly been peaches and cream for me.'

'How are your peaches, by the way?'

'Oh, ha-bloody-ha. Can we get back to the matter in hand? You remember? The red stone?'

'Of course I remember,' Greg said.

'Well, I've been thinking. How hard can it be to locate a half-blind hay salesman? Why don't we spend the rest of the morning looking for him? He's bound to be staying in one of the inns on the King's Pass, isn't he?'

'What makes you say that?'

'Greg, the guy can barely find his own nose to blow it, you really think he could wander off down the backstreets of Lower Calver to find a place to stay?'

'Good point. Finish your pastry. We've got a stone to find.'

Chapter 8
Needle in a Haystack Salesman

It didn't take Greg and Ralph long to find out where Keith Smart was staying. Just as Ralph had predicted, he was staying at one of the more obvious establishments on the King's Pass. This particular inn, The Flying Dishcloth, offered a bathroom on each floor, a free wake-up call and for one night only – fresh from a sold-out conference tour, self-made businessman and entrepreneur – Jerry Gushingham.

'Of course this is where he's staying,' Greg said. 'Keith wouldn't pass up the chance to meet a fellow businessman, now would he?'

Ralph and Greg went into The Flying Dishcloth and informed the young man behind the desk that they had a meeting with their colleague Keith Smart about their hay-making business. The clerk wasn't aware that Greg and Ralph had used the same line in three previous inns further down the Great Hill.

This time it worked and the clerk apologetically informed them that Mr Smart was out for the day, conducting business elsewhere in Lower Calver, but would be returning by five p.m. as he'd booked a front row seat at Jerry

Gushingham's 'Empower your Earning Potential' seminar.

'Is it possible to leave Mr Smart a message? We're just so sorry we missed him. We had so much hay to discuss,' Greg said.

They left Keith Smart a message which Ralph then watched the clerk place in the pigeon hole for Room 34. They thanked the clerk for his time, walked out of the front door, followed the building around until they were stood outside the kitchen door at the back.

'Right, what's the plan?' Greg asked.

'Go in through the kitchen, up to Room 34, get our stone back and leg it.'

'Really? That's it?'

'Greg, sometimes you need to keep it simple. Besides, I want to get a move on; there's rats back here the size of dogs and they look like they're up for a mugging.'

Ralph pushed open the back door and stepped directly into the kitchen. As was the same with any inn along the King's Pass the day before the market started, the kitchen was the busiest room in the building.

Pots bubbled, pans clanged and all manner of people moved around the place with a practised ease. This was more than could be said for Greg and Ralph. First the heat hit them like a slap in the face and then it seemed wherever they turned they ended up in someone's way. They managed to manoeuvre their way over towards the cavernous fireplace where two small boys dressed in nothing more than ash-stained undergarments were turning four different pigs on spits held over a roaring fire.

As they were about to reach the fire, a cook grabbed them, clamping one meaty hand on each shoulder.

'Where do you think you're going?'

Greg froze, thankfully Ralph didn't.

'Are you the head cook?'

'What's it to you?'

'Because,' Ralph said, folding his arms. 'We're from the Sanitation Health Inspection Team.'

The cook looked puzzled, which, on his face, produced the effect of someone trying to force out a square poo.

'The Salutation Health Inception Team?'

Greg, following his brother's lead, shook his head. 'Oh dear, oh dear. Looks like this one has never heard of us. This could spell trouble.'

'Big trouble,' Ralph added.

'Why? What you talking about? I ain't never heard of a Health Team.'

'Looks like you've never heard of soap either, Scruffy McSlovenly,' Greg said.

Ralph ran his finger along one of the wooden benches used to prepare the vegetables. He inspected his fingers, then rubbed them together.

'You see, my good man,' he said. 'We're a newly formed bureaucratic department. It's our job to ensure that all premises within the service industry provide their customers with the highest level of hygiene.'

'Hello!' shouted the sous chef chopping carrots on the bench next to them.

'Excuse me?' Greg said.

'My name's Gene,' said the sous chef.

'Sorry,' Ralph said. 'We weren't talking to you. Carry on.'

'Not a problem,' he said and carried on dicing carrots.

'Anyway,' Greg continued, 'we're here under strict orders to inspect this property to see it meets our high standard of cleanliness.'

'Well, I dunno about that,' said the cook, the small eyes in his round face darting left and right.

'Of course, if you'd rather we start our inspection somewhere else in the inn, I suppose we could pop back later, give you a chance to tidy up,' Ralph said.

'I'd be much obliged,' the cook said and sprinted over to where a waiter had dropped a plate of food and was in the middle of licking it clean.

'Righty-ho!' said Greg, as he and Ralph made their way through the kitchen. 'We'll see you shortly.'

The cook turned and waved to them, a grin plastered across his face, and then turned back and grabbed the waiter by the lapels. Greg and Ralph could only guess what he was saying to the pale waiter as he gestured in their direction.

On their way out of the kitchen, Greg and Ralph grabbed one of the room service keys which hung near the door, granting the staff access to any room at the inn.

***

'So far, so good,' Ralph said when they had made their way up to the third floor.

'Don't get carried away. We've not got the stone yet. And remember, don't get too close to our friend Mr Smart; you saw the damage he did in The Hairy Apple.'

They walked along the hall of the third floor, doing their best to avoid the creaking floorboards but failing miserably. When they came to the door of Room 34, Ralph put his finger to his lips, knocked four times in quick succession and called, 'Room Service!' in a high falsetto.

Ralph winked at his brother. 'Just adding a bit of realism to the situation,' he whispered to Greg.

'You sounded just like that after Eve kicked you in the plums. And besides, we know he's not in.'

'You can never be too careful. Now, open the door.'

Greg took out the key, turned it in the lock and slowly opened the door.

'On three,' Ralph said. 'One, two, THREE!'

Greg and Ralph jumped into the room, fists clenched, teeth bared. Which ultimately left them feeling quite silly as the room was clearly empty. The bed had been made and Keith had left his

72

bag on top of it as if ready to make a hasty exit. Aside from the wardrobe in the corner and a chair and small table by the bed with an empty candlestick, the rest of the room was bare.

'I suppose it's what we were expecting,' Greg said.

But Ralph was already rooting through Keith Smart's bag, throwing his clothes over his shoulder as he delved deeper.

Finally, he picked the bag up and shook it upside down.

'Dammit!' he said. 'It's not here. Greg, check the rest of the room with me.'

For the next ten minutes Greg and Ralph tore the room apart but the red stone was nowhere to be found.

'It was a bit of a long shot to think he'd leave it lying around in his room,' Greg said.

'I know,' Ralph said, slumping down on the bed.

Greg flopped down on the bed next to his brother and for a moment they both sat in silence, the only sound that of their breathing.

That and a very faint creak from one of the floorboards in the hallway.

So faint, in fact, it was as if someone was trying to make their way along the hall without being heard. Greg and Ralph looked at each other and then the door. There it was again. The slightest of creaks and then, only just audible: a whispered curse.

Slowly, very slowly, Greg and Ralph stood up from the bed, flinching each time a spring boinged. Greg picked up the candlestick and tiptoed over to the wardrobe, carefully shutting the doors once inside. Ralph moved to behind the door. Although they couldn't see each other, at the sound of the door handle turning, both Greg and Ralph held their breath.

***

Albert Fotheringhamshire cursed again under his breath as the door handle turned. It seemed to him as if this building was full of noises. He knew he was supposed to be quiet, like a ghost in the wind, but stealth had never been his forte. He wasn't exactly sure what his forte was but, as this was his first, proper job, he guessed he'd find out.

When he'd told his parents he intended to be a spy, they'd laughed. Laughed so hard in fact that his dad had suffered a stroke and later died. This wasn't his fault, even though his mother clearly blamed him.

Albert knew in his heart of hearts, one day, she'd start talking to him again. He'd thought it would be when he told her he was going to graduate from the Academy, but all she'd done is up his board, now he would be earning, and about time too.

His sister had said he would make the worst spy ever, but what did she know? After seventeen attempts at his final exam and fifty-two failed final practical tests, he'd eventually proved her wrong.

So here he was on his first official mission. He didn't care that no one else at HQ had volunteered for this mission; it was their loss as far as he was concerned. All he needed to do was get a few, nice easy missions under his belt and then he could call himself experienced. But he mustn't get ahead of himself. Rule number one: get in, get out and if possible, kill someone.

Albert didn't fancy killing anyone, not just yet, he wasn't sure he had the stomach for it, but should the opportunity arise, he'd certainly had more training than most.

It seemed like a straightforward mission but then Rule number 14 said: there are no easy missions apart from those which are finished.

Albert braced himself. This was a private contract, not worth much in itself, but it could lead to bigger things. Everyone knew that the private sector was where the big bucks were. His brief was simple: get in, subdue the individual, question him and find out if he really did have a valuable stone. It should be pretty straightforward, although the subduing part sounded tricky, but he had enough weaponry located about his person to start a small war, and he was only dealing with a travelling hay salesman after all.

**

The door swung open and in a move halfway between a forward roll and a cartwheel, a small man dressed only in grey entered. 'Ha!' he announced to the room, his hands held up in a karate stance.

Greg tried to peer through the gap in the wardrobe doors but could only make out shapes.

Ralph had seen the man enter but then had to grab hold of the door as it swung towards him and so he was now hidden too.

'Oh,' said the small man.

Greg leant closer to the gap and pushed his eye right up to the crack. Still he could see nothing of any clarity.

Albert Fotheringhamshire looked around the room. It was empty. Or was it? Rule number 33: suspect everything and everyone, including yourself.

'Well I guess there's no one here,' he said in a louder-than-normal voice. 'Suppose I'll be off then...' He pretended to walk out the door by clomping his feet on the spot.

'Ah-ha!' he said as he crouched down to look under the bed. Nothing.

'Oh well,' he said in an even louder voice, 'this time I'll really be off...' and he clomped on the spot again, only this time he made his steps softer and softer.

'Gotcha!' he said as he flung back the door.

Ralph let go of the door just as the little man flung it shut. For a split second, they came face to face. Ralph was surprised by how little like a spy this man looked. Sure, he was wearing all the gear: grey outfit, soft boots, belt with a hundred and one different weapons attached, but if this was the level of killer Keith Smart had sent to get rid of them, then he was insulted.

Albert's eyes shot open wide at the sight of the man behind the door. He'd honestly thought the room was empty and was only going through the motions. Maybe the person behind the door was actually a fellow spy; it wasn't unheard of for two spies to compete for the same job. But no, the man behind the door wasn't a spy. For starters he wasn't wearing the right clothes and he was far too obvious to be a spy. Which meant only one thing: the man behind the door must be some sort of assassin.

Albert froze.

'Boo!' said the man behind the door.

Ralph watched as the little man nearly jumped out of his skin, let out a high-pitched squeak, stumbled backwards, tripped over the corner of the bed and clattered into the wardrobe doors.

Something hit the wardrobe doors hard. Greg was still unsighted but took this as his cue. He leapt out of the wardrobe, candlestick held above his head.

Albert bounced off the wardrobe doors as they flew open. Something hit him from behind, flattening him to the floor. He felt a sharp prick in his right hip and the room started to go blurry. He had just enough time to think that maybe his sister was right.

***

'I think we might have a bit of a problem,' Ralph said.

Greg was sat on the bed, looking down at the candlestick in his hands. 'Ralph, I didn't hit him. I just sort of fell on him. It was dark in the wardrobe, I couldn't see; I thought someone was attacking you.'

Ralph stood up and moved away from the little spy lying on face down on the floor. He walked around the bed, sat down next to his brother and carefully took the candlestick out of his hands.

'Greg,' he said. 'He's dead. I think you just killed a spy.'

'What do you mean, dead? Have you checked his pulse?' Greg said, standing up.

'I have, twice. Nothing.'

Greg sat back down on the bed. 'This kind of complicates things, doesn't it?'

Ralph patted his brother on the back.

'Yes and no.'

'Ralph, someone sent a spy to kill us and now he's dead. I don't think they'll be too happy about that.'

'If you're ticking off points in the minus column then the whole dead spy business goes straight to the top,' Ralph said. 'However, there are a few things which need adding to the positives column.'

'Such as?'

'First of all, we survived. Someone tried to kill us and we're still here,' Ralph said, checking

78

points off on his fingers. 'Secondly, nobody knows it was an accident. I have no idea how he died but it doesn't matter. Word will get around that you don't mess with the Hoffenbach brothers. And last but not least, I get to call you killer.'

'Why do you think he came here?'

'It's obvious, isn't it? Keith Smart hired him. Must've seen us around, known we weren't the type to give up, so he hired someone to follow us and get rid of us.'

'You think?'

'Absolutely.'

Greg stared down at the prone figure lying on the floor.

'So what now?'

'I say we stuff him in the wardrobe. Leave him for Mr Smart to find. Teach him a lesson.'

'Can we do that? It seems a bit undignified. He was just doing his job after all.'

'Which involved killing us!' Ralph said, standing up. He walked over to the body. 'Here, give us a hand. He might only be little but he's all floppy. I can't pick him up on my own.'

***

Keith Smart arrived back at his inn a full hour before the start of Jerry Gushingham's seminar. He'd spent the day getting in touch with a wide variety of people all of whom expressed an interest in helping him sell his red stone. Some even offered to take it away and get it valued but Keith Smart was nobody's fool. The stone had remained on his person right up to a half hour ago when he'd deposited it somewhere very safe. That way, he could afford to have a few drinks tonight and not worry he might misplace it.

As he approached his room, he took his front row ticket for Jerry's seminar out of his pocket. A smile spread across his face. He would be but a few feet away from the great man. Being that close, he'd probably absorb business acumen without even realising. Afterwards, he intended to buy Jerry a drink and see if he could pick up a few secrets.

Approaching his door, Keith fumbled for his key; it was somewhere in his pocket. He managed to grasp it just as he reached number 34. He had to lean in really close to see the numbers but with his nose pressed to the door, he could read them.

One minute the door was there, the next it wasn't. The wood of number 34's door was instantly replaced with a huge bulbous nose. Keith blinked hard, twice. The door had definitely been replaced with a face. Just as he was about to ask what someone was doing in his room, he was yanked inside and thrown onto his bed. The door slammed shut as he hit the bed.

'What the devil–'

'Shut it!' came a voice from behind him.

Keith tried to get up off the bed but instantly two pairs of hands threw him back down. One set tied his hands behind his back, the other his legs together. He was then lifted off the bed and sat on a chair.

Once his heart slowed to a steady thrum and he was able to focus his vision, as best he could, he realised he was in deep trouble. Obviously being accosted within your own room had hinted at this but he now realised it was much, much worse.

His first thought had been that someone who he'd talked to earlier in the day had chosen to pay him a visit and steal his stone (which was another reason he'd hidden it) but he instantly recognised the grey clothing and his heart sank.

'You're spies,' Keith said.

The owner of the bulbous nose moved closer, his arms folded across his chest.

'We can neither confirm nor deny such a statement,' he said with a grin.

Keith didn't like the grin. Something deep in the pit of his stomach did a little flip when it saw the grin.

The owner of the grin's two accomplices had positioned themselves over by the door.

'You realise I'm a reputable businessman,' Keith said. 'I think there's been some kind of misunderstanding.'

'You know something, sir; you wouldn't believe the amount of times I've heard that said.'

'Well it's true!' Keith said. 'I'm here to sell my hay at the market tomorrow. That and listen to Jerry Gushingham's talk this evening.'

'Is that so?' The grin was gone. He nodded once to one of the men by the door who moved so quietly across the room it was as if he glided. The spy with the large nose turned the chair Keith was sat on around to face the wardrobe.

'Tell me then, Mr Smart. How do you explain this?!'

The silent man pulled open the doors to the wardrobe and stepped back. The thing in the pit of Keith's stomach started doing somersaults.

Somehow, some way, there was a small man in grey hanging in his wardrobe. He'd been hung up with a coat hanger through the back of his clothes as if someone had hung up an outfit that just happened to contain a man.

The silent man prodded the man hanging in the wardrobe who slowly rotated around to face Keith.

The spy with the large nose bent down so his mouth was an inch from Keith's ear.

'As you can see, he's dead,' he said in a low whisper. He picked up the chair Keith was sat on as if it weighed nothing and slammed him down right in front of the wardrobe.

'Now then, Mr Smart. If you try to tell me that you don't know how this happened, or that he was like that when you rented the room or even that you sent your grey outfit to the cleaners and he came back with it, then I'm afraid I'm going to have to cut your fingers off.'

'But I—'

'Think before you speak, Mr Smart. The gentlemen in your wardrobe was, let's just say, a member of our club. He hadn't been in our club very long and quite clearly, he wasn't very good at being in our club, but nonetheless he was, until very recently, in our club. People in our club don't like it when members of our club are...' the nose bent even closer so his lips brushed Keith's ear and spoke very slowly, each word controlled, 'killed and then hung in a bleeding wardrobe!'

'I honestly don't know how this happened,' Keith said. 'I've never seen him before in my life. Honest.'

The Nose stood up. 'Fair enough, Mr Smart, fair enough.'

The room was silent for a moment. Nobody moved, or at least that's what Keith thought. He was about to say something when he heard the slightest rustle of clothing and then the man who'd been stood by the door said, 'Don't worry, Mr Smart. This'll only sting a bit,' as he jabbed a needle into Keith's neck.

Chapter 9
A Leap of Faith

Greg and Ralph did the only sensible thing they could do after leaving The Flying Dishcloth: they went to the pub.

The Halfway Barrel was just as famous as The Hairy Apple, but for very different reasons.

It was a proper pub. Named accordingly, it was located halfway between the gatehouses of Lower and Middle Calver on the King's Pass and had been in business for as long as people had lived in Calver. Whilst many of the businesses along King's Pass looked to accommodate those who came to Calver either for business or pleasure (or if you strayed into The Handmaiden's Drawers, both), The Halfway Barrel remained steadfast in its principles.

It was a place which served beer. Nothing more, nothing less. If you wanted music, go somewhere else. Food? No chance, it slowed down the drinking.

There were no 'artefacts' on the wall, no paintings to give the pub an identity and certainly no staff who greeted the patrons with a smile and a 'how are you doing today?'

If, however, you wanted somewhere to sit and enjoy some of the best beer in the Kingdom, then

The Halfway Barrel was the place to go. The owner, Eddie Prince, liked it this way. He'd owned the Barrel since his father had died, over forty years ago, and his son would own it after him. They poured the beer, threw out those who couldn't drink anymore and took money from those who could. It was a simple recipe, but the best ones usually are.

Greg and Ralph made a point of visiting The Barrel every time they came to the market and after the events at The Flying Dishcloth, it seemed like a good idea to continue the tradition.

They pulled open the front door and stepped into a fog. Smoke clung to the ceiling in great billowing clouds meaning that the top half of the room remained continuously hidden.

The conversation stopped as everyone in the pub looked at the newcomers.

'Two mugs of Hardstaff, please,' Ralph said to the barman.

The conversations resumed. Greg and Ralph got their beer, paid and found a seat in one of The Barrel's many alcoves. Even though it was midday, the pub was dark, due to the total lack of windows. Each table had a candle lit, the candle itself stuck in a beer mug. That was about as fancy as the interior design in the Barrel got.

Greg took a large pull of beer and sat back, his shoulders relaxing.

'I'd forgotten how good the beer is here.'

Ralph slurped down half of his mug, let out a satisfying belch and sat back too.

'How could you forget? Only place in the Kingdom you can get a decent pint of Hardstaff. Beautiful stuff.' He took another swig.

'Steady on,' Greg said. 'Don't get too carried away; we've got a lot to sort out.'

'You worry too much,' Ralph said, already a very slight slur to his words.

'Ralph, we both know you can't handle your ale.'

'That's not true!'

'Last summer when we sampled Reg Argenold's cider you made a right prat out of yourself.'

'I don't remember that.'

'Of course you don't, that's the point, and it's a good thing too. All I'm saying is, his chicken still walks funny.'

'All right, all right,' Ralph said putting his mug down on the table. 'Let's talk.'

'Well,' Greg said, leaning in closer. 'We've got no red stone, we've not found Keith Smart and we've managed to kill someone.'

'Like a man with a prostate problem, that's a lot of we's. However, we're in this together, so I'm prepared to overlook the fact that it was you who Keith stole the stone from and also you who killed a man not an hour ago.'

'Ralph. You took the stone in the first place. Without you doing that, we'd still be at home, with the stone!' Greg said exasperatedly.

'All right, all right,' Ralph said again, looking around. 'Keep your voice down, would you? Look, let's just say we both made mistakes and leave it at that. We need to deal with the here and now and get our stone back.'

'Maybe I can help you with that,' said a voice to their left, causing Greg and Ralph to jump. 'Sorry for the intrusion; my name's Art Rosebud. Most folks call me Bud, though.'

Art 'Bud' Rosebud extended a long, sinewy arm. He shook first Greg's and then Ralph's hands before folding himself into a chair next to them.

'Once again,' Bud said, smiling, 'I duly apologise for the interruption but I'm afraid I couldn't help overhearing what you were discussing and I've a feeling I may be able to help.' He smiled even wider, leant back in his chair and sailed one leg over the other.

'Erm, I very much doubt that,' Ralph said turning to Greg.

'Oh, I don't know,' Bud said, picking a piece of fluff from his jacket. 'A lot of people seem to think I'm pretty good at finding things.'

'Is that so?' Ralph said. 'Well I'm sure that makes you really useful in a game of hide and seek but we're fine. Thank you.'

Ralph turned his body to try and block their visitor from his vision.

'How about you, Sir?' Bud said to Greg. 'You of the same opinion as your brother here?'

'It's not that we mean to be rude,' Greg said. 'It's just that we don't really need any help. You see, we're a couple of farmers here for the market tomorrow, that's all. But thank you for your offer of help.'

'Not a problem, gentlemen,' Bud said, standing. 'It was a pleasure to meet you both, I hope you enjoy the market tomorrow and I'll bid you a good day.'

'Goodbye,' Ralph said, shaking his head.

'If you have a change of heart,' Bud said as he pushed the chair back up to the table, 'you let me know. I'll be around.'

'Goodbye,' Ralph said again.

Once Bud had left, Ralph and Greg decided to leave too. The idea of sitting in such a busy place discussing the red stone now struck them as a stupid idea.

'So, what now?' Ralph asked as they stepped out onto the street.

'We go back to The Flying Dishcloth,' Greg said.

'That's a splendid idea. You planning on bumping someone else off?'

'I don't mean go inside. Look, Keith's got to come back at some point, so, we find a spot outside where we can wait and then when he turns up, we can have a word.'

'Actually, that's not a bad idea. I've got a few questions I'd like to ask Mr Smart myself.

Starting with, "Why did you send someone to kill us?" and ending with, "Where would you like your testicles posting to Mole-man?"'

***

Greg and Ralph headed back down the King's Pass. The street was becoming busier as traders from the three corners of the Kingdom arrived in town, ready for the market.

'Tell you something,' Ralph said as they passed F. Chesterton & Daughters, 'I could go for another one of their pastries, they're certainly moreish.'

'Me too,' Greg said. 'Maybe later though. I want to try and catch Keith Smart.'

'Yeah, fair enough,' Ralph said, looking longingly at the pastries on display.

As they approached The Flying Dishcloth, they crossed the road to the other side and fell back amongst the people wandering along, gazing in the shop windows.

They came to a stop outside a sweet shop. Young children stood in a queue waiting to enter, their parents holding their hands, trying desperately hard to put the thoughts to the back of their minds about what would happen when their children consumed the sweets and the sugar kicked in.

Greg and Ralph pretended to peer in through the window.

'Can you see anything?' Greg said.

'They've got those apple ones I like.'

'No, you mug. In the reflection. The Flying Dishcloth behind us.'

'Oh, that. Nothing out of the ordinary. People going in, people coming out. Someone just fell out of a window.'

Greg and Ralph whirled around and were met with the dull thud of flesh on cobblestones.

What an odd sound, Greg thought.

He didn't know what he'd been expecting as he'd never witnessed someone hitting the floor from a great height before, but he'd certainly expected more squishing.

Someone screamed.

Ralph and Greg ran over to where the body lay. Already there was a crowd starting to gather but they managed to get a good look. Most of him had been smeared outwards from the centre but there was no mistaking the glasses.

'Looks like you found your Mr Smart,' Bud said from behind them, once again making them jump. 'Still think you don't need my help?'

***

Greg, Ralph and Bud were sat on one of the many wooden benches that surrounded the Square. They watched as traders made their way in through the gatehouse and looked for the Foreman of the Market who ticked them off his list, pointed to a space and left them to set up, ready for tomorrow.

Over half of the plots had already been allocated and stalls had been erected awaiting their merchandise, ready for the buyers.

Bud sat, one thin leg draped over the other, a soft smile on his lips as he took in the scene. Greg and Ralph both sat staring at nothing in particular, Ralph with his left leg bouncing up and down, Greg slowly shaking his head.

I just want a new plough.

Bud stood up.

'Pardon me, gentlemen. I'll be back momentarily.'

Greg and Ralph watched as he walked over to a man stood behind a tree on the opposite side of the Square. He was doing a very bad job of trying not to be seen.

Bud spoke to the man for less than a minute, nodded and then slipped something into his hand. The man behind the tree walked away in the opposite direction, very quickly.

Bud lolled back over to the bench but did not sit down. He looked off into the distance, possibly somewhere higher up the Great Hill, folded his arms and let out a long breath.

'Well, gentlemen. It looks like we're going on a little journey. Seems as if your red stone is creating a spot of interest.'

'And if we don't want to go?' Ralph said.

'Oh, you don't have to come with me. Not at all. Did I mention that Mr Smart thought he didn't need my help earlier today?'

Greg and Ralph stood up.

'Lead on, my good man,' Ralph said.

Bud led them onto the King's Pass. They walked past The Flying Dishcloth (Keith Smart had been quickly removed – nothing's worse for business than a flat ex-guest on your doorstep), past F. Chesterton & Daughters and past The Halfway Barrel. Past everything, in fact.

'Have you two gentlemen ever had the pleasure of visiting Middle Calver before?'

'With all due respect,' Greg said, 'we're farmers.'

'That you are,' Bud said, looking the brothers up and down. 'Don't worry, I won't hold that against you.'

The gatehouse at Middle Calver was very different to the one Ralph and Greg had experienced when entering Lower Calver. There were only three entrances, one marked 'trade', the other 'middle', and the final one 'upper'. There were just as many guards, but these were younger and better dressed than those down the hill. The message was clear: the higher you went, the better the service.

Greg and Ralph headed over to the trade entrance and a wide archway in the thick wall.

'Not this time, gents,' Bud said, smiling. 'This time you get to move up in the world,' and he pointed over at the middle entrance.

Greg and Ralph quickly fell in behind Bud. They walked into the archway and were greeted by a smiling guard. Well, he smiled at Bud and successfully managed to hold the smile in place as he looked over Bud's shoulder at the two farmers behind him.

'Good afternoon, Mr Rosebud,' the guard said. 'These two, erm, gentlemen with you?'

He asked the question with a slight turn of his head as if to say, *Please tell me these gentlemen aren't with you.*

'They most certainly are, Charles.'

Charles's shoulder's sagged but he recovered quickly.

'Very well, Mr Rosebud. Will you be heading into the gatehouse comfort suite for refreshments, or...'

Bud laughed.

'Don't worry, Charles. We haven't the time to stop. I'll be taking the gentlemen right on through.'

Charles practically beamed.

'Very good, Mr Rosebud. Oh, and Marge asked me to thank you for the gift. She reckons she hasn't a clue how some lucky lady hasn't snapped you up yet!'

'Well now Charles, you go on and tell her she's most welcome. As for my current lady situation, I do okay,' Bud said and winked.

Charles winked back. 'I bet you do, Mr Rosebud. I bet you do!'

'Come on, gentlemen,' Bud said and he waved Greg and Ralph onwards. They both couldn't help but notice that as Bud passed Charles he slipped something into his hand.

They both nodded and Bud carried on.

Charles's smile vanished as Greg and Ralph approached. 'Don't get used to this, farmer boys,' he said through clenched teeth.

'Whatever you say, Charlie-boy,' Ralph said, whistling as he strolled past.

It took Greg and Ralph a full minute to walk through the gatehouse in Middle Calver's wall; it was so thick. When they emerged, they were still on the King's Pass but this wasn't the same King's Pass which ran through Lower Calver.

Middle Calver was like the Sunday afternoon version of Lower Calver.

Shops, places to eat, places to drink and other businesses still adorned the King's Pass, but, everything was a bit less cluttered and a bit more thought out. The streets — which wound their way from the King's Pass into the various nooks and crannies of Middle Calver — seemed, by comparison, charming enclaves rather than dangerous backstreets. People moved about, continuing their daily business, but at a far more leisurely pace, as if they had the time of day to do so and weren't overly concerned about going anywhere in particular.

The main square in front of the gatehouse contained a lawn, flowerbeds and even a bandstand. Women with children chatted and walked together, whilst men carrying scrolls of paper nodded at each other as they crossed the grass and then turned down side roads.

'Little bit different up here, hey gents?' Bud said, watching Greg and Ralph taking the scene in. 'Down in Lower Calver, people work hard to scrape out a living, but up here in Middle Calver is where the business really gets done. You can work your life down in Lower Calver and not even get close to the kind of money that exists up here.'

Bud led them further up the King's Pass. They reached a road which crossed the King's Pass east and west and took the west road, now walking around the Great Hill rather than up it. Most of the buildings in this section of Middle Calver were houses, each built with the best wood, each a minimum of three floors high and each in its own plot of land.

'You'd be surprised at the rate folks up here build and rebuild. Down there,' he said, pointing in the vague direction of Lower Calver, 'space is a premium. You either build up, or on top of. Up here, the only restriction's money.'

They turned left then right and finally came to a stop in front of a huge four-floor-high house, each level decorated with dark oak beams.

Bud knocked on a gate cut into a twelve-foot-high wooden fence which ran around the property.

A viewing hatch slid open and a face peered out.

'Help you?' the face said.

'You most certainly can,' Bud said, smiling. 'You can open this door right now, before I poke your pickled-egg eyes out.'

'Bud? That you?'

'Course it's me, now open up!'

The viewing hatch slid shut. For the next few seconds, a series of locks, latches and bolts were systematically undone. 'Safety first,' Bud said over his shoulder.

The gate swung open. Bud stepped through the open gate, then turned back to Greg and Ralph.

'Come on in, gentlemen. I've got someone who'd like to meet you.'

Greg and Ralph stepped forward, through the gate and into the house's garden. The gate slammed shut behind them.

Awaiting them were five men of differing sizes but with two things in common. They all held a weapon and they all looked like they knew very well how to use them.

Chapter 10
It's All in the Numbers...

Greg sat very still.

Ralph didn't; his left leg bobbed up and down as he chewed his nails. Neither spoke.

Somewhere, in another room, a large clock ticked.

They'd been left alone in a downstairs room after being searched for goodness knew what out in the garden by the five men with weapons. Actually, only one had done the searching; the other four stood perfectly still, weapons raised. Bud had disappeared once they were inside the house. The men had ushered them into the room they were currently in, told them to sit down and left.

Greg looked around the room. It was the same size as his entire farmhouse. He and Ralph were sat on small wooden chairs over by one wall. In the centre of the room stood a huge mahogany table with eight chairs around it. On the walls hung different maps of the Kingdom.

Ralph crossed his legs to prevent them jittering.

'Hey, Greg,' Ralph said in a whisper. 'Who d'you reckon we're here to see? Me, I think it's got to be some high ranking officer in the King's Guard. What about you?'

'The five men who met us in the garden didn't look too much like they'd belong in the King's Guard.'

Ralph shook his head, uncrossed and then re-crossed his legs.

'Of course not. The King's Guard don't do security detail for anyone other than the King. No, this officer must be so important; he's got his own private security.'

'At this moment, Ralph, after the day we've had so far, I guess anything's possible.'

Ralph nodded and continued staring around the room.

'You nervous, Greg?'

'Yeah. You?'

Before Ralph had a chance to answer, one of the men from the garden opened the door and Bud stepped in, still smiling.

'My sincere apologies for keeping you waiting, gentlemen.'

Ralph was up like a shot. 'Bud, what's going on? Who lives here? It's an officer in the King's Guard, isn't it? That's what I told Greg. So, who is it?'

Bud held his arms up in front of himself.

'Whoa there, Nelly! All will be revealed. I've come to take you to the owner of this fine property. Follow me, boys.'

Bud turned and walked out of the room with Ralph close behind him. Greg stood up and followed. The man from the garden who'd opened the door for Bud closed it and then followed Greg.

They walked across the front hall, past a grand, sweeping staircase and came to a stop at a closed door. Bud knocked and a voice from within told him to enter. He did and beckoned Greg and Ralph to do the same.

Once inside, the door was closed behind them and Greg and Ralph were left staring at the largest collection of books they'd ever seen (which, to be fair, up to that point, was only three).

One wall, the one to their left, contained a window out onto the garden. The rest were covered from floor to ceiling in shelves stacked with books. Each shelf was arranged meticulously so that the books seemed almost a part of the walls. The room itself had been extended upwards to accommodate more books. At the height the old ceiling would've been ran a rail circumventing the three walls upon which was attached a thick wooden ladder on wheels.

Under the window was a cow's leather sofa, which itself was sat on a rug made from the hide of an animal. The rug covered most of the floor and led to a cherry wood desk, behind which sat a man reading a book. In front of the desk were two chairs.

Greg studied the man reading the book. He was leaning back in his chair, feet up on the desk, his brow wrinkled in concentration. His grey hair was cut short, and he kept a short beard too, just long enough to be fashionable.

The man reading the book closed it, sighed and placed it carefully on his desk. Greg could see that it looked almost new. The man seemed to notice for the first time that he wasn't alone.A smile lit up his face and he stood. 'Please, sit.'

He gestured to the two seats in front of his desk as he collected his book and turned to find its spot on a shelf behind him.

Greg and Ralph did as they were told.

'Welcome to my humble abode, boys,' the man said, his voice thick with an accent. 'My name is Augustus Malvern.' He turned to face them. 'I'm also known as 'The Collector', but you may call me either Gus, or if you're not ready for such familiarity, Mr Malvern.'

Augustus Malvern sat back down in his chair. He laced together his long-fingered hands and leant forward, elbows on his desk.

'What do you think of my study?'

'It's very impressive,' Greg said.

'That it is, son. That it is. There are books in here that cost more than you'll ever make as a farmer in your entire life. Or maybe that should be, *would've* made in your entire life until you stumbled across that red stone of yours.'

It didn't come as a surprise to Greg that Mr Augustus Malvern knew about the red stone. Bud already knew a fair deal so it stood to reason that the owner of the house he'd brought them to would too.

Apparently, though, it came as a surprise to Ralph. It was either that or he was simply unaccustomed to keeping his mouth shut for such a lengthy period of time.

'How did you know about our red stone?'

Augustus Malvern turned his attention to Ralph, seemingly pleased someone had given him a reason to explain himself.

'Come now, boys,' he said, leaning back in his chair, lacing his fingers behind his head. 'I'm a businessman, just like your associate...' Augustus Malvern sat forward and consulted the papers on his desk. 'Your associate, Mr Smart.'

'Now hang on,' Ralph said. 'Mr Smart isn't, well, wasn't is probably the correct term, he wasn't our associate.'

'I should think not!' Augustus Malvern said, eyes wide. 'If that's how you boys treat associates, then goodness knows how you'll treat a business partner.'

At this point it seemed Ralph's mouth had dried up. He sat with a quizzical frown on his face as he tried to read between the lines of the last statement.

Greg didn't need to. He sat forwards and looked directly into the eyes of his host. 'Mr Malvern. I would introduce myself, but you seem the sort of person who never enters a conversation at a disadvantage. I wouldn't ever claim you were wrong but it does seem you've been given some false information. We didn't know Keith Smart before he gave us a lift to the market on his cart. He's certainly wasn't an associate of ours. You said it yourself: we're farmers. We grow things, then we sell them. Simple as that. The other day, I did find a red stone that might be worth some money but all I'm looking to do is sell it so I can replace my plough which, unfortunately means my brother and I just aren't looking for a business partner.'

'Although you'd be a great one,' Ralph nodded.

Augustus Malvern nodded his head in return.

'You said they were good, Rosebud.'

'Never judge a book by its cover, Mr M.,' Bud said from the back of the room.

'Okay boys,' Augustus Malvern said. 'Here's what we'll do. We'll cut through all the talk and get right to the point. How's that suit you?'

'I really don't think there's any need.' Greg said.

'There's a need if I flaming well say there is!' Augustus Malvern said, slamming his hands down on the desk. Ralph jumped, but Greg kept looking into his eyes. There was something in there, something barely contained. Something which frightened Greg very much.

Greg realised what was bothering him about the house. It wasn't the obvious show of money, nor the things wealth brought. It was the oppressive feeling of power. Power over things, yes, but more importantly, power over people.

102

Greg didn't want to spend a second longer in this house than he had to. He just had to think of a way to get out.

He held his hands up in mock surrender.

'Okay, Gus. You got us.'

'He has?' Ralph said, giving his brother the 'who are you and what have you done with my sensible brother?' look.

'Yeah, he has. You'll understand, Gus, that we had to be careful. Play our cards close to our chests and all that. Make sure we were dealing with the right kind of people. We made the mistake of choosing to work with people who didn't share the same vision as us; people like Mr Smart and that didn't end too well. So, cut to the chase, Gus.'

Augustus Malvern sat, stone-faced, only his eyes moving from Greg to Ralph and then back again. Then he leant back and roared with laughter.

'I like you two!' he said, slapping the desk. 'Rosebud, I like these two. They've got balls, I'll give them that much!'

Ralph leant over to Greg. 'Either you've suddenly become delirious after sniffing too much book dust,' he whispered, 'or that bonk on the head back on the farm is kicking back in. What the hell are you doing?'

'Thinking on my feet,' Greg whispered back. 'If it works we'll be out of here in five minutes.'

'And if it doesn't work?'

'I think some of these books are covered in human skin.'

Augustus Malvern walked around to the front of his desk and perched on its edge.

'Okay boys, you've got my attention. Here's how we'll proceed: I know for a stone-cold fact that your red stone is worth a fair bit of money. You see, your friend Mr Smart didn't really live up to his name. As soon as he arrived in town, he started to make enquiries. Whilst I'm still in the process of finding out exactly who he spoke to, word on the street is that your red stone is the real deal and seeing as I'm being on the up and up with you, I won't bother with any more waffle. Here's how it works. I'll say a number and if it's acceptable to you, we're good to go. If not, then we'll barter till we reach an amicable arrangement. Does that sound good?'

'Well, Gus, my boy,' Greg said, feigning boredom. 'That depends on the level of your offer.'

Augustus Malvern laughed and looked at Bud, still stood by the window, although he didn't look as relaxed as before. 'You believe these guys, Rosebud? Talking to me like that, in my own house. These guys got some intestinal fortitude. I like it. Reminds me of the old days.'

'They got a lot of something, Mr M.'

'Okay, boys,' Augustus Malvern said, turning his attention back to them. 'How does ten sound?'

'Twenty,' Ralph said before Greg could answer.

'Fifteen,' Augustus countered.

'Seventeen and it's a done deal,' Ralph said.

'Boys, I like your style, it's a deal!'

Augustus Malvern shook Ralph's hand and then Greg's.

'So, you'll toddle off and when we next meet, you'll bring me the red stone. Rosebud, see these gentlemen out, would you?'

Their business finished, Augustus Malvern sat back down behind his desk and selected another book from the shelf. By the time Ralph and Greg had made it to the door to his study he was already reclined and lost in the text.

***

As Bud closed the study door behind them, Ralph let out a huge sigh and clapped his brother on the back.

'Phew! That was a bit intense, wasn't it? But we got through it, didn't we? The old Hoffenbach brothers, doing what they do best. Kicking ass and taking names!' He held his hand up for a high five but quickly brought it back down again when he saw Greg's face.

'What in the blue hells did you do?' Greg asked.

'What do you mean, what did I do? I'll admit it took me a while to get up to speed in there, old Gus is a little intimidating, but I came through in the end.'

'Came through? *Came through!* You complete berk!'

'What are you talking about, Greg? You set it up and I clinched the deal!'

Greg looked at the space between his feet, took in a deep breath and counted to ten. He let it out very slowly. 'Ralph. What exactly do you think just happened in there?'

'Well, it's obvious, isn't it? You pretended to have the red stone and when the boss man wanted to talk numbers, I — being the more astute member of the family — took over.'

'When you took over, what numbers did you think you were discussing?'

'Days, of course. Don't you get it? I bought us seventeen and a half days to find the red stone.'

'Oh, you're dead,' Bud said, appearing behind them.

***

After Greg and Bud had managed to explain to Ralph that it was money numbers not days numbers, things moved along quickly. Ralph quickly fainted.

Between them, they managed to get him stood up again.

'Why didn't you stop me?' Ralph asked.

'You didn't exactly leave much room for interruption, Ralph.'

'So, he's going to pay us seventeen gold coins, for the red stone?'

'No,' Bud said. 'He's going to pay you seventeen *thousand* gold coins.'

Ralph's legs wobbled.

'For a stone I'm pretty sure you don't have. Which means you're in a whole heap of trouble.'

'How long have we got?' Greg said.

'Until Mr M. gets bored of waiting for his stone. Which will probably be tomorrow night; he's not the most patient of men.'

Greg had to reach over and grab Ralph before he fell over. His face had completely drained of colour.

'Gregory,' Ralph said, clinging on to his brother, 'what did you let me do?'

Upstairs there was the sound of a door opening and then closing.

'We should go,' Bud said, looking at the top of the staircase. 'Sounds like Mrs M. just got up. We don't want to be around when she comes downstairs.'

Bud led them to the door, although Greg had to help Ralph. They made their way out into the garden and then back onto the streets of Middle Calver.

'Right, suppose I should escort you two gentlemen back to Lower Calver,' Bud said.

Greg grabbed Bud by the arm.

'Before we take one step further, I want to know who you just got us involved with.'

Ralph seemed to perk up.

'Yeah,' he said, 'you're the one who brought us up here to meet with your *Mr M.* You set this thing up.'

'Hold on now, gentlemen,' Bud said. 'It's not what you think.'

'Why don't you tell us what we should think then?' Greg said.

'Listen, we'll head on back to Lower Calver, I know a place we can talk.'

Chapter 11
A Plan, of Sorts

Greg and Ralph had no idea where they were. They knew in general terms: on one of the many backstreets linked to the King's Pass in Lower Calver. But once they'd followed Bud down a dark passageway between a tobacconist's and a funeral parlour, they'd immediately lost their bearings.

The sun had instantly disappeared as the buildings on either side hung over them like the interlocking branches of a tree. The temperature dropped too, giving the shadowed aisles the feel of a damp February morning. As they stumbled onwards, Greg tried to peer in through the windows of the passing buildings but almost all were covered with a thick layer of grime and he suspected most had been purposely covered so.

Occasionally, they heard a noise, often behind them but neither Greg nor Ralph turned to see. They simply quickened their pace. They both knew they couldn't lose sight of Bud who turned left and right, seemingly at random yet his pace never slowed.

One more right turn, down an alley no wider than one man could walk, and then Bud stopped. He'd reached a dead end. The grey bricks on either side of them curved round at the end of the alley in a filth-laden embrace.

'You enjoying the backstreets, gentlemen?' Bud said.

'It's got a certain element of charm,' Greg said.

'Yeah, if ominous is a charm,' Ralph added.

'You gentlemen are lucky; not many out-of-towners get to experience the backstreets.'

'I wouldn't plan on setting up a tour,' Ralph said.

'Maybe not,' Bud said, chuckling. 'Now, if you'll just take a step back, gentlemen...'

Greg and Ralph did as they were told and stepped back. Once they'd moved, Bud stamped on the floor, three times in quick succession.

'Cockroaches?' Ralph said.

Bud stamped again, this time twice, then stepped over to where Greg and Ralph stood. From where he'd been stamping came the sound of metal grinding on metal. The cobblestone floor slowly rotated anticlockwise as the grinding sound intensified. With an almighty crunch, a large, round portion of the floor lifted up and slid to the side. Out of the hole in the ground a head slowly rose up.

It was the kind of head which looked as if it had been trapped in a vice: long, pointed features on a head which was longer than it was wide.

'What do you want?' the person in the hole said.

'It's me, Marvin. Let me in,' Bud said.

'Why should I let you in? This is a secure location, cleverly designed to keep out those who are unwanted. We are completely self-contained and as such, incredibly secure,' Marvin said.

'Because,' Bud said, 'whilst being underground provides you with a level of security, you're now stood with your head poking out of a hole at street level, a fundamental flaw in your security procedure. Therefore, if you don't step aside, I'm going to kick you in the teeth.'

'Fair enough,' Marvin said, shrugging. 'It was worth a try. Come on down.'

Marvin's head disappeared. Bud walked towards the hole, stepped in and bit by bit also disappeared.

Ralph looked at Greg.

'Suppose this trip couldn't get any weirder, so why not follow someone we only just met today down a hole in the backstreets of Lower Calver?'

Greg just shrugged and followed Bud.

'That was sarcasm, you know!' Ralph said to no one in particular.

***

The hole in the street turned out to be a spiral staircase. Once Greg and Ralph had followed Bud down, Marvin pushed past them, ran back up the stairs and secured the lid over the hole.

111

Greg wasn't sure what he'd expected, maybe some dark and dank cavern or possibly a disused basement but he certainly wasn't ready for what he saw.

In fact, that he could see was the first surprise.

They were stood in a long passageway, lit every few feet by glowing instruments in metal casings which were attached to the passageway's brick walls. At the end of the passageway, Greg could just make out the dim flicker of more light.

'Come on then,' Marvin said, pushing back past them as if important and earth shattering business awaited him at the end of the passage. 'You'd better follow me. Just be warned, don't touch anything. I cannot be held responsible for personal injuries. Again.' Marvin loped off down the passageway with Bud not far behind.

'You know, he's probably a serial killer,' Ralph said.

Greg ignored his brother and looked at the lights.

'I wonder what makes these—'

'If you're wondering about the lights,' Marvin shouted without turning or slowing his pace, 'it's a chemical reaction. Involves lots of things mixed together including pigeon poo, earth from the swamps and some other bits you wouldn't understand.'

'Maybe not a serial killer,' Ralph said. 'Maybe more like a mad scientist. Prepare to be lobotomised, Greg.'

By the time Greg and Ralph got to the end of the passageway, Marvin and Bud had disappeared into a pool of light.

'Hang on,' Marvin said from somewhere within the blinding light. 'Let me just turn this down.'

There was a click, a fizz and shortly thereafter a bang and the bright light dimmed to the level of the lights in the passageway, revealing a room which would take a lifetime to explore. Granted it was pretty big, but its size was hard to gauge due to the inordinate amount of *things* within it.

Looking around, Greg realised that unless its owner knew exactly where everything was located, then the simple task of making a cup of tea could take anything up to four weeks, the first two of which would be consumed with finding the kettle.

In the centre of the room stood five circular wooden tables, pushed together, all covered with different equipment. On one, a series of tubes connected bubbling glass containers, some with coloured liquid in them, others with unidentifiable parts of animals in them and still others with what looked like a combination of the two. On the table next to it, strewn in all directions, were thousands of pieces of clocks. It looked as though an army of suicide bomber clocks had marched onto the table and simultaneously exploded covering the table with springs, cogs and bits of wire.

Each of the five tables contained its own oddity.

This theme was continued throughout the rest of the room. Tables were pushed up against walls with bookcases crudely nailed on top of them, each shelf overflowing with more *things*.

Every available space on the floor was also used to pile up objects with only a single, one-person-wide pathway leading through to the various areas of the room. From the room itself, a series of smaller passageways led out and on into darkness as these passageways were not lit.

'You certainly have a lot of things,' Greg said, unable to do anything but state the obvious.

'Not *things*,' Marvin said with a grimace. 'Everything you see in here has a use. Therefore it is classified as *equipment*.'

Ralph picked up what looked like a shrivelled baby's arm.

'So, you're telling me that this *thing* is equipment?'

'Well actually, not that. I'm not sure why I thought it would be a good idea to preserve my faeces.'

Ralph dropped the poo onto the table.

'Good grief man, what did you have to eat that day?'

'That's quite irrelevant,' Marvin said, hunching down so he could reach under one of the tables. After some serious scrabbling around and dragging out various parts of a push-bike, he eventually pulled out three stools. Of the sitting variety.

Bud took them and placed them around the edge of the furthest of the five tables. It appeared that he'd chosen this one as it had the least amount of equipment on, around or under it. He motioned for Greg and Ralph to sit with him.

'What about you, Prof? You joining us?' Ralph asked.

Marvin shot Ralph a look of pure disdain.

'Don't call me that.' His voice came out in barely a whisper but there was more force in those words than if he'd shouted them from the top of his lungs.

'Why don't you two hurry up and sit with me,' Bud said, patting the stools, but keeping his eyes firmly fixed on Marvin. 'I'm sure our new friend Ralph meant nothing by it, Marvin. Slip of the tongue.'

Marvin kept his eyes on Ralph for a moment longer, enough for Greg to see the ferocity in his stare and then he abruptly turned and marched off down a path heavily walled on either side with equipment and then disappeared down one of the many unlit passageways. All three could hear him chuntering to himself as he echoed further and further away.

'What was that about?' Greg said, taking the stool nearest to Bud.

'It's a long story,' Bud said. 'When I've got more time, I'll tell you. All you need to know right now is that Marvin is a special kind of guy. Don't let all of this,' Bud waved his arms to encompass the whole room, 'fool you. There's no one smarter than Marvin in the entire Kingdom. Of that I'm certain.'

'Just don't call him Prof,' Ralph said.

'Exactly.'

Greg glanced around the room. As a farmer through and through, he'd never really met anyone other than other farmers. Some were of course pretty smart themselves and he was no slouch in the brains department, but Marvin seemed like a totally different species. Sat surrounded by all these things, most of which he'd never seen before in his life, under the streets of Lower Calver, with a man he'd known less than twelve hours; it was a long way from home, that was for sure. All of this for a broken plough.

He'd certainly have a few stories to entertain Mollie.

One of the clocks on the table behind him bonged twice, tried for a third but a spring shot out across the room and then all the clock could manage was a somewhat lacklustre three more dinks.

'Ralph, it's six. We've got to be back at the First Inn for seven. Otherwise we'll be sleeping on the streets.'

116

'How time flies when you have no idea what's happening,' Ralph said and turned to face Bud. 'Okay, Mr Rosebud. Start talking.'

Bud's shoulders sagged. For the first time since they'd met him, his smooth style disappeared.

'I brought you here,' he said, 'so I could guarantee that no one else would be able to hear what I've got to tell you.'

'What about Marvin?' Greg asked.

'Don't worry about Marvin. He kind of exists on a whole different plane to everyone else. He considers normal conversation a waste of time.'

'Yeah, I can see that,' said Ralph. 'On you go.'

'I'm going to make this as brief as I can, but I need to tell you some things, so please don't question or interrupt me. It's all relevant to where you're at right now.'

Ralph started to say something, but Bud shook his head.

'Like they say, questions at the end. I don't doubt you'll have a few, but please, for the first time in a long time, Ralph: keep your mouth shut.

'Okay, here goes. I was born and raised on the streets of Lower Calver. Now, I know plenty of people make statements like that, but they're full of horse shit. I truly was raised on these streets. I have no idea who my parents were, could've been any of about twenty

117

different folk who were kind enough to take me in. My childhood was spent sleeping in different places, anywhere there was food or a bed. I soon realised that to survive, I needed to specialise. Who's going to want to help out some punk kid who eats your food and takes up space on your floor unless you're getting something in return? Well, my return was finding things. Doesn't sound like much, does it? Let me tell you, if you know someone who can get something for you, no matter what that thing is, they're a pretty useful person to know. So, for a small charge – sometimes food, other times a roof over my head and occasionally money – I found things for people. You name it, I could find it. As I grew up, I became so good at finding things, I was able to elevate my status in society. I made myself a bit of money, bought a nice little building right out on King's Pass, moved from the shadows to the light. That's when I met 'The Collector', or Augustus Malvern as you two know him to be. Think about it: one collects, the other finds. A perfect set-up. At first it was pretty straight forward. As you've seen, books are his thing. Everybody's got a thing and books just happen to be his. As fast as I'd find them, he'd want more. And he paid a good price too. Made me a whole pile of cash, which, as a kid from Lower Calver, should've set the alarm bells ringing, but when you've come from nothing, a bunch of money tends to cloud things somewhat. Next thing I know, Mr M. is asking me to move from finding books to finding people. Nothing too strange about that, I'd found plenty of people in the past, the only difference now was a pattern was starting to emerge. I'd find someone for Mr M. and then, a short while later; they'd find themselves dead, if you'll pardon the oxymoronic nature of that statement. I've never really been one to claim I operated hand in hand with the law but there's a big difference between making a profit on the sale of illegal tobacco and helping someone meet their maker. So, I did the only thing I could and I went to see Mr Augustus Malvern. Boys, let me tell you, I'll never forget that meeting. It was the moment I realised what a monumental mistake I'd made and that I was trapped like a fly in a web. I told him I was happy to keep finding things for him but not people. I said I couldn't carry on helping him kill people, it just wasn't my style.'

'What did he say?' Greg said, unable to stop himself interrupting.

Bud managed to smile yet look desperately sad at the same time. 'He said my style was to do as he told me to. He said that he was surprised it had taken me so long to confront him, but then I was just some dumb street punk, raised by the scum of Lower Calver. All of this he said in that quiet whispering voice of his. He said he knew who the people were who had helped to raise me, said he even knew who my real parents were, although I doubt that

119

very much. He said that if I ever came to him like this again, he'd kill everyone who'd ever put a roof over my head or given me food. And you know something? I looked into his eyes, deep into his eyes, and I knew it to be true. Then he smiled at me, put his arm around me and walked me to his door. Told me to keep doing my thing and everything would be fine.'

'Jeez,' was all Ralph could muster.

'Jeez indeed,' Bud said. 'Now here's the bit you're really not going to like. Part of doing my thing is letting Mr M. know when I find something that might interest him. You boys and your stone are something that definitely interests the likes of Mr M. And don't go thinking I could've just kept my mouth shut and not told him, because it doesn't work like that. If he'd found out about you boys and your stone from someone else, he'd have known I was holding out on him.'

'Well, you could've warned us!' Ralph said, standing up. 'Do you realise you pretty much led us into the hands of a... a... whatever the hell he is!'

'A very powerful man is what he is,' said Bud. 'Who's very influential in lots of different places. But that doesn't mean he's untouchable.'

Ralph plopped back down onto his stool and kicked out at ball of rags at his feet. It sailed across the dimly lit room and crashed into a bookcase. A few items fell off and landed on the floor. Once the dust had settled, it wasn't at all clear that anything had actually moved.

Bud waited. He'd expected Ralph to react in this way, the little he knew about him, but it was Greg he watched. A farmer he may be, but Bud knew smart when he saw it.

Right on cue, Greg smiled. 'Oh, I don't think so,' he said, shaking his head.

'What?' Ralph said.

'Way I see it,' Bud said, 'you don't really have much choice. I am sorry for that, by the way.'

'What?!' Ralph said, turning to Bud.

'Look, I'm sorry too, Bud,' Greg said. 'I wouldn't trade places with you for one minute, but there's no way it's going to happen.'

'No way what's going to happen?' Ralph said, turning back to his brother.

'It wouldn't take much,' Bud said. 'I've got most of the details already worked out, all you'd need to do is to play along.'

'Play along with what?' Ralph said.

'Bud, there's a difference between playing along and being dead. One is active, the other is terminally passive.'

'Right!' Ralph roared. 'If someone doesn't tell what in the blue hells is going on and I mean right now, then I'm going to...'

It was at that moment that Marvin returned, his arms full of what looked like suitcases.

'It really is quite simple,' he said, placing the cases on the table in front of the three of them.

'Although when it comes to simplicity, it seems Ralph here is somewhat under-qualified. What your brother and Mr Rosebud here are discussing is whether there's a way to use your red stone to bring about the demise of Mr Augustus Malvern.'

Ralph turned to Bud who smiled at him. Then he turned to Greg who patted the stool next to him.

Ralph sat down.

'Let me get this perfectly straight, so that it's one hundred per cent clear and out there in the open,' Ralph said slowly whilst staring down at the table in front of him. 'You, Bud, who we only just met this morning, want me and my brother to use a stone, which by the way I should remind you we don't have, to somehow take on, outsmart and ruin a wealthy criminal and known murderer, who just happens to be in charge of a vast and villainous faction, in order to release you from his clutches and potentially save the lives of people who may or may not be your parents.'

Bud's smile widened. 'Now you're getting it.'

Chapter 12
A Hard Night's Night

Greg and Ralph returned to The First Inn at two minutes before seven. They'd ran most of the way back, partly because they thought they were going to be late but partly because they didn't like the thought of being on the backstreets of Lower Calver once it got properly dark. Bud had given them precise directions on how to get out (he was going to stay and spend some time with Marvin), but, as Ralph pointed out, bumping into a local on the backstreets of Lower Calver, carrying directions and a map was the quickest way to get dead he could think of.

So they'd run.

Which was probably a good thing as it had meant they couldn't talk.

Ralph had left Marvin's underground whatever-it-was, determined never to speak to Bud again. Greg wasn't so sure.

As they pelted down the cobbled backstreets, Ralph occasionally calling out a left or right turn, Greg couldn't stop thinking about what Bud was asking them to do. Not that they'd hung around long enough to listen to what he wanted them to do, but he would find them later. That is, after all, what he did. And when he did, he would have a plan.

Yet, everything so far had happened so fast, Greg hadn't a clue what they'd say to Bud once they saw him again. Truth be told (as it should on but a few occasions), Greg had no idea what the next five minutes would bring, let alone the next day. It was hard to believe he'd only found the red stone a few days ago.

As they left the cold shadows of the backstreets, Ralph and Greg slowed to a fast walk.

They crossed the King's Pass, just as Ronald Freepepper was finishing his shift. Greg and Ralph tried to look as if they were just wandering past but after dashing out from the backstreets and then scuttling across the road, the impression they gave was that they'd just stolen something.

Without a word, Ronald Freepepper nodded to the brothers, tilted his head to the left slightly and then disappeared down the side of The First Inn.

Greg and Ralph waited a few seconds, each suddenly very interested in the cobbles at their feet and then, after glancing over both shoulders like professional ne'er-do-wells, followed the doorman into the gloom.

'You two cut it a bit fine!' Ronald Freepepper said, loosening his neckerchief.

Ralph leant back against the wall.

'You wouldn't have wanted us hanging around outside, now would you?'

'And what were you doing in the backstreets, or maybe I shouldn't ask!' Ronald Freepepper touched the side of his nose and winked at Ralph.

'You know us, Ron,' Ralph said, touching his nose and returning the wink. 'We get about a bit. We're the kind of individuals who know how to handle ourselves.'

Greg shook his head. It was like being trapped in a very bad play.

'You want to be careful, fellas. Anyone'd think you're a pair of assassins!'

'You got the first three letters right,' Greg said.

'Oh, good one, sir!' Ronald Freepepper pointed at Greg.

Ralph, illusion shattered, leant forward from the wall.

'Okay then, Ron. We're here, as promised. What's the deal?'

Ronald Freepepper brought his finger to his lips in a shushing gesture and waved Greg and Ralph further back into the passageway.

The further back the passage between The First Inn and its adjacent building went, the narrower it got. Ronald Freepepper moved so far into the vice-like darkness that when he finally turned to face them, all three were no more than a nose hair apart.

'Well this is cosy,' Ralph said.

'Has to be, sir. You see, if anyone, how shall I put it, undesirable in nature, should overhear our conversation, then, well the consequences could prove catastrophic!'

'You don't by any chance have a Masters in Understatement, do you?' Greg said.

'Another good one, sir! My, we are the witty one today. Full of wit, you are!'

'Can we just get on with this?' Ralph said. 'I'm starting to feel a little claustrophobic.'

'Sorry, sir. Just needed to impress upon you both the seriousness of the task at hand. Anyway, here's what I'm offering. For the opportunity to spend one night at this fair inn, free of charge, all I need you two to do is to unlock a room at ten in the evening and then lock it again at four in the morning. Two tiny acts of simplicity for a free night's accommodation. How's that sound?'

'Too good to be true,' Ralph and Greg said at the same time.

'Ah-ha!' Ronald Freepepper said, smiling. 'I can very well see that I'm dealing with a couple of sharp ones here!'

'First you tell us that the task at hand is incredibly serious and that something catastrophic will happen if anyone should overhear us talking,' Ralph said.

'Then you tell us all we have to do is something as simple as unlocking and then locking a door,' Greg said.

'You see the very complexity of the situation then boys? On the one hand the task is but a simple one, on the other it is extremely important and on the other it could have catastrophic consequences should it all go wrong.'

'That's three hands,' Ralph said. 'What's so important about unlocking and locking a room?'

'Glad you asked, sir!' Ronald Freepepper said. 'It's not the locking and unlocking per se, it's what'll happen in the room once it is open.'

'I don't like the sound of this,' Greg said.

'Hold on there, sir. Before you make any rash decisions, let me explain, although, due to the sensitive nature—'

'For the love of the Gods, get on with it!' Ralph said.

'Sorry, sir. Right away, sir. Tonight, in the room I require you to unlock, a group of like-minded individuals will converge for a few hours, discuss some matters of business and then part company. These people are in the business of keeping themselves to themselves and wish not to be interrupted. They sought me out as I am a man of many means, and I then sought you gentlemen out.'

Greg was puzzled. 'Why don't you just open up the room yourself? Save all this secrecy and entrusting matters of a delicate nature to two strangers.'

'Actually, yeah! What my brother said,' Ralph said.

'There's the real kicker, sirs! Whist I may be able to provide the room, if I were to turn up to unlock it, especially when I never work nights, well then, that would immediately arouse a level of suspicion I am unwilling to rouse. You see my predicament. These people trust me to make the necessary arrangements yet my hands are tied when attempting to carry them out.'

Greg turned to his brother. 'I don't like this one bit. It's got disaster written all over it, especially the way our day's gone so far.'

'True,' Ralph said, nodding. 'However, it's a room for the night and our alternatives aren't exactly looking good. Most places worth staying in will be full of people ready for the market and those that do have room, well, we probably wouldn't make it through the night anyway. What've we got to lose?'

Whilst Greg pondered the many possible answers to his brother's question, Ralph shook Ronald Freepepper's hand and took the two keys from him.

I just want a new plough, Greg thought to himself as the deal was done.

***

As they walked back up the alley and onto the street, Ronald Freepepper filled Greg and Ralph in on all the details, so by the time he bid them a good night and walked away whistling, they knew exactly what they were expected to do. However, none of the knowing what to do had persuaded

Greg this was a good idea and besides, who walks away whistling? People up to no good, that's who.

Ralph clapped his brother on the shoulder. 'Fear not, oh brother of mine, for I have a plan.'

'Well that's settled me right down. Everything's going to turn out just peachy, so long as Ralph's got a plan.'

Ralph shook his head. 'O ye, of little faith. You should have more confidence in me. If you're not careful, this lack of confidence in my abilities will end up giving me a complex. It's a good job I'm thick-skinned.'

'What's your plan, Ralph?'

'Simple really. We head on into the First Inn. Go on up to—' he pulled the keys out of his jerkin's front pocket, '—up to Room 179. Have a look around, you know, case the joint. Then we head over to—' he looked at the keys again, '—Room 181, where the meeting is. If either of the rooms — or the situation itself — looks in the slightest bit ropey, we head on out of there. By the time Ronald finds out we didn't do as he asked, we'll be long gone.'

'That's actually quite a sensible thing to do.'

'I know. I shocked myself, actually.'

'Just one problem,' Greg said. 'If we don't like the look of Room 179, where are we going to sleep?'

'Now you're just putting up barriers, Greg. One problem at a time. Come on Mr Negative, let's go check out the room.'

***

If Greg and Ralph worked their entire lives and then took the money they'd made, gambled it on a 100-1 shot at the Kingdom races, they still wouldn't have had enough money to afford a room like Room 179 for one night at The First Inn.

The minute they opened the door (very carefully; one encounter with an assassin was enough to instil a healthy level of caution in anyone), they knew they'd be staying the night.

The room itself was huge, nearly five times the size of the room they'd been attacked in at The Flying Dishcloth and it was clearly furnished to the highest standard. In the centre of the room stood an immense four poster bed, with enough room to sleep a large family. Over by the window, which stretched from ceiling to floor, a large table occupied most of one side of the room. Around it, ten thick, wooden chairs stood sentry. The room came with not one but four wardrobes and an exquisitely hand-carved wooden bath which, much to Greg and Ralph's confusion, had been positioned in one corner of the room.

There were three doors leading from the room, upon inspection they discovered they led to a bathroom, a closet and a storage space.

Ralph launched himself onto the bed.

'I see you've bypassed the bit about checking the room out to see if it appears ropey,' Greg said, walking over to the grand table in front of the window.

'You know something, Greg? I think I was born to stay in rooms like this, I really do. Somehow, somewhere down the line, I ended up as a farmer when really I should've been a rich merchant or maybe even someone like our Mr Augustus Malvern.'

'You'd really want to be someone like Augustus Malvern?' Greg said, wandering over to the bath.

'Well no, not really. But I certainly could see myself as a leader of men, you know?'

'Ralph, you struggle leading the chickens from their coop. Why do you think there's a bath in the main room?'

Ralph got up off the bed and walked over to his brother.

'It's what you do isn't it?'

'What, put a bath in the same room as a desk?'

'If you've got money, of course,' Ralph said. 'Listen, it's a hard and fast rule that the more money you've got, the less sense you have. Rich people are always doing stuff like having a bath in full view of anyone else in the room. They don't care; they're rich.'

After Greg and Ralph had finished exploring Room 179, they sat down at one end of the table.

'So here's the plan,' Ralph said. 'We spend the night in Room 179 – let's face it, we'd be mad not to – but at the first sign of something not right, we scarper. Either back out the way we came in, or, if the worst should happen, out the window. Same deal once we check out Room 181.'

Greg wanted to disagree, he really did. He wanted to point out all the possible flaws in Ralph's 'plan'. Like the fact that climbing out the window of a second-floor room in the middle of the night would probably end very badly. He wanted to talk about all the things that had happened to them since they left the farm and how something was bound to happen because no one just gave you the keys to a room like this for nothing. He wanted to talk about the bad feeling he had growing somewhere deep in the pit of his stomach but sometimes all the 'want' in the world can't beat plain old tiredness. It had been a very long day with enough packed into it to last a lifetime and Greg felt tired.

Really, truly, deep in his bones tired.

As he laid his head on his arms on the table in front of him and slowly drifted off, just for an hour mind, he could hear Ralph's voice getting further and further away. Something about checking out the room they had to unlock. Greg knew this to be important but try as he might, he couldn't fight the darkness as it overwhelmed him.

There really is no pleasant way of waking up when you've fallen asleep at a table. Tables were not designed for sleeping at. So, when Greg awoke, it wasn't pleasant. His neck hurt all down one side, both his arms had gone numb and, as he sat up, a globule of drool connected his mouth to the table.

None of this was very useful as he tried to remember exactly where he was. He looked up at the huge window in front of him and saw that it was night. Outside, lamplights glowed softly, casting a faint light into the room. Then he remembered.

Room 179 of the First Inn.

Slowly, and very carefully, he got up. One of his legs threatened to cramp but he shook it off quickly. There was a clock on the table by the side of the bed. Greg hobbled over and in the dim light from outside, could see enough to pick it up. The tiny cogs whirred and whirled inside the glass casing as Greg brought it over to the window. He held it up so he could see the time.

Midnight.

'Ralph!' Greg shouted. 'Room 181! It's midnight, we're late!'

No sooner had the words come from his lips than Greg knew he was talking to an empty room. He lumbered around the room, checking the other, smaller rooms, all the time his body returning to normal. Each room was empty, only confirming what Greg had first thought when he'd called out.

Ralph was gone.

***

Out in the corridor, the way was lit by a series of candles placed at convenient intervals along the walls of The First Inn.

It was entirely likely that Ralph had gone on ahead, unlocked Room 181 as Ronald Freepepper had instructed them to and then headed down to the hotel bar. Or off out to some other place in Lower Calver, living it up. Which was all good and well but when it came time to lock the door, would Ralph remember or, more likely, be in any fit state to do so?

Greg offered a silent prayer to the god of good fortune that his brother would return in good time, so he could properly strangle him. Greg knew what he had to do: check Room 181 was unlocked, then find his idiot brother.

The first-floor corridor was deserted. It was, after all, midnight in a respectable inn. Greg walked as quietly as he could as he made his way to Room 181. The last thing he needed was to wake up one of the other guests, given that he wasn't even a guest himself.

He made note of the room numbers and worked out that Room 181 was going to be the last room before the stairs down to the ground floor. As he rounded the corner, a group of people stepped out from the stairs and one of them knocked on the door to Room 181.

Quickly, Greg turned and darted back around the corner. He realised the last thing he needed wasn't to wake up one of the other guests, it was to be spotted by one of the four large men from The Hairy Apple.

***

Given the choice, Greg would've turned back to Room 179, gone inside, locked the door behind him and tried to forget the last three seconds of his life.

Actually, given the choice, Greg would've happily run all the way home to Mollie and never left his farm ever again.

But – such is life – he wasn't given the choice, because as he stood with his buttocks clenched and his back against the wall, trying to control his breathing, all choice was taken away from him.

He heard the door to Room 181 open, then:

'Evening all,' one of the large men said. Greg recognised the voice. It was the largest of the four, the one who'd been hit in the face with a flying beer tankard at The Hairy Apple. 'Before we set foot in this room, anyone says anything about the state of my face and I'll ram their teeth...'

It went quiet for a moment. Then the same voice burst into fits of laughter.

'Well, well, well,' the largest of the large men said. 'If it isn't Mr Outside now! Seems like we've got a spot of unfinished business, me and you.'

'Now, steady on,' Ralph said. 'Let's not be—'

The end of his sentence was cut off as the door to Room 181 slammed shut.

135

Chapter 13
When in Rome, Leave

To say that Greg acted without thinking is not entirely true. He quite clearly thought, *what on earth am I thinking?* as he knocked on the door to Room 181. He'd decided, quite quickly, that thinking about what to do whilst hiding around a corner with clenched buttocks, wasn't going to help Ralph in the slightest. So, taking a leaf out of his brother's book, he just went for it and hoped everything would turn out alright in the end. It had served Ralph okay for most of his life, so why not?

The door seemed to open by itself until something at Greg's navel made an odd grunting noise.

Greg looked down. The owner of the voice was only about four feet high but at least five feet wide. In fact, he looked like a normal person who'd been squashed downwards. His shoulders filled the doorway so that, unless Greg was prepared to dive headlong over the answerer of the door, he couldn't get in.

'Step aside, short and stumpy, I have pressing business to conduct,' Greg said in a voice he hoped commanded authority.

Short-and-Stumpy did not move. Greg rolled his shoulders.

'Now listen here, junior. My name's Randolph Hoffenhymer. I'm here on behalf of Mr Augustus Malvern. You may have heard of him. He's somewhat influential around these parts. Now if you don't let me in I'll rip your ears off and stuff them up your nose.'

Short-and-Stumpy's left eye twitched; he looked like someone who longed to meet Randolph Hoffenhymer under other circumstances. Someone inside the room told him to step aside and he did, allowing Greg in.

Room 181 was of a similar size to Room 179 but all of the furniture, apart from the huge table, had been pushed to the sides of the room. The table had been moved from under the window and now occupied the centre of the room. Just like in Room 179, there were ten chairs but in Room 181 the ten chairs were occupied. There were other people in Room 181, but they had to make do with perching on the edge of things, like the bed or a chest of drawers. It was clear that the most important people in Room 181 were sat around the desk and what a collection of people it was. The largest of the large men was joined by eight other men, of varying shapes and sizes as well as one woman. Most of the men looked like they'd spent a great deal of time helping to rearrange faces, breaking bones and generally inflicting large amounts of pain. Of the nine men, only two had straight noses. Some were smaller than the large men, others were bigger. All looked like they'd have no problem ending Greg's life and sleeping as sound as a baby afterwards. Only one of the men around the table looked out of place. He wore the finest robes, deep purple in colour, wore his dark hair short and had a scar which ran the length of the left side of his face.

Greg scanned the faces sat at the table as each one turned to face him. Clearly, they hadn't expected to be interrupted further. Each looked at Greg as if he'd just interrupted a pleasant meal with a dirty smell.

'May I ask who you are?' the woman said.

She was sat at the furthest end of the table from where Greg stood, with two enormous men stood at each of her shoulders. She was dressed head to toe in blue, blue high-necked cloak, blue robe underneath, even blue pearls around her long, thin neck.

'You may ask, madam, and I will tell you the same thing I told Old-Vertically-Challenged at the door. I am here on behalf of Mr Augustus Malvern. My name is Randolph Hoffenhymer. I believe you have something in this room that belongs to us.'

A faint smile played across the lips of the woman in blue.

'And what might that be, Mr Randolph Hoffenhymer, who is here on behalf of Mr Augustus Malvern?'

138

'Him,' Greg said, and pointed at Ralph who was sat on the bed, squashed in between two of the four large men from The Hairy Apple.

'Wait a minute!' the largest of the large men said, pushing his chair back from the desk and standing. 'I recognise you! You were at The Hairy Apple too. With him!' the largest of the large men pointed at Ralph.

'No he wasn't!' Ralph said, trying to stand but completely unable as the two large men on either side of him placed their hands on his shoulders.

'Yes, he was!'

'No he wasn't!' Ralph said.

'Yes, I was,' Greg said.

'Sorry, my mistake — yes he was,' Ralph said, sitting back down.

'I was there under orders from Mr Malvern and you four numpties nearly cost me dearly.'

'What?' the largest of the large men said. 'I don't understand?'

'Look,' Greg said. 'I don't have time to explain all of this, especially to someone like you. All you need to know is that he belongs to Mr Malvern, which means I need to take him. So if you don't mind...' Greg walked over to Ralph who once again tried to stand up.

The largest of the large men turned to the woman in blue.

'Let him stand,' she said.

Ralph stood and brushed the shoulders of his jerkin where the two large men had been holding him in place.

'Thank you,' he said. 'Next time, wash your hands; you've left your greasy paw-prints all over my nice clothes. Now, Mr Hoffenhymer, lead on!'

Greg and Ralph started to walk towards the door.

'If you'll just wait for one moment,' the woman in blue said.

Greg and Ralph halted. Both winced. So close.

'Won't you join us for a drink before you leave?' she said. 'We so rarely meet and when we do it's even rarer for us to entertain guests and guests of Mr Malvern, no less.'

Greg looked over towards the door which was now closed. Short and stumpy sidestepped in front of the closed door. He was wearing a look which said, go on, just try it and give me a reason.

Ralph turned on his heel and walked over to the table.

'I never could resist an invitation for a drink with a beautiful woman,' he said, leaning over and picking up the flask of wine.

'Whilst your flattery is amusing, if completely uncalled for, I do find you interesting, Mr...'

'Ralph. Well, not Mr Ralph, that would be silly. My name is Ralph. I think we're at the first names part of the evening, don't you?' Ralph raised a toast to the woman in blue. 'And what might your name be?'

140

The woman in blue smiled. It achieved something Greg thought not possible. It seemed to be both truly beautiful and truly venomous. Of course, Ralph could see none of this.

'My name is Evangeline.'

'What an enchanting name, if I may say so,' Ralph said, walking over to where Evangeline sat. He was well and truly in the moment which meant he was completely oblivious to anything or anyone other than himself and the woman in blue sat at the end of the table. Greg, however, wasn't in the moment. He wanted the moment to be over so that he could spend many more moments somewhere else. As Ralph sauntered down the length of the table, wine glass in hand, all bar one of the men shot him daggers with their eyes. If looks could kill then Ralph would be nothing more than a squidgy pile, staining the rug. Only one of the men looked as amused as Evangeline.

The man with the scar.

His eyes danced in the flickering candlelight and a smile curved at the edge of his lips. He worried Greg more than any of the other eight sat around the table. The other eight were men who met a challenge with a fist. They pounded their way through a problem. They were men who could be out-thought. The man with the scar looked like the type of person who was used to out-thinking people. He looked like someone who gained a lot of pleasure from out-thinking people. And right now, it looked like he was about four steps ahead of everyone else in the room.

'As much as we'd like to stay and indulge in a few social graces,' Greg said, taking a step towards the table, 'we really do have to be going. I've got to get this one to Mr Malvern and I'm sure you know how he hates to be kept waiting.'

'Indeed,' the man with the scar said. His voice had an amused lilt to it and came out in a quiet, clipped manner. 'Just before you whisk Ralph away, would you permit me but one question?'

'Certainly, Mr...' Ralph said. 'I'm sorry, I didn't catch your name.'

The man with the scar smiled once more. 'You're right, you didn't, but you needn't be sorry about it. I didn't give it to you.' He stood up and moved from the table. Or rather Greg thought he must've done because one moment he was sat with the others and the next he was stood. Then he stepped out from behind the table in one, fluid motion and glided over to stand next to Evangeline. 'Now for my question, if you please.'

Ralph, who was finally starting to slip from within the moment, faltered.

'Erm, yes, of course. One question, why not?' He slowly backed away from the end of the table and towards Greg. 'Although you'd better make it quick, my good man, Mr Hoffenhymer here needs me.'

'Oh, I don't doubt that,' the man with the scar said. 'My question is this: what were you doing in this room when Evangeline arrived?'

142

'Doing?' Ralph said.

'Yes, doing. She informed me that she found you hiding behind the curtains over there.' The man with the scar pointed to the large windows where the table had originally been positioned.

Greg made yet another mental note to strangle his brother.

'Well, it's like I told Miss Evangeline: I was cleaning the windows.'

'Cleaning the windows?' the man with the scar said.

'Yes.'

'On the inside?'

'Yes.'

'With no water?'

'Yes.'

'And no cloth?'

'Erm... yes.'

'Come now, Ralph, you really expect all of us who are such sticklers for privacy to expect that you're a window cleaner who cleans without the use of water or a cloth?'

If the eyes in the room were shooting daggers at Ralph before, they'd now switched to full-blown swords, spears and anything else incredibly sharp they could find.

'I think I might be able to help,' Greg said, 'although I must reiterate that time is of the essence.'

'Of course. Mr Hoffenhymer, I'd forgotten all about you and your little task for Mr

Malvern. Please, proceed with a viable explanation.'

Greg stepped forwards. 'Firstly, it will come as no surprise to anyone in this room that Ralph here is a bit simple. The wheel's still spinning but the hamster's dead, if you catch my meaning. So, I guess this is all my fault, because I sent him up to our room whilst I sorted out some other, pressing business. Now don't ask me how he ended up in your room, but he did. Like I said, he couldn't pour piss out of a boot even with the instructions written on the heel. Anyway, I spent the last hour looking for him and it was only by chance I saw the four beauty contestants over there knock on this door and then whose voice should I hear but Ralph's! And that, lady and gentlemen is that. Now if you don't mind...'

Greg waved Ralph over and they both made for the door, which this time was open and unguarded. Without slowing, they both walked straight out the door, turned left instead of right, ran all the way down the stairs, past the main desk and out in to the cold night air.

***

Hargaard dutifully closed the door to Room 181. They could all see from his posture that he wasn't happy. He loved nothing more than giving out a good slapping and was certain it was going to happen but, as the two streaks of piss had made for the door, Evangeline the Blue had motioned for him to let them go.

'I know you're annoyed, Hargaard,' Evangeline the Blue said, 'but we've matters to discuss and sometimes violence isn't the answer. Yet.'

Hargaard smiled at Evangeline the Blue. He couldn't tell her that he got her meaning because he had no tongue, so instead he just smiled and nodded.

'I thought you'd understand,' Evangeline the Blue said.

'Well I bloody don't!' the largest of the large men said. 'We just let them walk away. Do you really believe the horseshit they spouted?'

'Of course I don't, Johnson,' Evangeline the Blue said. 'But as Hargaard now understands, thinking with your fists doesn't always guarantee the best results.'

'It's worked okay for me over the years,' Johnson said.

'Oh, really?' the man with the scar said. 'How's that nose of yours?'

A couple of the other men sat around the table laughed, some into their hands, the braver ones made no attempt to hide it.

Johnson looked at the man with the scar as he touched his recently broken nose, courtesy of a flying tankard. For a moment he looked like he'd like nothing more than to wring his neck, but then he burst out laughing instead.

'I like you, Rothchild, I really do. You make me laugh. And you've got balls.'

'Yes, I collect them. They're in jars at home,' Rothchild said, smiling.

This time everyone around the table laughed. All apart from Evangeline the Blue who shook her head at Rothchild who in turn shrugged his shoulders as if to say it's what they expect.

'If we could gather ourselves and return to the matter in hand?' Evangeline the Blue said.

Johnson sat back down and the others around the table turned to face the woman at the head.

'I don't doubt that one of us needs to have a word with our useful hotel employee, Mr Freepepper,' she said. 'Hargaard, I think you could handle such a situation.'

Hargaard nodded enthusiastically.

'Although,' she continued, 'we still may require his services at some point so it would be a shame if you got carried away. I'm afraid I must limit you to sending a warning.'

Hargaard smiled. To a man of his considerable talents, sending a warning presented a world of opportunities.

'Now, with that out of the way, all of you sat around this table can surely see how seriously I take this breach of our privacy.'

Most of the men around the table nodded but a few seemed unconvinced. At the end of the table, someone stood up. He was wafer thin, and his eyes moved quickly about the room as he spoke.

'You all know who I am. Some of you know me because you've met me on the Blood Wastes, others have only heard about my reputation, but to a man, you know who I am. I don't like meeting like this, in the city, away from the fresh air and I certainly don't like meeting in secret in some poxy inn. It took a lot of persuasion to get me here and one thing you said to me,' he pointed at Evangeline the Blue, 'was that this meeting would be completely private. In fact, if I remember rightly, you *promised*.'

'Evangeline,' Rothchild said, 'if I may...'

Evangeline waved for Rothchild to continue.

'You are right, Granger, I know who you are. Granger Fearbringer. A name earned the hard way, when names like Fearbringer were not easy to earn. Your reputation is one of near legend. Some say you've fought in every war, battle and conflict that the Kingdom has seen for the last forty years. As a mercenary, you've killed more than your fair share which makes you a very dangerous man indeed. Some say that the mere mention of your name, whispered across the Blood Wastes, can cause an army to turn and flee. Which is why your presence at this meeting is so valued.'

Granger Fearbringer sat down. He picked up a glass and poured himself some wine.

'You can save the flattery for the whores, Rothchild,' he said. 'I don't need an arse-licker like you to tell me what I already know. What I do need is for someone to tell me how, in a meeting I was promised would be secret, two bumbling idiots were allowed to wander in and get a good look at my face.'

Rothchild glided from behind Evangeline and moved along the table until he was stood next to Granger.

'I understand your frustration, I really do. However, I do believe Evangeline has identified the weak link in our chain as the hotel doorman and she did, did she not, just say that he will be dealt with? That, for me, is good enough.'

'Well, it's not good enough for me!' Granger shouted as he stood to face Rothchild. 'If word gets out that Granger Fearbringer, the warrior mercenary who cuts out the eyes of his victims, was spotted meeting with—'

A strange thing happened. There was a blur of movement, almost too quick to be seen, and then Granger looked like he was trying to work out a really hard riddle. He moved his right hand down to his stomach and then brought it up to his eye level. It was a deep red.

'Oh,' he said.

Rothchild took a step back. Slowly and deliberately he wiped his knife on Granger's sleeve and then placed it back in its sheath on the belt around his purple robe.

Granger looked down at his stomach and the gaping hole his intestines were now protruding out of.

'Shit,' he said, and collapsed onto the floor.

A few of the men around the table started to rise, hands already on their weapons but Rothchild cut them off.

'Granger Fearbringer was one of the most feared men sat at this table. Yet he was a man of the past. You were all asked to be here to help forge a new future, one filled with forward thinkers. I took no pleasure in ending Granger Fearbringer's life but I will tell each and every one of you this now: reputations and past achievements hold no weight in the future.'

Most of the men sat back down.

'How do we know you won't stab us when we least expect it?' Johnson said, his hand still on the hilt of a huge axe. 'After all, we're all used to fighting the proper way, man to man. None of us ever poked someone in the stomach when they least expected it.'

This drew a chorus of grunts of approval, some even banged on the table. Rothchild looked over at Evangeline the Blue. She nodded at him. It was time.

'I would never claim to be the kind of man any of you may be,' said Rothchild, 'but it's time for a few home truths. Johnson, you say that none of you ever poked someone when they least expected it.'

'No way,' Johnson said. 'Just ain't right. A man should be afforded the correct death. Not a coward's one.'

'Is that so?' Rothchild said.

'That's so,' Johnson said and once again the men around the table grunted their approval.

'And let me ask you, how's that course of action working out for you?'

'What do you mean?'

'Take Granger Fearbringer. Who could question his reputation on the battlefield? I'd be prepared to bet he gave each of his foes the chance to die like a man.'

'Too bloody right!' Johnson said. More grunts.

'Yet here he lies, his guts hanging out and, if I'm not mistaken, nothing to show for it.'

Evangeline played with the blue pearls around her neck. It had gone exactly as her and Rothchild had planned, but this was the most crucial part. They would either lose them or have them until the bitter end.

'As tonight seems to be a night for questions,' Rothchild continued, walking around the table, looking each man in the eye in turn. 'I have but one question for you all. Once I've asked my question, you can, if you choose, get up, walk out and never have to see myself or Evangeline again.'

Here it comes, Evangeline thought. She hoped Rothchild was as good as they said he was otherwise this could prove a very costly mistake.

'So here's my question. After all the battles that you gentlemen have fought in, after all the small and large victories you've helped secure, after all the bloodshed and pain, if you died tomorrow, what would be left behind? Because let me tell you, I see one of the greatest mercenaries this Kingdom's ever seen lying in a pool of his own blood and faeces on an inn floor and what's left behind? His reputation? What's that worth to him now?'

There were no grunts.

No one stood to object. In fact, total silence reigned.

Rothchild moved over and stood next to Evangeline the Blue. Carefully, he took her hand. She stood.

'All we ask, gentlemen,' she said, 'is that you go away from tonight's gathering and think. Before tonight, you've not been given that option. In many ways you've been treated like pieces of equipment, hired out, used and then returned. Some of you have made a nice amount of money from doing so, others have not been so fortunate. Some of you only have to answer to yourselves, others have a band of mercenaries who will follow you to the ends of the Kingdom. For what? Glory? Honour? A warrior's reputation? Join us. Let us together form a group more powerful than anything this Kingdom has ever seen. Then you shall have more than mere words to honour you. You shall have power beyond your wildest dreams. Together, we can own this Kingdom.'

***

Room 181 stood empty apart from two figures sat at the table. One dressed in purple, one dressed in blue. It had been a night full of unexpected events but they had made it through.

'I think that went reasonably well, all things considered,' Rothchild said.

'I'm just glad we made it through alive,' Evangeline said.

'It was touch and go for a minute there.'

'Do you think the rest of them really believed that those two idiots were who they said they were?'

'Probably not,' Rothchild said. 'Doesn't matter. They think we're doing something about it and sometimes all people want to know is that someone else is handling the problem.'

'Speaking from experience, Rothchild?'

'Absolutely.'

Evangeline chuckled. 'To think that, after all this planning, two farmers could wander into our meeting and nearly ruin the whole thing. Although, I must admit, my ears pricked up when they said they were working for Augustus Malvern. I wonder where they got *his* name from?'

'Just goes to show, sometimes blind luck trumps meticulous planning.'

'And you're sure there's no way anyone could've found out about our meeting?'

'Oh, they could've found out, no problem. But the seeds I planted made it sound like a group of dodgy businessmen were meeting in Room 181. The worst we could've encountered was a band of hopeful thieves barging in.'

'They'd have gotten a shock. Expecting ten wide-boy businessmen but coming face to face with some of the most hardened mercenaries in the Kingdom.'

'Quite,' Rothchild said. 'Which presents us with our next problem. Even if only half of them decide to join us, it's still going to cost us a pretty penny. Mercenaries are, by their very nature, bloody expensive.'

'That they are, my dear Rothchild. That they are.'

'You're smiling that smile again, Evangeline.'

'I am? Why, I'd not noticed.'

Rothchild stood and stretched. It had been a very long night and he had to get back to work soon. 'If I know you as well as I think I do,' he said, 'you've been holding something back.'

Evangeline also stood, also stretched.

'I may have stumbled across the answer to our financial problems.'

'Now I am interested. I was starting to become concerned that the money you'd been squirrelling away wouldn't be enough.'

'Whilst we do have a considerable amount, this new discovery will mean we can think bigger; much bigger.'

'I like the sound of that.'

'You should. It's been brought to my attention that within the boundary of Lower Calver resides a very precious and incredibly valuable red stone. Some of my sources say it could bankroll an entire army.'

Rothchild allowed his air of good nature to slip slightly. He wasn't used to not knowing things. 'I've not heard of such a stone. Are you sure your sources can be trusted?'

'Oh Rothchild, I do believe you're cross!'

'I'll admit, it's not often someone knows more than me.'

'It's living at the top of the hill, you're out of touch. And besides, my sources are impeccable. This one in particular.'

'Who?'

'My husband.'

'Well in that case, I suppose you're right. That is good news. Just think what we could do with the right level of funds.'

Rothchild and Evangeline both made their way to the door of Room 181.

'A good night's work, Rothchild. Give my regards to the King.'

'Very droll. I'm quite sure the King has no idea what's about to hit him. I'd ask you to pass on my regards to your husband but I don't think he'd be too happy to know we'd met.'

'Indeed, it's one of his shortcomings. Augustus is so temperamental.'

Chapter 14
Everybody Loves a Good Bargain

Ralph was having a lovely dream.

It was one of those dreams in which the person in the dream knows they're dreaming, but that doesn't stop the dream from being completely amazing. He dreamt that he was in a room, high above the city of Calver, a room draped in the very finest things: furniture, jewellery and women. In fact, there were women everywhere. Women from all across the Kingdom; different colours, builds and features, each one as beautiful as the last. They were there for one reason and one reason alone: him. Ralph. Or King Ralph as it was in his glorious dream. He rose from his throne and strode regally over to a window in his palace. Looking down, (because that's what kings did, they looked down), he saw the city of Calver stretch away before him and he was pleased with what he saw. It pleased him that the others, all those ants beneath him, were scurrying about their daily business whilst he, King Ralph, watched over them, his ever-protective gaze keeping them safe and out of harm's way. In his dream, King Ralph knew without a shadow of a doubt that his people loved and respected him. He was, after all, King Ralph the Beloved. With a contented smile he strode back across the room and lay on his royal bed. Upon the waving of his royal hand, a beautiful dark-skinned woman, dressed in very little (he was pleased to see), swayed over to him, carrying a flagon of the finest wine money couldn't even buy.

She leant over him and slowly, very carefully, poured the wine into his mouth. Something wasn't right. King Ralph the Beloved wasn't much of a wine drinker but he was pretty sure that fine wine wasn't supposed to be warm. And salty. In fact, it tasted like—

Ralph awoke with a start. He opened his eyes and came eye to eye with a horse's dripping winky. Ralph retched as the horse pee dribbled from his face. He sat up and smacked his head on the underside of a cart as the horse moved forwards, pulling the cart behind it. The bang on the head slammed him back down and he duly smacked the back of his head on the cobblestone floor.

Ralph lay still. Partly through choice, partly through necessity as the cart rumbled over him, the wheels passing within inches of his sides.

As far as starts to the day went, this had to rank right up there with one of his worst.

In his dream he'd been King Ralph the Beloved, ruler of the entire Kingdom. In reality he was a peed-on farmer who'd spent the night sleeping under a cart on the outskirts of Lower Calver's square.

Once the cart had moved on, Ralph stood and tried to iron out the kinks, strains and knots in his body that had come from sleeping on a burlap sack laid over cobbles. He needed to wash. His hair, face and neckline stunk of horse piss and three hours' sleep on a cold floor hadn't been anywhere near enough to leave him feeling refreshed. He turned to see if he could find a bucket of water when one came to him. Or at least the contents did. Freezing cold water hit him in the face, causing him to stumble backwards.

'Ooh, that felt good!' Eve Manslayer said.

'Urgh-flump gah!' Ralph replied.

'What's that Ralph, you want another one?'

'Nargle!'

'I'll take that as a yes!'

Eve picked up a second bucket of water and once more, threw it over Ralph, who, this time, couldn't maintain his balance and sat down on his rear end with a thud.

'You know, after the first bucket of water, I didn't think the second would feel as good, but it did!' Eve said.

Ralph stuck his head between his legs and threw up half a bucket of water.

'Well, now there's gratitude for you,' Eve said.

'Okay, you've had your fun,' Greg said leaning over his brother. 'Give him a minute to sort himself out. How are you feeling, Ralph?'

Ralph groaned.

'I'm seriously reconsidering my policy of not hitting girls.'

'I'm sorry, Ralph,' Eve said. 'But I wouldn't fight you for all the gold in the Kingdom. You stink of piss.'

Greg helped Ralph get to his feet.

'I'd forgotten we were supposed to meet her,' Ralph said.

'Yeah, me too,' Greg said. 'But I got kicked off the cart I was sleeping on at first light this morning and bumped into Eve when I went looking for some water.'

'Sleeping *on* a cart?' Ralph said. 'Yeah, I can see how that would've been a good idea.'

All around them the market was starting to spring to life.

The open space of the square was no more as stalls of various shapes and sizes were erected, ready for the day's business.

A steady stream of people flowed through Lower Calver's gatehouse each one directed according to their business by one of a growing number of officials, distinguishable by their brown outfits and clipboards. Everyone knew a clipboard made you official.

The majority of people who entered were all ushered to the same area, known as the holding pen. These people were those who came to every market and always got there far earlier than necessary. They were serious bargain hunters and they were a stall-holder's worst nightmare. The minute the market opened they would dash from the holding pen and swarm the market like crazed wasps, poking, prodding and generally disturbing everything on sale. If they did buy anything they refused to pay full price and seemed convinced that *they* were doing *you* a favour in buying it. Each trader who arrived to set up his or her stall gave the holding pen a wary look and hoped to the Gods that the market official wouldn't give them a pitch too close.

To Greg, the square already looked full but as he watched, more and more traders walked down the King's Pass from wherever they'd been staying the night before, collected their cart and somehow managed to crow-bar themselves into a spot that hadn't been there before they'd arrived.

The market was split into different sections and Ralph, Greg and Eve were stood behind the food section. Not all of the traders selling food had started cooking their wares yet, but enough had for the smell of fresh-roasted meat to grab them by the nose.

'Good grief, that smells good,' Ralph said, standing up.

'Three seconds ago, you were honking all over the cobbles,' Eve said.

'Yeah, well, I've made room for breakfast, haven't I?'

'Let's see if we can grab something to eat,' Greg said. 'I've a feeling it's going to be a long day.'

King Siguld the Watcher had chosen the window of his palace which afforded him the best view of the growing market, far, far beneath him and he did as his name suggested.

He watched.

He cast his gaze across the sprawling expanse of Lower Calver, confined between the lower and middle walls. It was not lost on him how much it had changed. When he had been a young boy and his Great-great-grandfather, King Paeter the Bold had ruled the Kingdom, Lower Calver had been little more than one street (the King's Pass) with but a few places of business for the weary traveller to make a quick coin or two.

By the time King Siguld was in his teens, his grandfather had died and his father was King, and what a reign that had been.

King Freydar the Short, was, in actual fact, well over six feet high. His name was given to him posthumously and based on the length of his time in office.

He was King for a glorious two years.

In those two years, depending on who you talked to, King Freydar was either the greatest King the land had ever seen, or the worst. For it was King Freydar who had thrown open the gates of Lower Calver and invited anyone and everyone to come and reside in the city. Most of the newcomers only made it as far as Lower Calver, but a few managed to climb the social ladder into Middle Calver. Those who chose to move and live in the city were, supposedly, allowed to live where they chose and gifted a grant to see them through their first year.

Unfortunately, King Freydar didn't make it through his second year.

Rumours flew about Lower, Middle and Upper Calver as to how the King had met his demise in a ladies' establishment deep within the newly built and ever-expanding backstreets of Lower Calver but one thing everyone did agree on: they had a new king, one who was fourteen years of age.

Many predicted total and utter chaos during the young king's first years on the throne. After all, the gates of Calver had been well and truly thrown open by his father — an act which brought about rapid expansion, overcrowding, corruption, murder and all manner of illicit activities.

Yet, thirty years on, Siguld was still king and the Kingdom had never been as stable as it was now.

Many attributed the young king's success to the people he surrounded himself with. After all, one so young couldn't possible have the maturity to rule a Kingdom during such a period of unprecedented change.

This was only partly true.

Of course, King Siguld was clever enough and humble enough to realise he couldn't possibly rule a Kingdom on his own at the tender age of fourteen, so he did indeed surround himself with the best minds in the Kingdom and paid them handsomely to advise him.

However, there was another reason he'd lasted so long.

Siguld knew he'd been given the name 'The Watcher' as a kind of double-edged sword.

Yes, it meant he was patient and deliberate in his actions, but he also knew there were those on his council and within the walls of Middle Calver who maintained the name represented his lack of action and reliance on others. That he couldn't, or wouldn't, act before watching to see what his highly paid advisors would do.

That they thought this bothered Siguld not one bit.

Being someone who was good at watching others and situations unfold had been Siguld's greatest blessing. It meant that his decisions were always informed and that he was rarely caught by surprise. King Siguld the Watcher had always been of the opinion that in a world of snakes, the man who observed where the big sticks were would always have half a chance at survival.

So he stood at the window and watched. He watched the steady stream of people arrive at Lower Calver's gatehouse and then funnel through into the square below. He could see them as they moved along the main route through the

Blood Wastes and, if he trained his eyes carefully, could even see beyond the Blood Wastes as groups emerged from over the hills and made their way towards the city. His city.

A knock at the door brought his attention back up the hill and into the room in which he stood.

'Enter,' King Siguld said.

The door creaked open – King Siguld did not like doors which opened quietly – and an old man shuffled in. He was dressed in the long, brown robe of an official and walked stooped over as if the very weight of the Kingdom rested solely upon his shoulders.

However, as soon as the door noisily shut behind him, the old man became a different person. He stood up straight and whisked the robe off, casting it on a nearby chair.

'I see you're an official this time, Perenholm,' the King said, walking over to a small table in the centre of the room.

Perenholm dusted himself down, straightened his hair and joined the King at the table.

'Proves to be careful, boss,' he said. 'I'm not a fan of muslin-cloth brown but it gets the job done.'

'Indeed,' the King said. 'I know I ask every time but...'

'I wasn't followed, don't worry.'

'That's good. I'd hate for people to think we got along.'

'The way you keep raising taxes, I don't think that'll be a problem.'

'Perenholm, you've never had it so good and don't try to tell me any different.'

Perenholm reached into the pocket of his padded jerkin and pulled out a thick notebook and pencil.

'Yeah, suppose I can't complain. Certainly better than when your dad was in charge, Gods rest his soul.'

King Siguld shook his head and smiled. It was his father who'd made it possible for men like Perenholm to sit where he was now sitting. At a table across from the King and talking as if they were equals.

Perenholm was, in fact, King Siguld's greatest secret. Not even his closest advisors knew of their relationship, mainly due to Perenholm's innate ability to hide in plain sight. He'd known Perenholm almost as long as he'd been King and not once had he seen him in the same outfit.

But it was more than that.

After Perenholm's visits it took the King a long time to even remember what he looked like. Perenholm was a master of not being seen. He was also a master at getting things done. Those two qualities were what had attracted the young king to Perenholm when they'd first met, shortly after his father's funeral.

He'd approached the new king and explained that he'd worked his way up from the backstreets of Lower Calver and now ran a very reputable and very profitable import and export business from his place of business in Middle Calver. He'd said he could help the new king in ways he'd never imagine and then turned on his heel and left.

Little over a week later, Perenholm sent a letter to the young king, informing him of a plot to kill him that very day. The letter went on to detail how and where the act of treason would take place. At half past eleven that night, four of King Siguld's personal guard snuck into his quarters and stabbed his pillows to death, after which King Siguld killed each of the four after leaping from the wardrobe he'd been hiding in. The rest, as they say, is history. Perenholm had remained his closest advisor ever since.

Perenholm flipped through his notebook until he found what he was looking for.

'Right then, Your Royal High and Mighty, you're not going to like this very much.'

'You know you're supposed to sandwich bad news in between two pieces of good,' King Siguld said. 'It makes it easier to digest.'

'Oh, really?' Perenholm scratched his thick blonde hair which the King was sure had been short and black the last time they'd met. Or maybe it was auburn. 'Righty-ho then, here goes. On the plus side of things, it doesn't look like it'll rain tomorrow which is great news if you're planning on going outdoors at all. On the minus side, our little venture didn't quite pay off. To finish with a spot of good news, you look lovely today.'

'When you say our venture didn't quite pay off...'

'I mean it failed miserably. I was trying to be diplomatic.'

'How miserably?'

'Well, one of them got killed and then the others had to kill the one who done it. That miserably.'

'Really?' the King said, sitting up straighter. 'How did he kill him?'

'Which one? Remember, two ended up meeting their maker.'

'The one we hired. How was he killed?'

'When I spoke to the rest of the lads, they said it was too soon to know for sure, but they seemed to be of the opinion that the target used one of our guy's own weapons against him.' Perenholm consulted his notes. 'Needle in the upper thigh is what they thought.'

'You said the others had to kill the one who did it? The target.'

'Yeah, that's right.' More consulting of notes. 'When I spoke to the boss man, he said they hadn't heard back from their colleague and, as it was his first job, they went to check up on him. When they got there, they found him hanging in the target's wardrobe. So they waited for the target to return, questioned him and then, well, then they killed him. After that they killed him some more.'

'Killed him some more?'

Perenholm once again checked his notes.

'They threw him out of a window, just to send a message. Nobody gets away with killing a spy.'

'Effective, if a little dramatic.'

'I got the impression that in their line of work, they don't get many chances to be dramatic what with all the sneaking around and stuff.'

The King rattled his fingers on the table. It was something he did whilst thinking. Perenholm knew to sit and wait. The King was very good at thinking and it wouldn't be long before an idea came along.

'Did they say why they chose to give this task to someone who had never done a job before?'

'They did. They said that because it seemed a simple enough task; break in, find an object, minimal chance of conflict, they'd decided to give the new boy a chance to earn his stripes. They seemed a little embarrassed by the whole escapade to be honest.'

'Did you express your concern that the matter was still unresolved?'

'Of course, boss. I said that whilst I was sorry for the loss of one of their colleagues, I was left with a sense of disappointment that a task I had personally paid handsomely to be completed was anything but.'

'And?'

'They said they understood, that reputation plays a big part in their line of business and that the next job they did for me would be handled in a more professional manner.'

'You must put a lot of work their way,' the King said.

'You know me, chief, I like to support the local economy.'

King Siguld stood up and walked back over to the window. He remained still, hands clasped behind his back. Perenholm waited. Finally, the King turned and walked back towards the table but he did not sit.

'You're sure this red stone is worth all this trouble?' he asked.

'If my sources are correct, and might I add they usually are, then this kind of red stone is worth more than all the trouble you could ever imagine and then a bit extra thrown in on top. You could buy this Kingdom and the next three, just with a tiny chunk of it.'

King Siguld shook his head.

'It's not the wealth that interests me. I'm a king, after all. I do okay when it comes to money. No, what interests me is what something like that red stone would mean to the wrong kind of person. Someone with the wrong ideas about power could, if you're right, destroy this Kingdom and everyone in it. I want that stone because I don't want it to fall into the wrong hands.'

'And I suppose you've thought of our next move,' Perenholm said.

'I've thought of our next three,' King Siguld the Watcher said.

***

Although the start of the day wasn't very good, it was getting much better. Greg, Ralph and Eve sat on one of the many wooden benches surrounding the market and finished their breakfast. One of the few advantages of spending part of the night sleeping in the market was that you were at the head of the line when the food stalls started serving breakfast.

Once finished, they tossed their bones to the growing pack of dogs at their feet and moved on into the market. When Ralph had asked why they were wasting their time wandering through the market, Eve had replied that three people wandering in and out of the stalls of a market setting up for business raised far less suspicion than three people huddled on a street corner, quite obviously up to something. Greg had to agree. Besides, there were so many people hustling about that they practically went unnoticed.

'So, did you boys have a pleasant night?' Eve said.

Greg and Ralph looked at each other. Both looked like they'd spent half the night trying not to get killed by a bunch of bloodthirsty mercenaries and the other half sleeping on the streets.

'Yeah, not too bad,' Greg said. 'Pretty uneventful, really.'

'Dull as dishwater is the way I'd put it,' Ralph added.

'Which would explain why you both look like you got eaten by a dog and puked up this morning. Too much ale?'

'You caught us,' Greg said. 'Us farmers aren't used to the strength of ale they serve in The Barrel.'

'I guess you could say we drank them dry!' Ralph said.

'The Barrel?' Eve said. 'That's funny, I was in there for most of last night, catching up with old friends, and I didn't see you two at all.'

'Oh, I'm sorry, you must've thought we meant that we'd spent the whole night in The Barrel!' Greg said.

'The whole night?' Ralph said. 'Good grief no, we like to spread ourselves around a bit, mix with the locals, you know how it is.'

The three carried on walking in between the stalls as the traders hurried around, transporting their goods from their carts onto display.

'So you went to other pubs?' Eve said.

'Oh yes!' Ralph said.

'Like what?'

'Like the...'

'Hanging—' Greg said.

'Scrotum!' Ralph said.

'The Hanging Scrotum?' Eve said, stopping and turning back to face Greg and Ralph.

Greg too turned to face his brother. 'The Hanging... Scrotum?' he said.

'Yes, Greg, The Hanging Scrotum. You probably don't remember it because it was much later on in the night and as we all know, you're a lightweight when it comes to ale.'

'I've never heard of The Hanging Scrotum before,' Eve said. 'Where is it?'

'Oh, I'm afraid I can't tell you that,' Ralph said. 'It's a very select establishment and they're very strict about who they let in. You, in particular, wouldn't stand a chance getting through the front door.'

'Is that so?' Eve said.

'Yes,' Ralph said. 'It's a gentlemen-only establishment. A place where important men from the far reaches of Calver society get together to discuss the finer things in life.'

'You went to a gay pub,' Eve said, turning and resuming walking through the market.

'We most certainly did not!' Ralph said, running after her. 'I'll have you know that me and my brother are red-blooded males who enjoy nothing more than giving a woman a good—'

Eve spun around and stepped to within an inch of Ralph.

'Why don't you tell me exactly what you enjoy giving women, farm-boy?'

'Well, I don't think now's the right... it's just that it's probably best to... I... erm... Greg?'

Greg stepped in between Ralph and Eve.

'Why don't we swiftly change the subject?' he said. 'Did you manage to find anything out about our red stone?'

Eve stepped back from a rapidly blushing Ralph.

'As a matter of fact, I did,' she said. 'But first, I need to ask you something.'

'Okay,' Greg said.

'When were you going to tell me that Keith Smart's dead and that you've struck a deal with a low-life scumbag like Augustus Malvern?'

'Ah,' Greg said.

'Ah,' Ralph said.

'I think we need to have a serious chat,' Eve said.

The Hoffenbach brothers did exactly as they were told.

Chapter 15
All that Nearly Glitters

When Rothchild entered the throne room he liked to do so through a different door each time. Yes, they all squeaked, creaked and generally made a gods-awful noise, but if he had to enter through a ridiculously noisy door, at the very least it would be one of his choosing. In this instance, he chose the door which opened straight in front of the King. He had been summoned to the throne room immediately after he'd awoken at seven. It wasn't anything out of the ordinary to be summoned by The Watcher at such an un-godsly hour – Siguld regularly requested his presence, the vast majority of the time to help make a decision any idiot could make – but this time felt... different.

Rothchild couldn't put his finger on it what it was that felt different. He'd survived twenty years as an advisor to the King, and those twenty years had taught him to trust his instincts. The Royal Court was as vicious and filled with as much villainy as any of the backstreets in Lower Calver and at least down there they'd look you in the eye as they stabbed you. In the Royal Court you were lucky if you felt the knife twist, let alone got a good view of its owner.

Surely the good King couldn't have found out about his meeting with Evangeline and the mercenaries – it had only been last night. No, that was preposterous. King Siguld the Watcher would only know something if Rothchild himself had told him. He was the King's eyes and ears and he missed so very little (although not knowing about the stone Evangeline mentioned last night had rankled him), so the chances the King knew were slim to none. Besides, who else did the King trust? Rothchild had always been and, if he played the game right, always would be his most trusted advisor, right up until he realised that all was lost. If Evangeline was right and this red stone was as valuable as she believed, then their plan could be sped up by anything up to six months. *In six months*, Rothchild thought as he flung open the door into the throne room, *I could be sat where you are, Watcher*. Rothchild smiled as he greeted the King. His King.

For now.

***

The market had begun.

People from all over the Kingdom had descended on Lower Calver, some to sell, others to buy and a few to steal. They moved around the stalls in a swirling mass amidst the shouts of the traders, the smell of the food and the clatter, clink and rustle of money changing hands. There

174

were bargains to be had and there was money to be made.

Greg, Ralph and Eve saw none of this.

The three had moved away from the market and back out through the gatehouse of Lower Calver. They moved against the tide of people as they pushed their way back towards the Blood Wastes. Eve had suggested they go there as, on Market day, it would be deserted.

They quickly found a patch of ground, a small hillock, large enough for a small army to gather and, if the notion called for it, stand their ground from up on high.

From their vantage point, Greg could see the steady stream of people heading towards the first huge wall of Calver and the gatehouse beyond.

'You know, it's funny,' he said as they sat on the damp grass around a space that had been cleared for a fire.

'What?' Ralph said.

'Less than a week ago, we would've been in that crowd, heading into Lower Calver, hoping to buy a few things, maybe trade other bits and now... this.'

'Less than a week ago, the market wasn't on. We'd have been a week early.'

'You know what I mean, Ralph. More's happened to me in this last week than in my entire life.'

'Me too,' Ralph said.

Eve said nothing, just looked off into the distance at the people crossing the Blood Wastes, her Blood Wastes. A place where her people had, in the distant past, made one last stand. She herself had spent many years moving from place to place, fighting to make a name for herself and against those who thought she didn't belong as she forced them to take her seriously. She'd been doing it for so long, she'd almost forgotten about who she used to be. And here she was, sat atop a grassy knoll with two farmers, who she'd only just met, yet when she'd located them this morning, she'd actually been happy to see them.

How strange.

'Enough reminiscing,' Eve said. 'Let's get down to brass tacks. You boys still haven't got your red stone.'

'Nope,' Ralph said.

'And you're not really much closer to finding it.' It wasn't a question.

'Nope,' Greg said.

'So, in the time that we've been apart, what exactly have you done?'

Ralph found that now was the perfect time to inspect his boots.

***

Rothchild left the throne room through the same door he'd entered, although he wasn't thinking about doors anymore. He walked quickly back to his chambers, his purple robe billowing behind him, his scar burning the left side of his face. Once inside, he closed the door and locked it. His chambers were vast; he had earned such a room through years of service, but he crossed them quickly and sat at the desk under his window. He pulled out a clean sheet of parchment and dipped his pen into the inkwell. With his pen poised above the parchment, he paused.

Maybe he needed to think for a moment.

He'd always been decisive but there was a world of difference between being decisive and being rash.

He thought back to the conversation he'd just had with the King. Rothchild had greeted the King as normal and then stood awaiting instruction. Normally, the King would ask him a question, maybe some form of Kingdom business he was unsure about, maybe just ask for advice. But this time was different. His instincts had been right.

'Rothchild,' the King began. 'I need to ask you something.'

'Certainly, your Grace.'

'Rothchild, you do this every time. It's Siguld or nothing. We've known each other for twenty years.'

Inwardly, Rothchild smiled. It was a game he liked to play.

'Sorry, Siguld.'

'That's better. Now, have you been made aware of anything out of the ordinary?'

'Out of the ordinary?'

'Yes.'

'So much happens within our walls, Siguld, it's sometimes hard to distinguish what's out of the ordinary.'

'Quite,' the King said.

'And with the market in town, odd things happen all the time. Why, just the other day, I overhead a woman claim she'd pay five gold coins for a flagon of cider.'

'I've never really got your sense of humour, Rothchild.'

That's not the only thing you've not got, you clueless fool.

'Sorry, Siguld.'

The King moved on.

'No, what I mean is that you're normally the first to know about anomalies within any of our three walls. It seems to be a gift you have. That and the ability to cut through to the very core of a decision.'

'That's very kind of you to say so, Siguld. I try to keep on top of things so I can keep you informed.'

'Yet...'

'Yet? I'm sorry, Siguld, I'm just not following you.'

The King looked at his most loyal subject. Looked him directly in the eyes. 'So you didn't hear anything about a small occurrence yesterday lunchtime?'

For once, Rothchild didn't need to keep his cards close to his chest. He had absolutely no idea what the King was talking about. He'd been incredibly busy yesterday putting the finishing touches to the meeting at The First Inn, a task which had meant he'd been in and around the establishments of Middle Calver all day. He couldn't even remember if he'd seen daylight at all yesterday.

'Yesterday lunchtime? A small occurrence?'

'Rothchild, are we holding this meeting in a cave? It certainly seems that way. Everything I say seems to just bounce back at me. The last thing I'd have you down for was prattling on like some useless echo.'

Rothchild let that one go. He needed to know what the King knew and, more to the point, why he didn't.

'Sorry, Siguld. It would seem you have me at somewhat of a disadvantage. I'm afraid I was a little under the weather yesterday and didn't manage to stray far from my chambers.'

'Well if you had, you'd have undoubtedly heard that a visitor to our fair city was unceremoniously thrown out of a window of The Flying Dishcloth yesterday lunchtime.'

Rothchild relaxed.

'Well, whilst that's certainly an undesirable occurrence, I'm not sure it qualifies as particularly newsworthy. People get thrown through windows all the time in Lower Calver, usually after consuming far too much ale and picking a fight with the wrong local.'

'It was an upstairs window,' the King said, leaning forwards. 'And he was already dead before he hit the ground.'

'Oh... really.' Rothchild didn't like where this was heading.

'Really. The word out there on the streets is that the gentleman in question had on his person something really rather valuable. Or rather he did have. Seems the item is no longer in his possession.'

Rothchild cleared his mind, relaxed his shoulders and forced himself to smile.

'Like I said, Siguld. I was feeling a touch under the weather yesterday, so I'm afraid this is all new to me. Seems like I've missed quite a bit. I don't know, you take one sick day and then... I shall return to my chambers and send word that we would like to be kept informed should any valuable items arise.'

'Very good, Rothchild.'

Rothchild stood, turned and walked towards a door, any door.

'Oh and one more thing,' the King said, causing Rothchild to halt.

'If you should come across something so valuable that others may offer you vast sums of money for it, you will remember your loyalties, won't you?'

'Were it not for you, my King, I would not be in the position I am now. You shall always have my loyalty.'

Rothchild turned and walked from the room and now sat pen poised, ready to write. No, he could not wait, he had to send the letter. It was worth the risk.

***

Back in the throne room, Siguld stared at the door Rothchild had exited through not five minutes ago. He'd known Rothchild long enough to know that he was lying. About what, he wasn't sure, but he was definitely lying about something. This made the ruler of the Kingdom uneasy. He was no fool, he knew exactly what Rothchild was and had only kept him on as his advisor for two reasons. For one he was very good at his job. This was because, up until now, his loyalty to the King had meant that Rothchild had prospered. Secondly, people like Rothchild needed to be kept close. Not too close, but close enough.

Movement behind the throne caused Siguld to reach for his sword. It was drawn in an instant and just as quick, Siguld leapt from his seat.

'Put it away, you jumpy bugger,' Perenholm said, emerging from the shadows.

'You know, you could knock, or cough,' Siguld said, sheathing his sword. 'I could've sliced you in two.'

'And then you'd have had to live with the guilt for the rest of your life.'

'Maybe, maybe not.'

'I'd come back and haunt you, anyway. You couldn't get rid of me that easily.'

'I'd noticed. Two visits in less than two hours. How long have you been back there?'

'Long enough,' Perenholm said.

'What did you make of my most trusted advisor?'

'Your most trusted advisor? I'm well and truly offended. I thought we had a special kind of relationship, your Grace.'

'You can bugger off with your special relationship. No, I'm serious. I want to know your opinion on what you just heard.'

'Well,' Perenholm said, perching on the edge of the throne, 'way I see it, your boy Rothchild wouldn't know the truth if it pulled down his britches and slapped him on the arse.'

'Perenholm, I knew that the minute I met him all those years ago.'

'See, I knew you weren't as daft as you looked. In terms of that conversation you and him just had, I'd say he either knows absolutely bugger all about the red stone or he knows a whole heck of a lot more than he's prepared to tell you.'

'In all the years I've known Rothchild, he's never known absolutely bugger all.'

'In which case, he's purposely keeping something from you.'

'Which means?' the King said.

'Which means,' Perenholm said, 'we've got a bit of a problem.'

It didn't take Greg as long as he'd thought it would to tell Eve about what they'd done in the time they'd been apart.

As a summary of events, if you kept to the bare facts, it was reasonably easy to remain brief. The problem was the actual facts themselves. They held a certain negative quality.

Eve looked off into the distance. The steady stream of people arriving for the market continued.

'And here's me thinking you'd spend the day and night enjoying the sights and sounds of Calver,' she said.

'In a way, we kind of did,' Ralph replied.

'Which way was that then?'

'The way that involves us getting to see parts of Calver most people never get to,' Ralph said, brightening. 'In fact, if you look at it in a certain light, we really have had an enthralling and invigorating twenty-four hours.'

Eve shook her head.

'The only light you could use to put a positive spin on the enormous mess you've made of the last twenty-four hours is the light a recently snuffed out candle gives in the darkest cave beneath Calver Hill.'

'I'll have you know,' Ralph said as he stood up and brushed off the seat of his jerkin, 'us Hoffenbach brothers have had a very trying time of it, thank you very much. And, as a couple of farmers, unused to the callous, devious and often downright nasty goings in inside the walls of Calver, I feel we've acquitted ourselves admirably.'

'Finished?' Eve said.

Ralph flopped back down.

'Yes. Just thought I'd give it a bit of a go.'

'Well,' Eve said, placing a hand on Ralph's shoulder, causing him to flinch, 'if it helps, I liked the part about quitting admirably.'

'Acquitted, not quitted. But thanks anyway.'

Good grief, things really are in a poor state, Greg thought. *Ralph and Eve are starting to get on.*

This time it was Greg's turn to stand. He felt a moment such as this required standing. He could imagine leaders of Tribes in years gone by, standing on such a mound before battle, delivering inspiring speeches as their men (and women) awaited the chance to prove their loyalty.

He looked down at his own troops – a smart-mouthed farmer and a half-pint mercenary – turned away and braced himself. There was no going back now.

'It seems such a long time ago that I broke our one and only plough. As farmers, we live by the plough and die by the plough. Which means that it's time to stand up and be counted. We can't go home. Augustus Malvern will find us. This means we have to go back in to the dragon's lair, face our destiny and do what's right.' Greg raised his fist into the air and stood with his eyes closed. He had expected a resounding and hearty cheer, but his troops remained silent. Maybe awestruck with his rousing speech. He'd especially liked the part about 'live by the plough, die by the plough'.

Someone whistled. Greg opened his eyes and turned around.

Ralph and Eve were halfway back across the Blood Wastes, heading away from Calver and towards the large group of mercenary tents over towards the edge of the great expanse.

'You coming? Or are you going to stand muttering to yourself, you great berk!' Ralph shouted.

They'd probably left just as he started to speak. Greg ran down the small, sloping terrain, feeling somewhat of a hillock.

Chapter 16
All You Need is Love (and a Really Big Sword)

Greg caught up with Ralph and Eve as they neared the edge of the mercenary encampment and the bridge they'd crossed when they'd met 'Death Knoll' two days previously.

'If you'd bothered to hang around and listen to me,' Greg said, panting 'you'd realise that we can't go home. Augustus will find us.'

Ralph put his arm around his brother.

'Greg, my dear boy, we're not going home.'

'Where are we going?'

'Our little mercenary friend, Miss Manslayer here, has come up with a bit of a plan.'

'Mercenary friend? Miss Manslayer? Two hours ago, you'd have gladly had her arrested!'

'Greg, Greg, Greg. Are we not like the ever changing seasons, not held prisoner in our own minds, but free to form new and more enlightened opinions?'

Greg pushed passed Ralph and drew level with Eve.

'Eve, what's going on? I'd ask Ralph but, well he's Ralph, and he's being odd.'

Eve smiled but did not stop walking.

'Whilst you were stood on your hill, doing goodness knows what, me and your brother had a little chat and I informed him of my plan. Even a turd like him knows a good idea when he hears it.'

'So...'

'So, we're off to see a man about a Wolf.'

***

It took the three of them a while to get to the edge of the mercenary encampment. There was still a great many people heading into Calver along the main road and as Greg, Ralph and Eve were heading in the opposite direction, they had to tramp along the uneven ground to the sides of the road rather than fight against the tide of people.

Eventually though, they reached the edge of what in essence was a small town of tents. Behind the tents the road wound its way invitingly across open countryside and off into the relative safety of home.

As they barged across the road, dodging carts and elbowing through groups of market-goers, Greg took a long hard look at the road home. How he wished to turn right and just walk. Just walk and not stop until he stood in front of his farmhouse, with his Mollie inside. He could do that. Just walk. Maybe they could run away, hide. It could work.

'He'd find you. You know he would,' Ralph said, appearing at Greg's side. 'Come on, let's catch up with Eve.'

Eve had already made her way clear of the throng of people and stood waiting. Once Greg and Ralph had caught up with her she pulled them to the side of one of the smallest of the mercenaries' tents.

'Right,' she said, turning her gaze first on Greg and then on Ralph, where it stayed fixed.

'These are my people. I wouldn't class many of them as friends and just about every one of them would happily slit my throat, if the price was right, but they're still my people. Which means that if you do anything which should offend them or humiliate me after the years of blood, sweat and toil it took me to earn my reputation, then a swift kick in the goolies will be nothing more than a warm up to the pain I'll inflict on you. Do we have an understanding?'

'You heard the girl,' Ralph said. 'You better be on your best behaviour, Greg.'

Eve stepped closer to Ralph.

'Just kidding!' he said. 'Jeez, you mercenaries, you can't take a joke.'

Eve maintained her close proximity to Ralph but turned to face Greg.

'You'd better gag funny boy. If he speaks out of turn, I won't be held responsible for what happens.'

With that she spun around and stomped off.

Greg and Ralph followed, at a distance. 'What did I say?' Ralph said.

They followed Eve along a line of tents, each one getting progressively bigger and more elaborately designed than the last. The first few in the row looked barely big enough to fit a man in and were made from a mixture of animal hide and vegetation. They were crudely made and smelt as if the animal hide was rotting from within.

Further along, the tents started to resemble places in which people could dwell, rather than providing barely adequate cover from the elements. Some of the middle sections of tents even had awnings stretching out from the main section, with the remnants of a fire glowing listlessly in the morning air. They passed these and moved further in towards the centre and a section of twenty or thirty tents. These clearly belonged to the highest paid and therefore most successful of the mercenaries. Able to command huge fees due to their fighting prowess and reputation for destruction, the owners of these tents lived as much of a luxurious lifestyle as living in a tent by the side of a battlefield would allow. These tents looked bigger than the average farmer's house, with multiple sections added on to the side and huge thick wooden fences marking the boundary of the property.

'Tell you what,' Ralph whispered to Greg. 'I reckon I could get used to living in one of those.'

'You'd have to get used to not fainting at the sight of blood first,' Greg said.

Almost all of the tents were fashioned from thick, colourful fabric, interwoven with gold silk. Almost all were festooned with jewels which sparkled and danced in the breeze.

Almost all had some type of elaborate flag sat atop their peak, fluttering in the breeze. Almost all.

Eve had stopped in front of the one tent in the final twenty which looked completely out of place. It was of a similar size to its neighbours but that was where the similarity ended. An estate agent would struggle to sell this tent as anything other than 'purposeful'. It had the correct amount of sides, a top and it was made of weatherproof material, therefore it served a purpose. It wasn't fashioned from colourful fabric nor was it interwoven with gold silk and it certainly wasn't festooned with jewels. It was brown. It had a flap for entering and that was that.

Purposeful.

Ralph opened his mouth as Eve shot him a look which contained a lot of unspoken words, words of the kind clumsy people will be familiar with when they're in the middle of a D.I.Y project.

Ralph shut his mouth.

Eve motioned for Greg and Ralph to follow her as she made her way up to the opening and then into the darkness of the tent.

Ralph's earlier swagger deserted him.

'Are you sure this is a good idea?' he said to Greg, tugging at his arm.

'What happened to "free to form new and more enlightened opinions"?' Greg said.

Greg walked on and into the darkness with Ralph close at his heels.

***

The inside of the tent, from what could be seen, was as plain as the outside. In the centre of a bare earth floor, a small fire burned offering a dim glow of the immediate area around it. Against the fire lay a bedroll and off to one side Greg could just about make out a thick wooden chest. Aside from those three items, Ralph behind him and Eve a couple of paces in front of him, the rest of the tent was empty.

Or at least that's what he thought.

'How do, Manslayer?' came a voice from the darkness. 'See you've brought fresh meat.'

'Mummy, Daddy, save me now!' Ralph shouted.

The voice in the darkness began to laugh, deep booming laughs which filled the space in the tent. Eve stood with her hand on her forehead, a look of shame barely concealed.

From the shadows across the fire the laughter moved closer. Its owner stepped in to the faltering light.

'Boys,' Eve said, shaking her head. 'Allow me to introduce Wolf Dangerpunch. Wolf, meet Gregory Hoffenbach and his chicken-shit brother, Ralph.'

'Right-ho, fellas,' Wolf Dangerpunch said, offering his hand to first Greg, who shook it, then Ralph who flinched. 'Fear not, o-ye-of-soiled-undergarments; I won't harm a hair on your head.'

Ralph visibly relaxed.

'It's your skin and the bones under it you should worry about.'

Wolf Dangerpunch sat himself down on the bedroll by the fire. He was of a similar height to Greg, which for a mercenary wasn't particularly tall. He wore no armour, and seemed to carry no weapons. Although his long hair was almost completely grey and his beard was likewise peppered with grey, Greg found it difficult to place his age.

'Okay then,' he said. 'Why don't we all sit on down on this here bedroll and have ourselves a little meeting of the minds?'

All three joined the mercenary by the warmth of the fire.

'First things first,' Wolf Dangerpunch said. 'As you're sat in my humble abode, around my fire, you might as well call me Wolf, that'll save us from getting all formal and you pair feeling like you might offend me. Last thing we need is Ralph McJumpy-Lumps getting all jittery on us again.'

'It's not that you scared me,' Ralph said, trying to recover from his poor first impression, 'more that, well...'

'More that you're like a coiled spring, ready to attack and anything could've happened?' Wolf said.

'Yeah, that's it!' Ralph said.

'Thought as much. I recognise a fellow dangerous human being when I see one. I shall remind myself to be more cautious around you, Ralph my boy. Don't want any uncoiling, do we? Now, who's up for a drink?'

All three accepted Wolf's hospitality and he busied himself with preparing a pan of water to hang over the fire.

'It's a lovely tent, you've got here,' Ralph said.

'If that's your honest opinion,' Wolf said, 'then I'd hate to see the state of wherever you call home.'

'I think my brother meant that—' Greg started to say.

'I know what he meant, Greg, and it's mighty kind of him to make the effort but you needn't bother. My tent is nowhere as fancy as any of the others,' Wolf said as he began chopping what looked like dried leaves on a wooden board he'd retrieved from the chest. 'It's not meant to be fancy. You know what I do for a living? I'm a facilitator. Did you know that?'

'A facilitator?' Greg said.

'Apparently so. That's what the rest of these mercenaries are now calling themselves. Facilitators. Can you believe it? The only thing

I help to facilitate is the parting of heads from their bodies.'

Wolf scraped the chopped, dried leaves into the now simmering pan over the fire.

'So they sit in their fancy tents, maybe travel around a bit, eat rich food and *facilitate*, every now and then. Whereas I sleep on the floor, eat food that nourishes me and only fight if I feel the cause is right. Call me self-serving and outdated, but that's just the way it is. If you can't fight with honour and a clear conscience, then you might as well stay at home and–'

'Take up knitting,' Eve finished.

'All right, all right,' Wolf said. 'I'll shut up. You've heard it all before, Eve.'

'Only about a hundred times.'

'Well, if you insist on coming round to see me, you'll have to listen to my ramblings. Right, who's for tea?'

The tea was unlike anything Greg had ever tasted. Admittedly, he was slightly concerned when Wolf passed him a wooden cup containing what looked like the remnants of a wet Thursday in October, which had been strained through an overused window leather.

Courtesy, and the fact he was sat across a fire from a mercenary, dictated he take a sip. He was surprised to learn that it tasted sensational. All three looked up from their drink to see Wolf staring intently at them.

'Well?' he asked.

'It's really good!' Ralph said.

'You're not just saying that?'

'It's really nice. I like it,' Greg said.

'Ah thanks, lads,' Wolf said, beaming. 'What about you, Eve?'

Eve took another sip. 'Yeah, this one's pretty good. Much better than the last one.'

'The last few were somewhat... experimental, I'll grant you that.'

'That's an understatement,' Eve said, finishing her drink.

'Well, some people feel a good vomiting session clears you out.'

'Do you make your own tea often, Mr Dangerpu– Wolf?' Ralph said.

'Oh, Gods, you'll get him started now,' Eve said.

'As a matter of fact, I do, young Mr Ralph,' Wolf said turning to face Ralph and Greg. Eve got up and walked over to the wooden chest. 'I'm something of a herbalist, you see.'

'How fascinating!' Ralph said with just a shade too much enthusiasm.

'Steady Ralph,' Wolf said, 'flattery's one thing but over-exuberance is off-putting.'

'Sorry. You were saying about being a herbalist?'

'That I was. You see, I was given the gift of killing people. Something I just happen to be naturally talented at. Don't know how or why and I certainly haven't worked hard at it. It's just something I can do very well, so I used my talent to make myself a spot of money but

195

more importantly; help those who I thought needed it most. Use my gift, so to speak.

'But I've become disillusioned. Because, back when I first started out as a mercenary, it was not long after the last big war. Oh yes, chaps. I'm that old. Back then, you took a job based on who you thought was in the right. As in, they had a valid grievance which required settling. In doing so, you stood by your morals, principles and ethics. That made dealing with the fact you killed innocent folk for money a little easier to handle. Now? Now it's become all about the money. What with peace in the Kingdom, these new mercenaries have sprung up. All these *facilitators* are interested in is who pays the most and how quick the job will be over with so they can get back to their fancy tents. Pop into Calver, bump off an old enemy for you and be back in time for supper and a nice pay cheque.

'But it's not just that.

'Nowadays, you so much as look at someone funny and they get all offended, which has to be dealt with because, as we all know, "being offended" is a grievous thing. All of this means that, more than not, mercenaries are employed to do a job for someone who's been looked at a bit funny or, Gods forbid, been offended.

'Nine times out of ten they're buggered if they can fathom why they're chopping some poor sod into pieces, just that they'll get paid at the end.

'To think, my ancestors fought in the Battle of the Blood Wastes for this.

'Short of it is, boys, I want out.'

'You're quitting being a mercenary?' Greg asked.

'He's been threatening to do it for years,' Eve said.

'Only this time I mean it,' Wolf said as he stood up and stretched.

'What would you do? I doubt someone like you would be happy sat doing nothing all day,' Greg said.

'You're a very good judge of character, Gregory my lad. There's no way I could whittle away my remaining years sat on my arse. Nope, I'm going to open a tea shop.'

Greg coughed and Ralph managed a high-pitch cough which, in some circumstances could be conceived as a stifled giggle.

'A tea shop?' Greg said, elbowing a coughing Ralph. 'That'll be a bit different for you.'

'I know what you're thinking boys. An ex-mercenary running a tea shop? Farting around in a little pinny, serving old dears cups of sweet tea and the occasional bun? How preposterous, eh?'

'Well, not exactly...' Ralph said.

'I'm not talking a quaint little tea room, no sir. My tea shop will be hardcore. It'll be a place where only the finest blends are available. No fancy little tables, no charming brass kettles dangling from the ceiling, just me, a counter and a rack of teas. More like a tobacconist's than anything else. It'll be great.'

Eve shut the lid on the wooden chest she'd been rummaging through.

'Look, I'm sorry to break up all the tea-related discussions, as fascinating as they are, but we're not here to discuss herbs and hot water. Remember?'

'Quite right, Manslayer,' Wolf said, sitting back down. 'Who am I to have dreams and ambitions and want to share my passions with visitors in my own tent? How very rude of me.'

Eve came and sat beside Wolf.

'Sorry, it's not that your dreams aren't important, it's more a case that we haven't got much time.'

'Fair enough,' Wolf said. 'Let's crack on, shall we? So, who do you want dead?'

***

Rothchild waited. Not like his indecisive employer, who seemed to dither and delay each and every decision, regardless of importance.

No, Rothchild's waiting involved patience, strength of will and the ability to sit very, very still. That way, people tended to un-notice you. Of course they saw you, which was the whole point. There was nothing more noticeable than a person doing their upmost not to be noticed. Not being noticed required effort and energy, which got you noticed.

Being un-noticed was more like hiding in plain sight. It never ceased to amaze Rothchild how often, if he sat very still on the edge of things, he went un-noticed.

So Rothchild sat on the bench at the edge of the grand pavilion in the centre of Middle Calver and waited.

How very different, he thought, this open space is to the tepid pool of human beings collected in the Lower Calver square, filled as it was with marker-goers.

He found the very thought of mingling, shoulder to shoulder, with the great unwashed as they pushed, shoved and bumped their way around the market like cattle in a pen, utterly disgusting.

Like many people fortunate enough to have been born into a position which afforded him clear distance from the average individual, he despised the average individual. He had no knowledge of their world, and certainly had no intention of finding out. That was what other people did.

Therefore, he liked that he, quite literally, looked down on Lower Calver.

As Rothchild waited he took the chance to review his latest actions. He was a man who liked to review his actions as often as possible, he felt it afforded him the chance to spot mistakes (not that he made many) and weed out the weak decisions (not that there were many) before others had a chance to. This way, he felt, he was always one step ahead.

Which is why King Siguld knowing about the red stone and the death of the person who'd reportedly brought it into Calver really annoyed him.

How the hell had he gotten hold of all that information so quickly?

It was Rothchild's job to determine what the King should and shouldn't know. A bit like an information filter. It was much easier that way and it had proved to work quite nicely up to now.

All of a sudden, the King knew more than he should. More than Rothchild would have let him know.

Now that was worrying.

Especially as things were moving along at such a nice pace.

His work with Evangeline had taken a long time to reach this point. They'd both been incredibly careful.

They'd had to be.

The risk was phenomenal. But then so was the reward.

Rothchild sensed someone approach from behind. She was good. He never heard her, more felt her presence.

Gracefully, with one fluid movement, Evangeline the Blue sat down next to him. However, for this meeting, she wasn't wearing her trademark finery of royal blue, but a dourer green. He too had left his colour of choice behind and selected a simple but well-tailored advisors' gown.

'Rothchild, my dear fellow, this had better be good. I'm sure you're fully aware of the difficulties involved in leaving my husband's premises undetected.'

'Evangeline, I apologise. Yet I'm sure for a woman of your talents it was but a mere inconvenience.'

'An inconvenience, yes. Difficult? no.'

Rothchild smiled. He'd always admired her self-confidence. They both watched as someone very official looking left one of the buildings on the right-hand side of the pavilion. With books tucked under one arm and a clutch of scrolls under the other, he strode purposely across the pavilion, cut past the band stand and entered a building on the left side of the pavilion.

'I often think of them as worker ants,' Rothchild said. 'They scurry about the place, all wrapped up in their important little tasks, feeling rather important about themselves, without seeing the big picture.'

'Which is?' Evangeline asked.

'That they're simply fulfilling a purpose. Instantly replaceable, instantly insignificant.'

'Would that be his Majesty's opinion also?'

'Good Gods, no. More's the pity. No, he rather annoyingly feels that everyone has the same worth, with each being as valuable as the last. Makes me feel a little nauseous to be honest.'

'Rothchild, you hold some very interesting opinions.'

'Quite,' Rothchild said, stroking his scar. 'I am what I am and it's served me pretty well so far. Let's not forget, my dear: you came to me.'

'That is undeniably true. Now, would you mind telling me what's so drastically important that you risked discovery by sending a letter to me asking to meet you.'

'We have a slight problem.'

Evangeline waited for Rothchild to continue. For him to say they had a problem, meant that he was rattled. Rothchild's entire being thrived on problems and solving them was his forte. He obviously felt this problem was serious enough or he wouldn't have summoned her to a hasty meeting.

'Our King is aware of the red stone. Which we can only assume means he's aware of its wealth. He is also aware that it is somewhere in his city.'

'Not such a big deal, Rothchild. It's inevitable he'd find out about it, that's the way this glorious city of ours works. Information passes up and down the hill faster than the wind. When that bungling idiot salesman arrived with it and set about getting it valued, word spread and it spread damned fast. Besides, the red stone is only a recent development. Admittedly, a rather large and, for our little plan, beneficial one, but it shouldn't derail our progress. We've done so much of the groundwork; the discovery of the red stone simply means we can think a little bigger. Less of an uprising, more of a revolution.'

Rothchild sighed.

Why was everyone so much, well, *less* than him? He liked Evangeline, he really did. She came about as close to someone he could respect as anyone he'd ever encountered. She was whip-smart, deviously ambitious and had more balls than any man he'd ever met. He just seemed to end up being disappointed in people when they weren't where he was, mentally. He had a knack for thinking four or five steps ahead, being able to not only see where a problem lay, but to look at its various outcomes in full and glorious detail. In this instance, that the King knew of the stone was, as Evangeline had said, inevitable but that wasn't the problem and it disappointed him that she hadn't seen that.

Once all of this was over he'd have to think long and hard about whether to keep her around or not.

Rothchild played the game.

'Of course you're right, my dear,' he said. 'Once something as priceless as the red stone arrived in Calver and those in the know got a good look at it, it was inevitable that word of its worth would spread. It is, of course, a concern that the man with the most money, the most influence and, more importantly, the most to lose, is now very much aware of its existence. I'd have rather liked him to find out a little later, if I'm to be honest.'

'So we're both agreed: the King knows about the stone and that's a little bit of a problem,' Evangeline said, starting to get up.

'But it's not that he knows that's the problem.'

Evangeline paused.

'If I know Siguld,' said Rothchild, 'now he knows it's out there somewhere and nobody knows quite where, then he'll have people scouring the city in search of the red stone so it can't fall in to the wrong hands.'

'Ah,' Evangeline said and sat back down. 'So, we need to find the red stone before he does.'

She still didn't get it.

'Up until this morning,' Rothchild said. 'I was very much under the impression, thanks to my network of helpers, that the stone was with the aforementioned visiting hay salesman, who was staying at The Flying Dishcloth.'

'Isn't it?'

'Given that most of him is smeared on the cobbles outside The Flying Dishcloth, I'd hedge my bets and say no.'

'So where is the red stone, Rothchild?'

'It pains me to say this but I have absolutely no idea. And nor do any of my helpers. Not one of them. It's as if the stone has completely vanished.'

'That could be a problem.'

Now she got it.

'It certainly is a problem. Initially, whilst a large number of people knew about our red stone,

I wasn't in the slightest bit concerned. That was because between us and our resources, they were our people. They knew that if they tried anything silly, like taking the stone for themselves or selling on the location of our rather flattened hay salesman, then, well, let's just say life would've become incredibly painful for them.'

'And now,' Evangeline continued, 'the King is not only aware of the red stone, which was to be expected — albeit a little sooner than we'd have liked — but he's aware it's somewhere in his fine city and he'll send people who don't belong to our network to find it.'

'Precisely. I've already caught some whispers on the wind that the King's got spies involved.'

'Ah. That complicates matters somewhat.'

'Somewhat. If the very worst were to happen and the King found the stone and either kept it in some vault somewhere—'

'Or,' Evangeline interrupted, 'he used its wealth to fund some project for the poor and needy...'

Rothchild slowly shook his head.

'It gives me the chills just thinking about it,' he said. 'Needless to say, our mercenary chums, who took some persuading to reach this point, might not be too impressed that we aren't as in control of things as we have led them to believe.'

'Sounds like we've got a bit of a problem,' Evangeline said.

Those were the words which she spoke to Rothchild.

What she wanted to do was slap the condescending look from his pointy face. It was his job to handle the information side of things. He was the one tasked with gathering information, gauging the mood of the royal court and digging up as much as he could on the people in the best position to help them achieve their goal of one day claiming Calver as their own. When they'd initially got together that moment had seemed a long way off. It had taken years of meticulous planning and constantly staying one step ahead of the different factions within Calver which could derail them and in some cases, destroy them.

Her very own husband for one.

And now, with the end in sight and potentially only a couple of meetings away from gathering a large enough group behind them, they had been presented with a gift horse.

One which Rothchild had allowed to bolt from the stable.

Evangeline had always considered him a self-important preener but had required his steady flow of information and close links to the King. Without him they couldn't get past the first royal guard, let alone take control of the Kingdom. So, she played the role of the feisty woman, just smart enough to be a cut above, but not quite as clever as the marvellous Rothchild who looked down from upon high. Once all of this was over she'd have to think long and hard about whether to keep him around or not.

***

Augustus Malvern put down his book. It was worth more than the entire takings of the market that day, so he put it down very carefully. It was a beautiful leather-bound volume, painstakingly hand-written on the finest parchment and bound using a special glue which would last until the book turned to dust. The book itself was about warfare. Augustus liked books about warfare.

He also liked books about botany, but that was a side of himself a man in his position could ill afford to reveal. So in the presence of others, as he was now, he read books about warfare. They spoke to him in a very visceral way. War was definite. Man versus man where tactics and planning held equal weight with aggression and ferocity. He ran his business empire (for that was what he considered it to be) in the same way.

Fail to plan, then plan to fail was one of his favourite sayings.

He also liked 'everyone has a plan until they get punched in the face' which is what he did to the person sat the other side of his desk.

He simply launched himself, like a spear across his desk and buried his fist in the man's face. Bones crunched and both men landed in a heap on the floor. Augustus rose to his feet, dusted himself down and sat on the corner of his desk. The man he'd just hit lay on his rug, clutching his nose, his eyes wide in shock. Once you've leapt across your desk and punched someone on the nose, they tend to lose all sense of security. They start thinking that if you're crazy enough to pull a stunt like that, what else will you do?

Which is exactly what Augustus wanted.

'Now then, Mr Freepepper,' Augustus said, helping Ronald Freepepper up and back into the chair. 'We have ourselves a baseline. I need answers and I'm prepared to hurt you to get them. So I'm really going to need you to think about the answers you give me, otherwise I'll have to tear your ears off. Can you do that?'

Ronald Freepepper started to nod, which hurt a lot, so he mumbled a yes instead.

'Good chap. Here comes the first question. Are you good and ready?'

'Mmph,' Ronald Freepepper said, hoping to sound enthusiastically helpful.

'Are you one of the doormen at the First Inn?'

That was an easy one and Ronald was only too happy to mumble in the affirmative.

'Thank you for your honesty. You see? This is easier than you thought it might be. Okay, here comes the second question. Have you, on occasion, let groups of people use rooms at the aforementioned First Inn for free? Before you answer that one, let me clarify, so we're on the same page. Have you let people "borrow" rooms for a few hours, without informing the management?'

Ronald Freepepper suddenly felt quite sick. It could be that he'd just swallowed a mouthful of blood containing some quite sharp bits which he could only assume were parts of his nose. More likely it was the image of that nasty bastard of a dwarf who'd warned him (through a series of gestures) that if anyone ever found out about him letting the rooms out at The First Inn then he'd pull his arms off. So far, all had gone swimmingly but Mr Malvern's latest question had caused his stomach to flip because it meant that he'd been found out; which meant the dwarf would be paying him a visit.

'Now Ronald, I thought we had an understanding. I ask a question and you answer truthfully.'

Augustus Malvern got up, picked up the ornamental silver thimble he had on his desk (it was a present from his wife, Gods knew why she'd picked a thimble), put it on his finger then whirled around and poked Ronald Freepepper in the nose.

The result was instant.

Ronald howled as a crackle of pain shot up his damaged nose, across his eyes and clamped into the nerves at the back of his mouth like a needle vice.

Sod the dwarf, this guy was the devil.

'Yeth, yeth, yeth!' Ronald said, his head threatening to implode. 'I get sthom-one thoo open up the room and then lock it! Godsth-damn that hurth!'

To be perfectly honest, Augustus Malvern knew all of this. He hadn't gotten to his position in life without knowing the right people who knew the right people who, in turn, knew some more of the right kind of people. The chain of right people regularly kept him abreast of the latest developments in and round Calver. Anything remotely interesting and he was pretty quick to find out. People either told him things because he paid well for information or because they knew that if he found out from someone other than them, then there'd be a price to pay. As a result, the good people of Calver, from the rodents of the backstreets to the movers and shakers in the King's court flooded to his door bursting to tell him anything and everything.

Consequently, he had his finger on the pulse which was a good thing for a man who liked to stop that pulse every now and again.

What bothered him was that he was missing some information.

For Augustus Malvern, that was unacceptable. Not one of his right people could tell him who was meeting in secret on a regular basis at The First Inn, in the middle of the night. It could be that they were a group of weirdos getting up to some strange and undesirable acts but he doubted it. Those kinds of people couldn't demand the level of silence surrounding their meetings and it bothered Augustus that someone could hold so much influence. He wanted to find out just exactly who could.

'Right then Ronald, I've got one final question for you and then you're free to go. Free to wander off and get some ice on your nose. You'd probably like that, wouldn't you?'

'Yeth,' Ronald said, wiping the tears from his eyes.

'Of course you would. Here comes the final question. Take a minute before you answer, because it's my most important question. Who uses the room?'

Now Ronald started to panic, his palms were already sweaty, as was his face and there was a trickle of sweat running down his back, settling in his undergarments.

Mr Malvern's last question turned the sweat to ice.

The reason he was panicking was simple; he didn't know who used the room.

The dwarf had approached him as he snuck in a quick ale before heading home after a double shift at The First Inn. He walked up to him, slammed down a piece of parchment on the table and walked off. The parchment instructed him to ensure Room 181 was unoccupied and left open between the hours of twelve and four.

Of course, Ronald thought this was ridiculous, screwed up the instructions and threw them into the fire.

Which was a big mistake.

As he stepped out into the crisp night air the dwarf was waiting for him. Although the dwarf never said a word – he hadn't spoken in all the time he'd known him – he made sure Ronald understood the instructions were non-negotiable.

Ronald winced as he remembered being unable to walk down the stairs for a month after the dwarf had helped him understand the non-negotiability of the instructions. In fact, Ronald's left leg still pointed slightly further outwards than his right.

This presented Ronald with a problem. If he told Augustus Malvern that he didn't know who used the room, he may as well sign his own death certificate. What else could he do?

Actually, he did what most men do when threatened with unbeatable odds and the very real prospect of extreme violence.

He did whatever it took to survive. Which in this case was to lie.

***

Ronald Freepepper walked home very carefully. Each time he took a step on the cobblestones he jarred his aching nose.

One of Mr Malvern's associates had very kindly escorted him to the gatehouse. After their little chat, Mr Malvern had been incredibly nice to Ronald and had even offered him some money so he might buy his wife something nice.

As Ronald exited the gatehouse into Lower Calver and counted the money he'd been given, he couldn't help but think that maybe Mr Malvern was alright after all. He had a reputation to live up to and sure he'd slapped him around a bit, but Ronald supposed that came with the territory. If Ronald had known how well he'd be rewarded for talking – albeit a web of lies – then he'd have talked so very much sooner.

Getting off with a busted nose seemed like a pretty good deal, considering what could've happened.

His composure returning, Ronald decided he might drop by the Dog and Ferret for a swift half before heading home.

Why not? It had been a heck of day. A heck of a day which instantly got a whole lot worse when the dwarf stepped out from the alley in front of Ronald. Ronald's already-stressed bladder let go as the dwarf walked forwards, smiling.

Chapter 17
Never Look a Gift Horse in the Backside

Sometimes in life, strange things happen. They happen for no apparent reason and as much as people would love to find the hidden meaning in these strange things, there just isn't one. It's the nature of people to try to find meaning in every detail of life, more so when the meaning seems so very hard to find. If only people would take these things at face value, shrug their shoulders and declare: "that was a bit strange, oh well, better get on with things" then life would be a whole lot less complicated. There'd be less fortune tellers for one which can't be a bad thing.

Sometimes strange things happen for absolutely no reason whatsoever when in actual fact, a woven intricate combination of happenstance, karma and divine intervention would sound much more impressive.

Sometimes shit just happens.

Which is the easiest way to describe how Greg, Ralph and Eve found the red stone.

They'd finished talking with Wolf Dangerpunch, proposed their next course of action (or rather Eve had whilst Ralph nodded along enthusiastically and Greg sat bewildered), then Wolf asked them to give him time to mull things over. What they were asking was quite a big deal, the kind of decision which couldn't be made until after a nice cup of tea.

Eve asked if there was anything they could do to help in the meantime and he'd suggested they mucked out his horse, which he kept round the back of his tent.

'When you asked if there was anything we could do,' Ralph said to Eve, 'I thought you meant give his tent a sweep or tidy out his storage chest.'

'Yeah, well,' Eve said, scooping up a pile of hay and throwing it over her shoulder, 'I've been dropping by Wolf's place for years now and it's as much home as anywhere else. He gives me some tea to sample, the occasional bite to eat and in turn I sit and listen to him talk about the good old days as well as doing a bit around the place to help out. Besides, you're farmers; this should be just like being back at home.'

'Well I for one think it's great that you help out around here,' Greg said. 'Oh, and by the way, when were you planning on telling me about hiring another mercenary?'

Ralph scraped a bundle of hay down from the cart and started to spread it on the floor.

'We tried to back on the Blood Wastes,' he said. 'But you went all peculiar so we decided to crack on.'

'And just how are you planning on paying Mr Dangerpunch? I'm assuming he's not offering us a freebee.'

Eve and Ralph looked at each other.

Just then, Wolf's horse, which was tied to the cart, let out a high-pitched whinny. Ralph, Eve and Greg stepped back. The horse began to stamp its hooves on the ground whilst shaking its head from side to side. It let out another high pitch whinny, which sounded much closer to a scream than anything else, shuddered, and then jumped forward as a large lump of soon to be manure plopped from its rear end.

'Crikey,' Ralph said. 'I reckon old Wolf needs to cut back on feeding his horse the spicy stuff. That sounded like it stung on the way out.'

'Ah yes, toilet humour,' Eve said. 'Thought that would be just about your level.'

'I'm just saying that poor old Dobbin here might want a bucket of water to sit down in; that one sounded like a proper ring-stinger.'

'If you two have quite finished,' Greg said, walking back over to the hay, 'we've got a job to do and, more importantly, you were about to tell me how we were going to finance a mercenary helpi—'

Greg stopped as his pitchfork clunked into something buried in the hay. He had just flicked a generous heap of hay over the horse's manure when he hit something much harder than a lump of sweetcorn.

As a farmer he was well aware of the noises pitchforks made when in contact with all sorts of materials. When working with hay and manure, they most certainly didn't clunk.

And of course Greg knew. He wasn't entirely sure how he knew, but he did.

So he bent down and – much to Ralph and Eve's disgust – scooped the red stone out from the slightly steaming horse manure.

He quickly dropped it into a nearby bucket, gave it a wash and then took it over to Ralph and Eve.

Well, he almost took it over to Ralph and Eve.

His first thought was, *that was a bit strange, oh well, better get on with things,* which was closely followed by, *oyou don't actually have to tell them you've found it, you know. You could hide it away and then come up with a plan in the meantime. It could work.*

But then Greg pushed that thought away and the horrible consequences acting upon it might bring, and took the freshly washed red stone over to Ralph and Eve.

'Listen,' Greg said. 'I've got something to show you and I don't want you freaking out when I do.'

'Wonder how many times you've said that to a girl,' Ralph said.

'Just come here and have a look at this.'

'Once again; wonder how many times—'

217

'Ralph!' Greg hissed. 'Stop being smart and come here. Now!'

Eve and Ralph leant in as Greg put his hand in his pocket.

'If you get your tally-whacker out...' Ralph said.

Eve shot him a look.

'Before I show you this, and I'm thinking of you Ralph, I need you to remain nice and calm. Can you be calm?'

Eve nodded impatiently, 'Can we just get a bloody move on? We've got things to do.'

'Sorry,' Greg said. 'It's just that I found out why Wolf's horse was making so much noise. I think it was this...' Greg pulled out the red stone.

Ralph's eyes widened. 'Holy mother of the Gods!' he shouted. 'It's the mother-trumping red—'

Ralph's words ended with the sound of fist on flesh.

Greg looked at his brother lying in a heap on the floor. Already the knuckle marks on his jaw were starting to turn a violent red.

Eve shook and flexed her hand.

'You've found the red stone then,' she whispered. 'That was a bit strange. Oh well, better get on with things. Shit happens. Or in this case, happened.'

***

For the second time in less than a day Ralph was awoken by a bucket of cold water which was unceremoniously thrown in his face.

He sat bolt upright, his eyes once again wide open.

Greg was crouched one side of him, Eve the other.

'Hey buddy,' Ralph said, the left side of his mouth starting to swell. 'I had the strangest dream.'

'It wasn't a dream,' Greg said. He held up the red stone for Ralph to see.

'Holy smokes!' he shouted, 'It's the red—'

Ralph flinched as Eve drew her hand back.

'Sorry,' he whispered, rubbing his jaw. 'You've got the stone back!'

Greg and Eve helped Ralph to his feet.

'Looks like we're back in business!'

'Who's in business?' Wolf said as he walked around the back of the tent.

'Oh, nothing!' Ralph said, standing in front of Greg. 'In fact, there's nothing much going on, really. In fact, it's pretty dull back here. That's one thing I could definitely say about back here: that it's most certainly quite dull.'

Wolf stopped, leant on the wooden staff he had been carrying and spat on the floor.

'That so?'

Ralph looked at Greg. 'That's exactly so,' he said. 'As a matter of fact, I was just saying to my brother Gregory here, that cleaning out a horse, whilst entirely useful and practical, is quite possibly one of the most uneventful tasks a man can undertake. Sometimes, if I'm feeling a little over stimulated, I'll head on out to the horses and give them a good mucking out, just so as I can level out.'

'Level out?'

'Yeah, you know, chill. Take it easy.' Ralph picked up a pitchfork and started frantically shovelling great lumps of hay. 'Ooh, I feel so relaxed what with this being so uneventful.'

'Looks like you found the red stone then.' Wolf said. 'Took you long enough.'

'What red stone?' Ralph said, feigning incredulity. 'As if, to say, for one and erm that is...'

Ralph trailed off in a staccato of unfinished statements.

'You knew?' Eve said, turning to Wolf.

Wolf smiled and rubbed his beard.

'Yeah, suppose I did.'

'And you did nothing?' Greg said.

'Looks like it, doesn't it?' Wolf said.

'I don't understand,' Ralph said eying up Wolf suspiciously. 'I get you probably didn't know how valuable it is, but still, you must've had some idea.'

'Oh, I knew how valuable it was,' Wolf said, walking over to his still-panting horse. 'Mr Smart told me.'

'Keith Smart, the hay salesman?' Greg said.

'One and the same,' Wolf said, stroking his horse's mane.

'He dropped by the other day, said he was looking to procure my services in a couple of days' time. Said he'd heard I was a good sort and

220

that he'd be coming into a lot of money, if all things went according to plan. Apparently, they did not.'

'So, he just left the red stone with you? For safe keeping?' Ralph said.

'Kind of.'

'Kind of?'

'Yeah, kind of. After we'd finalised the details of our business arrangement, he asked if he could pop out back for a tinkle. Now your hay salesman may very well be smart in name but by nature, he most certainly was not. I watched him rustle around out there in my hay pile for a good two minutes. Soon as he'd gone I went and had a look. That's when I found your red stone. Pretty little bugger, isn't it?'

'Wait a minute,' Ralph said. 'You found an incredibly valuable and rare stone and you left it in your hay pile for anyone to wander along and take?'

'Don't be daft, lad!' Wolf said, shaking his head. 'I fed it to old Rainstorm here!' Wolf patted the flank of his horse.

'Of course you did,' Ralph said. 'How very bleeding obvious.'

Eve shook her head and smiled.

'It's an old mercenary trick, Ralph. Anything valuable that's small enough, you feed it to your horse. That way your valuables walk around with you and...'

'Ultimately,' Wolf finished, 'they come out with interest.'

'So where does that leave us?' Greg asked, well aware he was stood less than three feet from one of the best mercenaries in the Kingdom whilst holding a very valuable item.

'Exactly where we were,' Wolf said. 'If you'd have listened to me properly back in the tent, I told you I'm a man of my word and that's what I'll stay until the day I die. You asked me to help you out, I'll help you out. Afterwards, whoever's still alive can negotiate my fee.'

'Why don't you just take the stone from us now?' Ralph said. 'You could use it to open your tea shop.'

'That I could, Ralph. I could slit your throats and take the stone from Greg's still warm hand, head into town, set up my tea shop and I wouldn't lose but a minute's sleep over it. But that's not the way things should be done. There are rules. A mercenary code of honour. Or at least there used to be, back when I started. You carried out the job you were hired to do. It was a mark of your character. And besides, based on everything you've told me so far, I reckon heading into Calver with that there red stone is going to provide me with plenty of excitement. So, what are we waiting for?'

***

'It's no bloody use, sir. We've tried every trick in the book and even some tricks which aren't in the book on account of how nasty they are. Nothing seems to work. If anything, the more

222

violent and depraved we get, the more he seems to like it!'

739 shook his head. He wrinkled his bulbous nose in a display of utter contempt. He could recall a time when an interrogation would last no more than a couple of hours and you'd be home in time to kiss the dog and put the wife to bed. That was back when being a spy had been a – relatively speaking – honest profession. A spot of espionage here, the odd interrogation there and only on the rarest of occasions would you have to kill someone. And that in itself was an art form. These days it was all so very different. The kind of individuals he dealt with now made him so very sad. There just wasn't the class of adversary available anymore. During the last few days one of his own had been killed and hung in a wardrobe, he'd had to deal with a half blind salesman and now... this. The problem with people nowadays was they just had no standards.

'Cut him loose.' 739 said.

'Really, sir?' 134 said.

739 turned to face the newest recruit. 'Did I stutter, stammer or in any way make my instruction somewhat unclear, 134?

'No, sir, it's just that...'

'134, how long have you been a spy?'

'Three weeks, sir.'

'And in those three weeks, how many missions have you undertaken?'

'One, sir.'

'Which was?'

'To fetch you coffee, sir.'

'Remind me how that turned out, would you, 134?'

'Well, it would appear that, certainly if you consider all the, also in all eventualities it would...'

'You brought me apple juice, didn't you, 134?'

134 hung his head in shame.

'So you'll pardon me, 134, if I don't take interrogation advice from someone who couldn't find his own arsehole with a torch and a mirror!' 739 bellowed.

739 took one last, long look at the dwarf hanging upside down from the rafters. He was a tough little bugger that was for sure. But there was more than one way to get what you wanted.

739 marched from the room, slamming the door behind him. He strode purposely along the dimly lit tunnel, towards the stairs.

As he did, someone fell in alongside him, not missing a stride.

'Bad day at the office?' Perenholm said.

'It never ceases to amaze me how you manage to get in here,' 739 said. 'And I don't want to know where you got the uniform from.'

'Probably best you don't,' Perenholm said. 'Old Short-and-Stumpy not talking?'

'Ha, bloody ha. Even if he had a tongue, he wouldn't say a word. I think he'd purposely drag it out, just to make sure he received as much pain as possible.'

Perenholm shuddered.

'Gives me the heeby-jeebies, that one does.'

'Me too.'

739 stopped and turned to face Perenholm, certain that, even after all of his years on the job, within five minutes of Perenholm leaving, he'd have no recollection of what he looked like.

'Tell me something,' he asked. 'Back in the old days, it wasn't like this, was it?'

'Like what?'

'I dunno. Maybe I'm getting too old for this malarkey. It just seems that the people I encounter now, well, they're not the same level of individual I used to deal with. They're more...'

'Unethical? Amoral? Unprincipled?'

'Exactly. Time was when you could rely on an adversary to have a little respect, you know?'

Perenholm patted 739 on the back as the two started walking again.

'Times have changed, my old friend. And they'll change again. Now, tell me, what's the plan with the dwarf?'

'Simple, really,' 739 smiled. 'He may be tough as old boots but he's as thick as them too. We'll let him go and I'll put two of my best on him. He'll lead us to where we want to be. I might be getting too old for this, but it'll take more than a stubborn dwarf to stop me.'

With a smile, 739 turned to Perenholm but he was once more alone.

'Smart arse!' he shouted to no one in particular.

***

Art Rosebud was starting to get slightly concerned. Only just slightly concerned but it was enough. He rarely allowed himself to move on over into mildly concerned and for someone who'd grown up on, in and often under the backstreets of Lower Calver, full-blown concerned was inconceivable.

He had found that slightly concerned kept you keen and more importantly, relatively free of trouble. So, yes, he felt slightly concerned.

As in most cases in Bud's life *what* had happened wasn't the slightly concerning part. It was *what to do* about what had happened.

Bud held to the simple philosophy that maintained it wasn't the things which happened in life that caused problems but your reaction to those things. Which meant that reaction became crucial in that moment between getting spotted with three loaves of bread up your jumper and legging it hell for leather before your twelve-year old self got a beating.

The reason for Bud's current state of slight concern was how to react to everything he'd just seen. For the most part, one of his other philosophies had served him incredibly well throughout his life: if you see something you shouldn't, keep your mouth shut, your head down and walk very quickly in the opposite direction.

Normally, he'd be inclined to follow his own advice, but in this instance he was starting to fit pieces together like a huge multi-layered jigsaw puzzle.

He'd been leaning on the corner of a building opposite Mr Malvern's house, hidden in the shadow of its eaves, hoping to spot Greg and Ralph. Of course he'd seen them leave the market and then Lower Calver with a small woman in furs but he knew they'd be back.

What choice did they have? If they ran away Mr Malvern would find them. It might take a while, but in the end he'd catch them. He always did. And besides, Greg was smarter than that. Ralph too, in a less obvious way.

So he was confident they'd return.

It was how they'd return and what they'd be planning to do which concerned him. He'd been waiting in the shadows for the last twelve hours and if needs be, he could wait for twelve more. He had no problem in waiting. He'd waited most of his life for an opportunity to be free. All he needed was Greg, Ralph and the red stone.

He'd been doing his damnedest to find the stone in the meantime but everyone he spoke to – and he had to be very careful who he spoke to, just in case Mr Malvern caught wind – had no idea where it was. He knew the right people and was therefore lucky enough to speak to a few who had actually seen the stone when that idiot of a hay salesman blundered his way around Lower Calver. All those who'd seen it could attest to its value. Some even went as far as saying it couldn't be valued, they'd seen nothing of the like before. They spoke to him in revered tones, speaking of the way the stone seemed to catch and store the light before sending it pulsing out in all directions.

Bud didn't give a nun's ass about dancing light, he just wanted the stone for what he could do with it. So he'd waited. Through the night and into the morning. He hadn't wavered once. It was as if he'd slowly melted into the brickwork of the building he leant against.

One event, followed by another, all requiring careful thought, all requiring some kind of reaction, each one added to the other causing Art Rosebud to become slightly concerned.

First of all, a doorman from The First Inn left Mr Malvern's. He had blood crusted under his recently broken nose and splashes of it on his uniform. He was also clutching a small bag of money. In and of itself, nothing too strange.

Within minutes of the doorman leaving, an incredibly short but very powerfully built man scurried from the shadows behind Mr Malvern's house and darted in and out of the spaces between the houses, seemingly following the doorman.

Again, nothing too odd about that; fresh blood and fresh money seemed to attract certain individuals in Calver, although they normally restricted themselves to the backstreets of Lower Calver.

For a while not much else happened. Bud had often found this to be the case when waiting and watching; there were sudden bursts of activity, followed by long periods of inactivity.

About an hour later, a member of Mr Malvern's security left the house and walked the perimeter of the garden, stopping periodically to talk to the other members of security. As he paused to talk to the two by the front gate, Bud caught wisps of words as they floated across the street to him. Two in particular grabbed his attention: 'brothers' and 'farmers'.

Before he had time to digest the words, something else happened. Or rather, someone.

Firstly, Mr Malvern left with four of his security staff. They left on foot and headed north up the King's Pass.

Shortly after that, Mr Malvern's wife, Evangeline, hurried from the back of the house, down a side street and off into the gathering dark as night fell. She was wrapped in a deep blue cloak with the hood raised and it was only when she turned to check she wasn't being followed that Bud was able to catch a glimpse of her face in the lamp light.

It would seem that it was a good time to be stood across the road from Mr Malvern's residence.

Part way through the night, Mrs Malvern returned, still with the blue hood raised to cover her face, still darting through the shadows. She re-entered through the back of the house and was soon gone from sight.

Mr Malvern had still not returned.

The final piece of action occurred just as dawn began to break. The dwarf was back. He hobbled across the road, favouring his left leg and rubbing his right shoulder. As he approached the rear of Mr Malvern's house he stepped out of the shadows.

Bud winced. He was pretty sure the dwarf had never been described as handsome, but after whatever he'd been up to tonight, he'd never get close. He looked as if he'd been dragged behind a coach across broken glass.

And the strange thing was, he seemed to be smiling.

Strange up until that point because strange is a relative thing. As it happened a smiling, battered dwarf became less strange as Bud caught sight of two spies crawling across the roof top opposite, clearly following the dwarf.

Slightly concerning but also very interesting. Very interesting indeed.

Chapter 18
The Often-Overlooked Swinging Headbutt

It was the last day of the market. By this point anything of any value had been sold, leaving behind worthless tat. Cheap, worthless tat.

Which is why the market was as busy today as it was on its opening morning.

When it comes to a bargain, you can't beat cheap, worthless tat. At least you know what you're getting. If, within minutes of getting it home, it turns out not to work then your expectations don't have far to fall.

The market had opened especially early today, with the hope that most of the products and produce would be shifted before lunch.

The people of Calver liked the market; they liked the money it brought to the city even more, but they were also happy when it was gone.

The King's Guard were more than happy to get back to their normal duties instead of policing the streets like common law keepers, the residents of Middle Calver were happy to be able to look from their properties and not have to soil their view with the masses drudging through the market and even the King was happy, as it meant he could relax, albeit just a little bit.

But, for now, the square of Lower Calver was all hustle with even a little bit of bustle thrown in for good measure.

Greg, Ralph, Eve and Wolf all entered through the gatehouse and into the open along with others desperate to grab a last-minute bargain.

Wolf was wearing a hooded short coat which appeared to be made of bits of sack. 'All these people!' he said, flicking his hood back and looking around. 'It never ceases to amaze me how many people come to the market. Just think if each one of them bought a bag of tea from my shop!'

A large shape, which could in all honesty have been a man, a woman or a well-trained farm animal barged past Ralph.

'And would you want any of these people in your tea shop?' he asked.

'Course not!' Wolf said, turning up his nose. 'Half of these folk couldn't tell the difference between a fruity autumnal blend and tepid rainwater!'

'If you're making it, the difference isn't that great,' Eve said under her breath.

'Besides,' Wolf continued, 'my establishment will only require the patronage of the more discerning individual. Any lowlife tries to come in, I'll poke their eyes out.'

'You should get that put above the door,' Ralph said.

'We should get a move on,' Greg said.

The weight of the stone in his jerkin pocket was an ever-present reminder of the job at hand.

'Yes,' Ralph said. 'I'm looking forward to meeting Mr Rosebud now that we've got our friend Mr Dangerpunch here. Maybe he'll be more inclined to listen to our side of the story and not just think of his own little plan.'

'He's just doing what he has to, Ralph,' Greg said. 'We've been over this. If, with Wolf's help, we can help Bud, then we'll do it. Dealing with the problem of Augustus Malvern is in our best interests too, you know.'

'Ralphy-boy just likes having someone to hide behind, that's all,' Eve said. 'It's probably not very often he has the chance to be all masculine and powerful.'

'As opposed to you, my dear,' Ralph said, 'who's masculine pretty much most of the time.'

***

Unbeknownst to Greg, Ralph, Eve and Wolf, they had been watched very carefully the minute they exited the gatehouse. Their every move had been scrutinised and most of their words duly noted and passed along.

Of course, some of the people doing the watching were very low level in their organisation and were merely instruments set the task of feeding information onwards up the chain of command. They were the kind of individuals who heard things, useful things, each and every day. They were known as the listeners. As a result, these listeners made a solid living from passing such information on. Some of them were even trustworthy. Some would pass anything on, regardless of the level of truth attached to it as they would be paid – albeit a nominal amount – for each and every piece of information.

Which then presented a problem. What information was useful and which could be dismissed out of hand? Hence, the next level in the information supply chain: the sievers.

These were the people who sifted the wheat from the chaff and passed on the good stuff. They were slightly better paid and acted as middle men (or women) in the dealings between the listeners and the more important people who required a steady flow of information.

Many an individual had risen to a position of importance merely through selecting good quality listeners and even better quality sievers.

What none of the listeners or even the sievers had expected was that as they went about their business of keeping tabs – literally – on the new arrivals to the market, was the presence of so many other listeners.

In fact, the market was crawling with listeners desperate to get close to Greg and his companions, and on just about every street corner around the edge of the market, the sievers did their best not to notice each other.

Such an occurrence was somewhat of an oddity and as a result, the listeners and sievers had no real plan for dealing with this sudden saturation of the marketplace; again, literally.

Normally the sight of another listener or siever would result in the latecomer moving on.

Today was different. Today the information wasn't being passed up the chain, it had been requested from the top of a number of chains.

Various listeners and sievers had been contacted in all manner of hush-hush ways and set the task of keeping an ear out for two individuals in particular.

Two farmers who fit the description of the two now wandering through the market accompanied by a pair of mercenaries.

As groups of listeners wandered in and out of the market, information was passed on to one of the many sievers stood at street corners. Occasionally, a siever would wander, ever-so-slowly from his position, take a couple of lazy and languid strides around a corner and then make a mad-dash for a backstreet. Moments later he would emerge and repeat the journey in reverse; a mad dash which would quickly turn into a wandering walk, often accompanied by a whistled tune and a glance skyward, in the time-honoured tradition of feigned innocence.

Information was passed onwards and upwards.

It was an odd situation, one which many listeners and sievers had never encountered before. They knew it meant the new arrivals must be important and they knew that a number of people wanted information about them. But the privilege of being low on the totem pole means that, so long as you're paid, you don't need to know any more than that.

***

'I think we're being watched,' Eve said to Greg as they pushed their way through a crowd towards the food section of the market.

'I was thinking the same thing too,' Greg said. 'Only I didn't want to say anything in case I came across as paranoid.'

'Paranoia is when you're unreasonably suspicious. Given that the bloke with the missing front teeth and the limp is about to pass us for the seventh time and this time he's got a notebook open, I'd say we've moved into the realm of reasonably suspicious. Wouldn't you?'

'So what should we do?'

'Well, just thinking off the top of my head...'

Eve bumped into the man with no front teeth and a limp. It seemed innocuous; that was until the man fell, howled and ran away clutching his right arm, the wrist of which seemed to point in a funny direction.

'Let's have a little look,' Eve said, flipping through the pages of the man's notebook. 'Interesting.'

'What's interesting?' Greg asked.

'It seems that our friend has in his possession a description of you and your brother.'

Eve flipped the notepad around to show Greg a very close likeness to himself and Ralph scratched onto the rough parchment in ink.

'I think it's probably time we left the market,' Eve said.

'Too late for that,' Ralph said, appearing at their side. He pointed over to the left where four huge men were pushing their way through the crowds like a plough through soft turf.

The very same four large men they'd first met at The Hairy Apple and then again in Room 181 of The First Inn.

'If I didn't know any better,' Ralph said. 'I'd think they were following us.'

***

Greg watched as the crowds parted and the four large men strode through the market, quite clearly with only one destination in mind.

'Don't worry, Ralph,' Greg said. 'I don't think they'll try anything, out here in the open.'

'And besides,' Ralph said, inching closer to his brother, 'we've got a couple of mercenaries on our side now, haven't we?'

Greg and Ralph turned to face Eve and Wolf who weren't there. They were nowhere to be seen.

'Oh bugger,' Ralph said, summing up the mood quite nicely.

Before Greg or Ralph had a chance to run, the four large men pushed through the remainder of the crowd and appeared in front of them, looming large in the early morning sunlight.

'Well, well, bleedin', well,' the largest of the four large men said. His nose was starting to heal but he still had deep purple rings under each eye.

'Three wells,' Ralph said. 'You'll be alright if there's a drought.'

'Oh yes,' the largest of the large men said. 'I'd almost forgotten how much of a funny guy you were, Ralph. A real funny guy.'

'You know me, fellas: a chuckle a minute at no extra cost. Anywho, it's been wonderful to catch up, but we really must be heading off. Mr Malvern... our meeting... you remember?'

The largest of the large men stroked the stubble on his chin and appeared to look into the distance.

'Mr Malvern? Mr Malvern? You know, I *do* remember. You both had to head off to meet him. That's right, isn't it?'

Greg could see the trap coming, but Ralph's mouth was already working.

'That's absolutely correct chaps. Now if you don't mind...'

Ralph performed a quick about turn and began to walk away. That is, his legs did. Unfortunately, the top half of his body refused to follow on account of the back of his jerkin being held by one of the large men.

'You see,' the largest of the large men said, turning to Greg, 'your brother here has presented me with a falsehood. An untruth. Which I feel has tainted our already rocky relationship. That presents me with a dilemma.'

'Really?' was all Greg could manage. At that moment his mind wasn't completely on the large man's words. Out of the corner of his eye he had caught sight of someone moving very quickly in between the nearest stalls.

'Really. You see, my dilemma is this. I have been given the task of apprehending you and your halfwit brother and escorting you to a certain location.'

Greg caught sight once more of a flash of movement. It was getting closer.

'So what's the dilemma?'

'It's this,' the largest of the large men said. 'Whilst I really do feel obliged to escort you to said location, I'd really like to slap your brother around a bit first.'

The movement slowed down.

'I find that most people do,' Greg said as the movement over to his left resumed, somewhat reluctantly.

'Don't I get any say in this?' Ralph said as he struggled to wriggle free.

'So,' the largest of the large men said, completely ignoring Ralph, 'how's about I give him a bit of a pasting now and then we can move on to you?'

'How about you don't?' Eve said as she stepped out.

'Who are you?' one of the large men said.

'Wait a minute, wait a minute!' the largest of the large men said. 'I know you! The fur, the mad, crazy eyes... you're Eve Manslayer!'

'That's right,' Eve said, drawing up to her full height, which still only came to the large men's middle.

'But, you're tiny!' the largest of the large men said. 'I thought you were supposed to strike fear into the hearts of all men? How the hell do you do that? By threatening to bite their ankles?'

Eve looked unmoved. 'Look boys, I'm a mercenary and you four are... mercenaries... of sorts. If you wander off now, we'll forget all about this.'

'We're going nowhere, sweet-cheeks,' the largest of the large men said. 'And what's this "we" business? Surely you don't expect this pair to help you out!?'

'These two?' Eve said shaking her head. 'Not these two. I was thinking more about him.'

'How do, numpties?' Wolf said stepping out from behind the nearest stall.

240

Greg had seen his fair share of fights. Farmers loved nothing more than a good old-fashioned dust-up, especially after a few jars of home-brewed cider, but this was no fight. It was more of a massacre.

It was as if Eve and Wolf had received a script beforehand, detailing every move the four large men would make over the course of the next ten seconds.

The first thing to happen was that the large man holding onto Ralph let him go and turned square on to face Wolf. Which turned out to be a poor choice of things to do as Wolf had already stepped in towards the man. He kicked him hard in the kneecap, as if kicking open a locked door. Something important snapped inside the large man's knee and he crumpled to the floor, clutching his leg in agony.

Two seconds. One down. Three to go.

As the other three stood, slack-jawed and gaping at their fallen colleague, Eve wasted no time. She dropped to one knee and punched the closet large man in the thigh. The resulting blow forced his leg to buckle and in one fluid movement Eve whipped her arm up and elbowed the man in the mouth. It took his body a moment to realise his brain was still crashing into the back of his skull before he too crumpled to the floor.

Six seconds. Two down.

Two to go.

Wolf winked at Eve as he pivoted on his left foot and shifted his weight as if to kick the next large man in the kneecap too.

The large man dropped his leg back in anticipation of the blow and only too late realised he had been duped. In shifting his right leg back, he had dropped his left shoulder which meant his face was now close to Wolf's. Too close.

Wolf's swinging headbutt caught the man clean on the side of the jaw and down he went.

Ten seconds.

Three down.

One to go.

'Ah, the often overlooked swinging headbutt,' Eve smiled. 'Nice work.'

'Why thank you, Manslayer. None too shabby yourself. Now, about this one...'

'Is there any chance I could ask you to go easy on the face?' the largest of the large men said.

'Of course,' Eve said. 'We're not animals, you know.'

They did go easy on his face.

Not so easy on his everything else, though.

Chapter 19
A Quiet Pint

Greg and Ralph left the market quickly. They found it was quite easy to do so with Eve Manslayer and Wolf Dangerpunch at their sides. Most of the market-goers seemed more than happy, desperate even, to move out of their way. There were one or two dedicated individuals who pushed forwards rather than slink out of the way. Most wanted a glimpse at what had just happened.

'Bloody rubberneckers,' Wolf said as he elbowed an overkeen onlooker in the teeth. 'And adrenaline junkies. The first lot are bad enough, they love a good bit of misfortune, but it's the second lot who bother me the most.' He carried on forwards, aiming kicks and punches at anyone stupid enough to get within his reach. 'These adrenaline junkies turn up at anything from a pub brawl to a full-on battle. They love a bit of violence. Taps in to something primal, I reckon. Bloody weirdos.' Wolf aimed a straight right at a man who'd leapt out from behind the rapidly parting crowd, his eyes wild.

'Yeah, man!' the newcomer shouted, pumping his fist into the air. 'You totally dominated th—'

There was a crunch as gnarled mercenary fist connected with adrenaline junkie teeth. The man plonked down onto his backside, looked up at the crowd and grinned a bloody grin.

'You shee thatsh?! I goth punshed in the faysh! Dat wozsh amayshing!'

'Idiot,' Wolf said simply, pressing on.

As they reached the edge of the market and thus the crowds of people, Eve slowed them down.

'Listen,' she said, grabbing hold of Greg's arm. 'We're going to need to split up. Pretty soon the whole of Lower Calver will be swamped with the King's Guard looking for the four of us. You take Ralph and find somewhere to hide. Just until tonight.'

'How will you find us?' Ralph asked.

'Don't you worry, Ralph,' Eve said. 'We'll find you. You won't have to pine for me for too long.'

With that she patted Ralph on the cheek, turned and was gone. Wolf, Greg noticed, had already disappeared.

Ralph brushed his cheek with his hand but stopped when he caught Greg looking at him.

'What?' he said.

'Nothing,' Greg said, smiling.

They started moving towards the edge of the market again, this time much slower and changing direction as many times as they thought they should.

'Fancy her thinking I'd be pining for her,' Ralph said as they stepped out of the market and tried to walk as nonchalantly as possible to a nearby shop window.

'Of course you won't,' Greg said, trying to check behind them in the window to see if they'd been followed.

'I mean, she's been nothing but horrible to me. Ever since she met me.'

'That she has.' It was also hard to make out if anyone was following them because the crowd was now moving back to their usual purpose of finding a bargain on the last day of the market. It took a lot more than a quick scrap to stop the bargain hunters.

'But she was pretty effective when it came to handling those four lummoxes. Did you see the way she moved?' Ralph said.

'I did.'

Eve had been right. Whilst the market-goers were returning to their business, the square was beginning to fill with King's Guards. They'd heard that there'd been a spot of bother in the market and were now happy for a chance to get stuck in instead of trying to present a more welcoming face of law enforcement. Might be they even got the chance to knock a few heads together.

Greg and Ralph moved further up the King's Pass and away from the market. They tried to act like tourists, pausing to glance in the occasional window, stopping to look up at the palace every now and again and do everything they could to disappear in plain sight. Neither of them knew whether this was working or not as the people who may or may not be watching them were probably very good at disappearing in plain sight too. Part of the job description.

Finally, they found themselves outside the entrance to The First Inn.

'You know something, Greg?' Ralph said. 'I reckon that Eve quite likes me.'

'You mean in between kicking lumps out of your lumps and throwing buckets of water over you.'

'Yeah. You see, I reckon what we've got going on there is a classic case of stifled emotions.'

'Is that so?' Greg said, taking the chance to glance back down the road towards the market.

'You've got Eve and you've got me. She's Eve Manslayer, the mercenary, and then I come along and I obviously intimidate her.'

'You do remember the part at the market when she elbowed that large man in the face and he fell down like a sack of potatoes?'

A look spread across Ralph's face that many a teenage girl would describe as dreamy.

'No, I don't mean intimidate physically, because as you know, I'm a lover rather than a fighter.'

'Is that knowledge widespread?' Greg said. 'Because this is the first I'm hearing of it.'

'Sod off, Greg. As I was saying, I reckon there's a bit of something going on there. I think she's into me.'

'All I ask is that when you put forward that theory to her, you make sure I'm in the room.'

'Will do, oh brother of mine, will...'

Ralph stopped mid-word.

'Hang on a tick, isn't that our good buddy Mr Freepepper?'

Greg turned to follow his brother's gaze.

Ronald Freepepper looked like he'd seen better days. In fact, his eyes were so swollen, it looked like he'd not been doing much seeing at all recently. He hobbled forwards out of The First Inn front door on legs that looked like they no longer bent at the knee. He was wearing his doorman's uniform and an expression of sullen rejection.

He glanced first left and then right, which was when he caught sight of Greg and Ralph. He attempted a quick about turn which ended up looking more like a straight-legged wobble and tried to shuffle back inside.

'Whoa there, Ronald!' Ralph said as he and Greg ran over. They each grabbed an arm and frog-shuffled the doorman away from the front door and down the side alley next to the hotel.

Up close, in the confined space of the alley, Ronald Freepepper looked even worse. In addition to the swollen-shut eyes, his forehead looked like it had been repeatedly pummelled with a small hammer and most of his left ear was missing.

'Please leave me alone!' Ronald Freepepper said, his head hung low.

'What's the matter, Ronnie, why the long and lumpy face?' Ralph said.

'You don't know what I've been through!' he wailed.

'Looks like a mangle,' Greg said. 'Backwards.'

'You two!' Ronald hissed. 'You're nothing but bad luck!'

'That's strange,' Ralph said. 'We had a similar opinion of you. You know, what with the whole unlocking a room for a bunch of cut throats and ne'er-do-wells.'

'You think you've had it bad? Look at me! They've sent me home,' Ronald jerked a thumb in the direction of The First Inn. 'Said they can't have someone looking like this, greeting visitors. They said it'll scare people away. Said I'm not getting paid either.'

'We're sorry to hear that Ronald, we really are,' Ralph said.

'Not as sorry as you're going to be,' Ronald said, a smile spreading across his swollen lips.

'What's that supposed to mean?' Greg asked.

'Do you know what happened to me? Do you? After you two totally messed up a perfectly good gig I'd got going on here, I got paid a visit. By a vicious and sadistic dwarf.'

Greg and Ralph looked at each other. There weren't too many dwarves in Calver.

'Go on,' Greg said.

'I don't think I need to go into too much detail but he made it perfectly clear he wasn't happy about our arrangement going belly up. It wasn't much of a leap to realise that you two morons must have ballsed up!'

'We didn't balls up,' Ralph said. 'We had to modify your instructions slightly when one of us ended up in Room 181 as the guests arrived.'

'You pillocks!' Ronald hissed. 'No wonder the dwarf was so... thorough. The vicious little bugger might not be able to talk but he left me in no doubt that his employers weren't too happy.'

Once more Greg and Ralph shared a glance. Short-and-Stumpy.

'Come on pal,' Ralph said, changing tact. 'It can't have been that bad.'

'Can't have been that bad? Can't have been that bad!' Ronald Freepepper spat. 'You see this?' He held up his left hand to show the middle finger missing from the knuckle.

'He bit it off and then he used it to poke me in the eyes. Again and again.'

'Okay, that's quite bad,' Ralph said, turning a strange shade of green.

'And there's things he did...' Ronald trailed off.

'Look,' Greg said. 'We're sorry we got you got into trouble. But I still think you should've told us about the kind of people who'd be in

249

Room 181 at that time of night. It would've been, well, courteous.'

'All things considered,' Ralph said quickly as Ronald started to shake, 'it might be best if we go our separate ways. It looks like our grievance with you is slightly negated by the tough time you've had as a result of our actions.'

'Oh, we're even, all right!' Ronald said, the smile returning to his lips. He shuffled away down the alley and back towards the street. 'I've had words with some very important people about you two,' he shouted back over his shoulder. 'That's right! Some very important people indeed. They were very interested to know who'd been using Room 181 at The First Inn. Naturally, I helped them to reach a desirable conclusion. Toodle-oo!'

'What on earth was he talking about?' Ralph said.

'I'm not entirely sure, but I don't think we came out of it looking very good. In fact, if I had to wager a bet, I'd say that our friend the hapless doorman has probably made things even more difficult for us.'

'Look on the bright side, oh brother of mine,' Ralph said as he put his arm around Greg's shoulders and led him back up the narrow alley and towards the street. 'As I've consistently found over the course of my life, you can only get in so much trouble. It's like being caught out in a rainstorm. Once you reach a certain threshold, then it's impossible to get any wetter.'

'You're wasted as a farmer Ralph, you really are. Was that supposed to cheer me up?'

'Not really, but I know something which might.'

They'd reached the entry to the alley and now stood looking across King's Pass at The Halfway Barrel.

'Pub.' they both said in unison.

***

'Now that's what I call a pint!' Ralph said, placing his mug back on the table. He let forth a hearty belch. They'd managed to find an alcove right at the back of the Barrel, one which was tucked away around the corner from the main bar area and, but for the pathetic flickers of flame from a few nearby wall-candles, in perpetual gloom. Normally, such seats would be taken, they were ideal for the kind of patrons who enjoyed either the solitude required by heavy, professional drinkers or the privacy needed for those who had a certain type of business to conduct. But, it was mid-morning on the last day of the market, so Greg and Ralph had been able to pick where they wanted to sit.

'You know something, Ralph?' Greg said, draining half of his mug.

'I know lots of somethings, Greg.'

Greg lowered his voice. 'I still can't believe it's been less than a week since I found the red stone.'

'It does seem a little surreal when you sit back and think about all the things we've been up to over the past few days. Certainly beats digging up turnips.'

'You think? I was just thinking about how it'll be great to get back to the farm. See Mollie, get cracking on the back field. With my new plough, that is.'

'You see, I was thinking the complete opposite. In fact, I was thinking about how everything you've just said sounds about as much fun as whipping yourself with a handful of nettles and then jumping in a bath full of leeches.'

'Really?' Greg was surprised. Not shocked, but still a little surprised. He knew Ralph wasn't a huge fan of working the land, Gods knew he moaned about it enough, and he'd always spoken about how he would one day move on, but most of what Ralph said needed to be taken with a handful of salt.

'I think I'm ready for a different kind of challenge,' Ralph said. 'One which doesn't necessarily include root vegetables.'

'What would you do?' Greg asked as he drank some more of his Hardstaff.

'That depends.'

'On what?'

It was Ralph's turn to lean in and lower his voice. 'It depends on how much the red stone is worth, doesn't it?'

'Yeah, I suppose it does,' Greg said as he sat back, thinking.

'Here,' Ralph said, beckoning Greg to lean in again. 'Over these past few days, has it ever crossed your mind that the red stone might not be worth as much as we think?'

'More than once,' Greg said. 'In fact, way back when Keith Smart took it, at one point I wondered if we wouldn't be better off just letting it go and returning home. But then, once we came to Calver and got wrapped up in things, it seemed like we just had to carry on. Now, with Mr Malvern involved, we haven't got a choice, have we?'

'Not really,' Ralph said.

'And back when we met Mr Malvern, he said he'd found out it was worth a bit after Keith Smart had started showing to people. Augustus Malvern doesn't strike me as the kind of person who makes too many mistakes. Anyway, what does it matter how much it's worth? As long as it pays for a new plough, that's all that matters, right?'

'Right, yeah of course. A new plough is all that matters.'

***

'And you say they've been in there for over an hour?'

'Yes, Sarge. Just sat at the back of the room, drinking and talking.'

'Drinking and talking? A regular pair of cool customers these two. We'll need to handle this one very delicately indeed.'

253

'You mean we won't get to do any clobbering, Sarge? Only it's been a slow week what with the market and all. Seems like ages since we got to clobber anyone.'

Sergeant Henry Renals shifted his weight. All these youngsters wanted to do was clobber people. You gave them a King's Guard uniform and they thought it gave them the right to wander about the place clobbering folk.

'Private Gresham. Being a good soldier is about more than just clobbering people. You'll never rise through the ranks by simply clobbering people. You need to use a bit of this.'

Sergeant Renals tapped Private Gresham on the side of his head.

'Oh, right you are Sarge,' Private Gresham said, smiling. 'I get what you're after. So we'll be mainly headbutting them then, Sarge?'

Sergeant Renals rolled his shoulders, closed his eyes and thought of his pension. After an internal count of three, he breathed out slowly.

'No Private Gresham, we will not be *mainly headbutting*. We will be using our brains. I realise this puts you at a slight disadvantage, but do not let that hold you back.'

'Our brains, right Sarge.' Private Gresham tried hard not to look crestfallen.

'As per our instructions,' Sergeant Renals said, 'we will attempt to apprehend the two individuals quietly and without drawing attention to ourselves. Which is why we are dressed in our

254

civvies and not the official uniform of the King's Guard.'

'I'm just saying, Sarge, that if we clobbered them both real quick, then they couldn't really cause a fuss, could they?'

'Private Gresham, go and get the rest of the men!' Sergeant Renals said, a tick developing by his left eye.

Private Gresham ran out from the side of The Halfway Barrel and back towards the Middle Calver gatehouse.

It was on occasions such as these that Sergeant Renals's mind tended to wander towards his retirement. He'd served on the King's Guard for all his adult life, had steadily risen through the ranks to the mid-level position of Sergeant which suited him just fine. He had three more years to go and then he was done. He'd already picked out a nice cottage for him and Mrs Renals in the countryside. It wasn't a big cottage but it had enough space for the two of them and an extra room in case the grandkids wanted to stay over.

Stood by the side of The Halfway Barrel, he allowed himself to be transported from the dark, dirty and rat-infested cobbled alleyway to the banks of the river which flowed past the end of the garden of his soon-to-be cottage. The water glided past like silk and he could already see himself sat on the bank, rod in hand, sandwiches by his side with nothing more to do other than fish. If he tried hard enough he could just about smell the wild flowers rustling in the breeze.

'You all right, Sarge?' Private Gresham said, shattering the moment. 'You look like you were miles away. Were you thinking about clobbering people?'

Three years, Sergeant Renals thought. *Three more years.*

***

'What took you so long?' Greg asked as Ralph returned with two more mugs of Hardstaff.

'Sorry, I got talking to a group of lads at the bar. They came in just as I was ordering. Nice bunch really. Here they come.'

Greg watched as a group of eight men walked around the corner and sat at various tables near to them. They were an odd mix. The oldest of the group looked as if he were taking a group of unruly teenagers out for their first pint. As he sat down he nodded over at Greg and Ralph. Ralph waved cheerily back.

'Who exactly did they say they were?' Greg said.

'They didn't,' Ralph said, returning to his drink. 'The older one came up to the bar as I was ordering. We had a little chat and then I came back over to you. Why are you looking at me funny?'

'You remember the part about keeping ourselves to ourselves? Trying not to draw attention? The whole, "stay out of the way" thing?'

'Of course I do,' Ralph said. 'I'm not stupid, and besides, there's no harm in having a chat with someone at a bar, now is there?'

'Ralph, have a look over at the group of them. Does anything seem a bit odd?'

Ralph looked over.

Aside from the older man, the other seven quickly turned their gaze away from Greg and Ralph, each one pretending to inspect a different part of the ceiling. The older one pinched the bridge of his nose and shook his head.

'Now you mention it, they do seem a little...'

'...obvious,' Greg said.

The older man sighed and started to stand.

Just then the door opened and even though Greg and Ralph were tucked away around the corner and therefore couldn't see who'd entered, whoever it was had a strange effect on the older man. He quickly sat back down, spat a few words to the rest of his group in hushed tones who all hunched down in their seats as if trying to hide away and then turned sideways in his chair with his back to the room.

***

739 was furious. This recent development furthered his theory that people nowadays had no real respect for the ancient profession of spying. Why the hell else would anyone send a bunch of bungling King's Guards to do the very same job they'd been assigned? The minute he walked into The Halfway Barrel, he knew

everything was about to go tits up. He'd been contacted directly with very specific instructions. Infiltrate, observe and, if necessary, apprehend. Yet his employer clearly felt he was incapable of getting the job done, otherwise the group of idiots pretending to be nothing more than paying customers wouldn't be here. He stomped over to the bar, his two companions trailing at his heel and ordered three mugs of Hardstaff.

'Looks like someone beat us to it, boss,' said the agent to 739's left. 'Wonder why someone would send in the King's Guard? Thought this was meant to be our gig?'

'So did I,' 739 said as he downed half his mug of Hardstaff.

'Can't understand why they'd send us and the King's Guard.' The agent to 739's right said. 'Unless, of course...'

'Of course what, 437?' 739 said staring straight ahead at a spot just above the bar. 437 had been with the service almost as long as 739 and he was one of the very few people 739 trusted. Almost trusted. He was a spy, after all.

'We got our orders from on high, did we not?' 437 said.

'We did,' 739 said.

'Which, you would assume, was where those sorry lumps of dripping sat over there trying not to look like exactly what they are got their orders from.'

'You would like to think so...' said 739.

'Of course,' 437 said, 'as the saying goes, if you assume something...'

'It makes an ass out of you and me!' Agent 231 at 739's left elbow said, glad to be joining in.

'It also makes you a bloody pillock,' 739 said.

'What if those members of the King's Guard weren't sent by the same people who sent us?' 437 said.

'That would make them quite keen not to be noticed,' 739 said, standing up and turning to face the room. 'Certainly by the likes of us. Coo-ee, fellas!'

739 walked over to where Sergeant Renals was doing his best to melt into the table.

739 tapped Sergeant Renals on the shoulder.

In all fairness, Sergeant Renals did his best impression of someone caught by surprise.

'Hello there!' 739 said in an exaggeratedly jovial manner. 'What brings you and your boys into The Halfway Barrel?'

'Just here for a drink, that's all.' Sergeant Renals said maintaining no eye contact whatsoever.

'Just a drink, is it?' 739 said.

'That's right. Just a drink.'

'Funny thing is,' 739 said, sitting down next to a clearly uncomfortable Sergeant Renals, 'you look suspiciously like a group of the King's Guard.'

'Is that so?' Sergeant Renals said, shooting a look at his men. 'You must be mistaken.'

'Oh, I doubt it,' 739 said. 'You see, I'm so very rarely wrong. No, what I think is that you're here for the same reason as us; the only difference is that you're not officially meant to be here. How does that sound?'

'Sounds quite fanciful, actually,' Sergeant Renals said.

'Looks like we might have ourselves a little bit of a dilemma then,' 739 said, standing back up.

'I think it's time me and my friends left,' Sergeant Renals said, also standing.

'I think that'd be a fine idea,' 739 said, stepping to the side.

The rest of Sergeant Renals men stood up as one.

As they did so, the door to The Halfway Barrel opened and in walked six mercenaries, led by Charlie 'Death-Knoll' McGowerty. The last one in closed the door and slid the bolt shut. The barman surveyed the scene before him, took off his apron, put it down on the bar and walked through a door behind the bar, closing it after him. There were a series of clicks and thuds as a variety of locks were slid into place. Then, silence.

Sergeant Renals turned to Private Gresham, who seemed to have lost all of his previous vim and vigour. 'Looks like you'll get to see some clobbering after all, lad.'

Chapter 20
If in Doubt, Hit It (Part 2)

The saying goes that you can cut an atmosphere with a knife. Sometimes sayings fit perfectly and are absolutely spot on. Other times the sentiment fits but it could use a little modifying. Therefore, within The Halfway Barrel, it would be fair and true to state that the atmosphere was so thick that it could be cut with just about anything. Including a stray word.

Up stepped Ralph Hoffenbach.

Before Greg could react, his younger brother leapt from his seat and strode purposely towards the centre of the room and a triangle which had a group of spies, King's Guards and mercenaries at each corner.

Greg was sure his brother had a plan and, given that he was currently running at around a forty-five per cent success rate when it came to poorly thought out plans, knew there was a chance it could all go terribly wrong.

'Well, gentlemen,' Ralph said, arms wide, turning to greet each of the three groups, 'and I use that term loosely. Looks like we have a little situation here.'

No one spoke. All of the three groups looked at Ralph as if they couldn't quite believe what he was doing. Greg joined them in that respect. 'It's apparently clear that someone somewhere has really messed up your diaries. All three groups here at the same time! How embarrassing!'

Greg shuffled over to join his brother. He smiled politely at the three groups of men.

'Ralph!' he whispered, still smiling. 'What are you doing?!'

Ralph continued to beam at the room in general. 'Simple,' he said through his shit-eating grin, 'divide and conquer.'

'Soooo!' Ralph announced to the room. 'Let's cut to the chase. On our left we have the always-deadly spies. How do, gentlemen?'

739 gave Ralph a look that could wilt milk.

'On our right,' Ralph continued, unperturbed, 'we have a group of poorly disguised King's Guards. At ease, fellas!'

The only movement Sergeant Renals made was to clip the saluting Private Gresham round the back of the head.

'And last, but by no means least, we have our old friends, the terrors of the Blood Wastes; the mercenaries!'

Ralph burst into spontaneous applause, something which no one else in the room joined in with.

'You finished?' Charlie 'Death-Knoll' McGowerty said, picking a bit of fluff from his sleeve. 'Only, me and the boys need to slap you around a bit now that your little protection crew aren't around.'

Ralph turned to his brother and winked. Then he turned back to the group of King's Guards.

'You know it's funny the way society's heading, isn't it?' he said, addressing Sergeant Renals directly. 'Turns out that nowadays, a bunch of mercenaries can walk into a pub, make threats of a physically violent nature and think they can get away with it, right under the noses of a group of King's Guards.'

'He's got a point, Sarge!' Private Gresham said.

'And as for you spies,' Ralph said, turning to face 739 who knew exactly what was coming. 'There used to be a time when no one, but no one, would mess with a spy. You chaps used to strike fear into the very hearts of anyone who had the misfortune of encountering you and your grey outfits. Now look at where you're at. Standing idly by whilst mercenaries and King's Guards make the decisions, carry the influence and generally laugh at you behind your back.'

Sergeant Renals turned to face 739. 'Seems like we have ourselves a little bit of a predicament, wouldn't you say?'

739 nodded. 'That it does. We all know why we're here,' he said pointing his thumb at Ralph and Greg. 'So how do you suppose we solve this?'

'Don't know about you nonces,' Charlie 'Death-Knoll' said. 'But we fully intend to take these two farmer chumps out of The Halfway Barrel and do as we please with them.'

'Yeah, I can't really see that happening,' 739 said.

'No, I really think that your suggestion is somewhat fundamentally flawed,' Sergeant Renals said, reaching for his sword.

'And why might that be?' Death-Knoll said, also unsheathing both his swords from their scabbards on his back.

'Well, for one,' 739 said, pulling a three-quarter-sized crossbow from under his cloak, 'there's no way you're leaving here with these two.'

'That's correct,' Sergeant Renals said. 'Because we will.'

'I'm afraid I can't allow that either,' 739 said. 'Although, for the record, if anyone other than me was to escort these two gentlemen from the premises, I'd rather it was you.'

'That's touching,' Sergeant Renals said. 'The feeling is, of course, mutual.'

'It would seem we have somewhat of a stand-off then,' 739 said.

'Not really,' Death-Knoll said, and threw one of his swords across the room striking Private Gresham directly in the chest.

Private Gresham stumbled back a couple of paces, let out a half squeak, half sigh and slumped forwards over a table.

The room erupted into a cacophony of shouts, clashing weapons and splintering wood. At which point Ralph and Greg hit the deck.

'What is it with people and fighting in pubs?' Ralph said. 'First The Hairy Apple and now here. You just can't go for a quiet pint anymore.'

All around them boots scuffed as men fought. Occasionally, someone would crash down on the floor next to them, more often than not with a sharp bit of metal sticking out of them.

'Ralph, we need to get out of here!' Greg said. 'Eventually, someone will be left standing and then they'll move on to us.'

'Fair point,' Ralph said. 'Right, after three, we stand up, turn around and head for the back door. Three!'

Ralph leapt up, turned, took two paces and then disappeared; the only sound his high-pitched scream as he fell down the open beer cellar door.

'You coming?' Bud said as he popped his head up. 'Only I think someone's going to need to give Ralph some first aid.'

***

As it turned out, Ralph's only injury was that he managed to twist his ankle as he landed amongst the many barrels in the cellar. Which was unfortunate as they had quite a bit of escaping to do and not much time to do it in.

It also meant that his mouth was in perfect working order.

'Ralph, we really need to speed things up,' Greg said as Bud led them out through a well-concealed doorway at the base of the cellar and along a series of tunnels beneath the streets of Lower Calver.

'Oh, I'm so very sorry to be of an inconvenience to you Gregory,' Ralph said, limping. 'It's just that I've sustained a serious injury in the midst of a very serious battle. A battle for our very survival, I might add. If it were not for me and my cunning plan to escape into the beer cellar, I have to wonder if we'd both be alive.'

'Ralph, you fell down a hole.'

'That I did, o brother of mine. That I did. I sacrificed myself for your continued survival. And what thanks do I get? None at all. My Gods, my leg feels as if it may fall off at any given moment.'

'That's probably because you're limping with the wrong leg,' Greg said.

'I was merely using my injured limb in an attempt to regain strength,' Ralph said, switching his limp to the other leg.

On they hurried, through tunnel after tunnel. If they'd found it hard to keep up with Bud when he'd led them through the backstreets of Lower Calver, down here in the dark and often winding tunnels, it was nearly impossible. All they had to guide them was the flame from his flickering torch which would suddenly disappear as he made swift left or right turns.

'Might I ask,' Ralph said, 'why we are following this man anyway? We don't need him anymore, remember? We have the stone, we have our two helpful mercenaries and therefore, what we certainly don't need, is Art Rosebud.'

Greg put his arm under Ralph and helped to hurry him along. 'We've been through this,' he said. 'We need to deal with Augustus Malvern before he deals with us. Bud's our link to do so. Plus, we didn't really have much choice back there at The Halfway Barrel, did we? Those three groups were there for one thing and one thing only. Namely, us.'

'Well, yes I suppose, but I still think we'd be better on our own.'

'Ralph, face facts,' Greg said, making first a left turn, then a right, all the while trying to keep his eyes on Bud's flame and also his balance on the wet floor. He did not want to start to think what it was that was so slippery on the floor of the tunnels. 'We are a couple of farmers. We don't belong in the city. Without the help of others; Bud, Eve and Wolf, we'd probably be dead by now. We need these people to help us.'

'But we're okay, aren't we?' Ralph said. His voice wavered. 'We're the Hoffenbach brothers. We can handle anything. Can't we?'

'We can handle more than some, you've got that bit right,' Greg said. 'But some things are a bit beyond us. Don't worry, though. We'll be okay. We always are.'

'Yeah, that's right,' Ralph said, the strength returning to his voice. 'Fall in shit, come up smelling of roses, that's us.'

'Apart from that time when the horse kicked you and you fell in that pile of manure. Then it was more a case of "fall in shit, smell of it for a week after"'.

Greg could see Bud's flame up ahead. It looked as if he'd stopped.

'A little more haste, boys,' Bud said, leaning on the wall.

Before Ralph had a chance to say anything and Greg had a chance to shut him up, Bud rapped on the wall three times in quick succession.

A stone slowly sunk away from the wall, replaced by Marvin's eyes as he peered through the hole. Or at least Greg assumed they were Marvin's eyes. His eyes were hidden behind two thick jam jars, each one with a candle burning on its end.

'Hey ho, fellas?' Marvin said. 'Like my night-vision goggles?'

'Sure, why not,' Ralph said.

'These are, of course, the mark two version.' Marvin said, as something clunked and gears ground behind the wall.

'What happened to the mark one version?' Greg asked.

'Ah. Well. Slight design flaw in that I put the candles on the inside of the jam jars. Burned my retinas and lost both eyebrows.'

The wall gave a final click just as Ralph started to say something.

With a deceptively smooth motion, the part of the wall Marvin had been peering through swung open to reveal another passageway.

'Come on then!' Marvin said, as he jumped out from behind the new doorway, waving them through. 'Don't stand there lolly-gagging. We don't want anyone to discover us, now do we?'

Chapter 21
Manoeuvres of the Out-espionaging Kind

'Well, I for one think it's a ridiculous idea,' Ralph said and stomped off to inspect a shelf upon which rested an old shoe, a belt, three bits of mouldy cake and what appeared to be half a dead cat.

'He won't touch anything, will he?' Marvin asked, his eyes darting nervously over to where Ralph stood.

'I'm pretty sure you're safe on that front!' Ralph shouted back.

They'd followed Marvin through another series of tunnels, the last of which had brought them back to his workshop. Once there, Bud had sat them down and explained what he wanted to do next. Ralph was yet to be convinced.

'You want to go and talk to your brother, maybe help him to see reason?' Bud said.

'Listen, Bud,' Greg said. 'I know you're only trying to help, but you've got to see things from our point of view. If we go through with what you're suggesting, we don't just risk losing the red stone, we risk losing everything.'

'Starting with our internal organs, shortly followed by our external ones!' Ralph shouted.

'You know,' Marvin said. 'Stomping away from the conversation to prove a point loses its impact if you carry on being a part of the conversation. In theory you're still part of the discussion, just a little bit louder. Besides, you clearly aren't thinking intelligently. Me and Bud have gone over the details. What is it your silly little brain is struggling with? Would you like me to draw you a picture?'

Ralph looked over at Marvin as he poked the dead cat.

'Maybe I'm not as smart as you, mole-man. But guess what? I'm touching your stuff, Marvy-boy! I'm touching your stuff! How's this for still part of the conversation?'

'Bud!' Marvin said, hopping up and down. 'He's touching my stuff! Tell him he can't touch my stuff. It took me ages to find that!'

'Really, Ralph?' Greg said. 'This is your rebuke to being told you have a silly little brain?'

Ralph picked the object up and began to rub it on his face.

'Bud! Tell him! If he wrecks that artefact, I'll... I'll... well, where am I going to find another genital wart that size?'

Ralph screamed and dropped the wart.

'If I could draw your attention to more pressing matters,' Bud said.

'I'll go and talk to him,' Greg said.

'I'd suggest you try and talk some sense into him, but I don't think we've got long enough,' Marvin said, clearly still agitated.

Greg paused as he got up from the table.

'My brother may be a bone-head at times, he also has a rather annoying habit of managing to find trouble when there seems to be none as well as rubbing people up the wrong way. In fact, once—'

'Is this going anywhere?' Ralph said.

'Sorry. Listen, he may be everything I've just said and a whole lot more besides, but he's my brother and that counts for something. Let's not lose sight of the fact that whilst you're clearly very smart, you haven't yet worked out how to exist above ground with all the normal people.'

'I choose to work down here!' Marvin said.

'I'm sure you do. Really, I am. I guess what I'm saying is, let's just try and get along so we can get this over and done with and I can get my new plough.'

'Plough?' Marvin said.

Greg left the table and walked over to Ralph. Or weaved given the amount of *things* in piles on the floor.

Bud and Marvin leant forwards and began a discussion. 'Thanks, I think,' Ralph said.

Greg smiled at his brother. Truth be told, he was tired. A great weariness draped over him like a heavy cloak. It seemed a lifetime ago when he'd set out from the farm in search of Ralph. He missed Mollie, he missed the farm and he missed his uneventful life. He just wanted this business with the red stone finished. He put his hands inside the front pocket and felt the rough edges of the stone. Back when he'd found it on the farm, he'd thought their worries were over. Now, he wished he hadn't found it.

It hadn't exactly brought him the pain-free existence he'd initially thought it would. So many people wanted the stone, and for what?

Money, power and everything in between.

If those things meant living this way — secret meetings, violence, death and constantly looking over your shoulder — then it was something Greg wanted no part of. Being a farmer may be a simple life but simplicity was good enough for at least one Hoffenbach brother. However, there was another Hoffenbach brother to consider and they were too far along the road to turn back and head home now. Greg knew they had to go ahead with Bud and Marvin's plan. It wasn't the best plan and they'd all be lucky if they came out alive but, right now, it was all they had.

So Greg smiled at his brother, put his arm around his shoulder and did what he'd done a thousand times before: he tried to talk some sense into Ralph.

***

The four of them spent the remainder of the day discussing the finer details of the plan. Not that there were many. Bud, Greg and Ralph

273

walked out of the backstreets of Lower Calver as darkness fell over the streets. Bud stopped them as they stepped out on to the King's Pass. Across the street a lamplighter opened a street light and lit the burner within.

'Okay boys, I'll set everything in motion. You get a hold of your mercenary friends and we'll meet back here in an hour.'

'An hour?' Ralph said. 'You think you can set it all up in an hour?'

For the first time that day, Bud smiled. 'Piece of cake. It's what I do.'

'Whilst I admire your self-belief,' Ralph said. 'I'm still not sure about this.'

'Well, tough,' Greg said. 'We've been over it enough times now and you said you'd go along with it and here we are, going along with it.'

Ralph mumbled something under his breath.

Greg gave his brother a long look and then turned to face Bud. He seemed to have aged considerably over the last few days. 'Be careful,' Greg said.

Bud nodded then melted back into the shadows.

Greg and Ralph stepped out onto the King's Pass. 'Suppose we'd better go and find Eve and Wolf, then,' Ralph said.

'Don't worry, Ralph. It'll all work out in the end,' Greg said, very nearly achieving a convincing tone.

***

Greg and Ralph sat down on one of the benches scattered around the edge of the market square. Most of the stalls had been dismantled, ready for the traders to depart tomorrow. A few still remained open, and even though it was now well into the evening, a few people still milled around. Initially, they'd thought about wandering around the remaining stalls too but had decided against that idea after visiting the first stall and seeing what it was they were selling.

'I had no idea they were allowed to sell those kinds of things,' Ralph said as they stared out across the market and towards the lower gatehouse.

'I suppose there's a call for that sort of thing. Somewhere,' Greg said.

'Well, I can't think where.'

'I don't *want* to think where.'

'Now I understand why they open at night. Hardly the kind of, erm, *merchandise* you'd be peddling in broad daylight.'

'Indeed. Anyway, on to more pressing matters,' Greg said. 'I reckon we've got about three more minutes before someone we don't want to spot us, spots us. I know Eve said she'd find us but we can't just sit here like this. One more minute and we'll move somewhere else. Somewhere less conspicuous.'

'Don't worry Greg,' Ralph said. 'If there's anything these last couple of days have taught me, it's that you need to be alert. We're safe for now. I've developed a sixth sense. Eyes in the back of my head and all of that type of thing.'

Which of course was the moment Eve stepped up and clipped Ralph around the back of the head.

'Oh, sorry Ralph,' Eve said. 'Did I get you in the eye?'

Ralph rubbed the back of his head. 'I knew you were there, you know.'

'Is that so?'

'Yes, I just felt it would dent your ego if a mere farmer like me out-espionaged you. That's all.'

'Out-espionaged?'

'Yeah, it's a phrase people like me use.'

'There are more like you?'

Wolf appeared from the night air and slid in silently next to Ralph on the bench.

'Think we can hurry things along? Wolf said. 'Only I'm not a massive fan of sitting here out in the open nattering like a bunch of old farts. Oh, and by the way, for the record, I like the word "out-espionaged". Has a nice old-fashioned ring to it. It would however, hold more weight, Ralph, if you hadn't nearly messed your britches when I sat down next to you.'

***

Eve and Wolf led Greg and Ralph away from the square and into the backstreets of Lower Calver once more. On their way, in hushed tones (punctuated with the occasional un-hushed tone from Ralph), Greg and Ralph explained Bud and Marvin's plan.

'So as you can quite clearly see,' Ralph said as they rounded a corner, 'this half-assed plan is useless but Greg thinks it's all we've got so I suppose we've got to go along with it.'

'Actually,' Eve said, 'I think it could work.'

'Me too,' Ralph said. 'I just wanted to be on the safe side.'

Wolf held up his hand as they came to the end of a backstreet. He waved them back as a group of the King's Guard patrolled past.

Greg and Ralph tried to push themselves further back against the building they were up against and instantly regretted it.

'Greg,' Ralph said. 'I'm not entirely sure what we're leaning against. I think it's a door but it feels kind of squidgy.'

'I'm trying not to think about it,' Greg said.

Eve stood across the backstreet from them, almost hidden in the shadows.

'Eve,' Ralph said. 'Can you see what we're leaning against?'

'Yes. Be quiet!'

'All I need to know,' Ralph said, 'is whether I can catch anything from it.'

'I think you're okay,' Eve said. 'I'll tell you what you're leaning against later. Although you'll probably scream like a little girl.'

'Coast's clear,' Wolf said. 'Let's go.'

Greg and Ralph jumped away from the building and spun around.

'What's that?' Ralph said. 'And what is this building. Who has squidgy things on their door anyway?'

277

'It's an abattoir,' Eve said as she walked off. 'Someone's left half a sheep to be gutted tomorrow. It's nailed to the door.'

Ralph did indeed scream.

***

They met Bud back at the edge of the backstreets where they'd left him just over an hour ago.

After a brief series of introductions they got down to business.

'It's all set up,' Bud said. 'Everyone agreed pretty quickly which shows they're on the back foot. All we need to do is see this through.' He looked at Ralph.

'Don't worry, my man. Everything will go swimmingly. I am not new to this kind of out-espionagisation.'

'Now you're just being ridiculous,' Eve said.

'Yeah,' Wolf said. 'That one was a bit of a stretch, even for me. But well done for giving it a go.'

'So, who's going with who?' Bud said.

'Wolf's coming with me,' Greg said, 'and Eve's going with Ralph.'

'You probably asked for that one,' Ralph said, smiling at Eve.

'Only so I could watch you die.'

'Okay,' Bud said. 'Greg and Wolf, you need to be there in thirty minutes. You okay with that?'

'Not a problem,' Wolf said. 'We'll be there in ten and have time for a quick look around.'

'Good luck,' Bud said. 'You got everything you need?'

Greg patted the front pocket of his jerkin and turned to Ralph.

'Listen–'

'Yeah, I know,' Ralph said. 'Don't go getting yourself killed either. I'll see you soon, okay?'

'Okay.'

With that Greg and Wolf headed off down the King's Pass.

'Just leaves me and you, snookums,' Ralph said turning back to Eve.

'I swear to the Gods, if you call me snookums again, I'll kill you myself.'

'Sorry, sweetpea,' Ralph said as he ran off up the King's Pass.

'You've got twenty minutes until you're expected,' Bud said as Eve turned to follow Ralph. 'And for the Gods' sake, make sure he doesn't talk too much.'

'More chance knitting piss,' Eve said and ran off to catch up with Ralph.

***

Evangeline didn't like this one little bit. Based on Rothchild's general demeanour, she could see he didn't either. He was, of course, a planner. Very rarely did he actually roll up the sleeves on that ridiculous robe of his and get his hands dirty.

But needs must.

Rothchild was sat in the very same chair he'd sat in the last time they were here as if it would give him the same sense of security he brandished so confidently before. Evangeline chose to pace the floor.

'Must you pace back and forth like that? It's wearing me out just watching you,' Rothchild said.

'Maybe you should stop watching me then,' Evangeline said.

'I try not to, but such a beautiful creature is so very hard not to observe.'

Evangeline stopped pacing.

'This all feels so very wrong. Us being back here again. Same room, same inn. It's got disaster written all over it.'

'Whilst I'll admit it's anything but ideal,' Rothchild said, 'it's all I could procure at such short notice. And besides, it may work in our favour.'

'How so?'

'Think about it. A meeting at such short notice means we're less likely to be discovered. If we didn't know about it until but a couple of hours ago, how will anyone else find out?'

'Yes, but summoned here. Told so little. I simply don't like the lack of control.'

Rothchild stood and walked to Evangeline. He placed his hands on her shoulders. It was supposed to be a reassuring gesture but to Evangeline it felt like being trapped in a vice.

'I've taken precautions,' Rothchild said, smiling. The scar on the left side of his face seemed to dance in the candlelight.

Before anymore could be said, there was a knock at the door. Rothchild walked over and opened the door.

Greg and Wolf walked in.

'Gentlemen, please do come in, we've been expecting you.'

As Greg and Wolf walked into the room Rothchild slid a piece of parchment into the catch-lock of the door and pushed the door shut. As he left the door and made his way back into the room, he paused long enough to hear the shuffling of many rather large footsteps moving along the corridor towards the room.

Rothchild smiled as he rejoined his guests.

**

'Now Ralph, you do realise how important the next few minutes are?' Eve said as they moved through the gatehouse and in to Middle Calver. Strangely, none of the King's Guards at the gatehouse seemed to be interested in them as they passed through. In fact most of them had found something far more interesting to do inside the barracks.

'Of course I do!' Ralph said. 'Look. I know that on the odd occasion, the odd, *very rare occasion,* my mouth sometimes runs a little faster than it should, but I get it. This is a crucial meeting which has to go well or we all may end up deader than that sheep nailed to the abattoir door.'

'Just so long as you understand,' Eve said.

'Sure thing.' Ralph said as they approached the outer gate of the large property.

Before they could knock, the outer gate swung open to reveal Augustus Malvern wearing little else other than a pair of cotton britches. He was holding a rather large spear, the pointy part of which ended very nearly where Ralph's nose began.

'I don't barter with bottom-feeding half-wits!' Augustus Malvern barked.

'Augy, baby!' Ralph said, pushing the spear to one side and stepping in to the garden. 'Why don't we put down the hardware and do a little business?'

Eve sighed and wondered if it was too late to swap brothers with Wolf.

***

'Gentlemen, please, have a seat,' Rothchild said.

Greg looked at Wolf, who nodded.

They both took a seat on opposite sides of the table. Rothchild walked back around the table, still smiling, still the ever-gracious host.

'Well now,' he said. 'Where to begin?'

'I often find the beginning just about does it,' Wolf said staring straight at Rothchild.

'Why, yes of course. What a blunt individual you are!'

'The sharpest blunt instrument you'll ever come across, sunshine.'

'I'm sorry,' Evangeline said. 'We were informed that Mr Hoffenbach here would arrive at Room 181 with a guest but unfortunately we were not furnished with a name?'

'Name's not important,' Wolf said, studying Evangeline's face, 'but if it'll help things move along, you can call me Fred.'

'Fred it is then!' Rothchild exclaimed and stood up to pour four cups of wine from the cask on the table. He passed them out to all around the table and held up his cup.

'A toast; to our future business venture. May we all prosper!'

Neither Greg nor Wolf touched their cups.

'Fair enough,' Rothchild said, unperturbed. 'I can see you want to get straight down to business. I can understand that. Strike while the iron's hot.'

Evangeline wondered why Rothchild was waffling. He wasn't one for unnecessary small talk.

'We all know why we're here,' Greg said, speaking for the first time. His voice held steady but inside it felt like his stomach was performing a tumbling routine.

'Not entirely,' Evangeline said. 'Whilst we have a rough idea, we know no more than you requested to meet us with regards to a certain valuable item. Normally we wouldn't entertain such a meeting at short notice but our information came from a very reliable source and so here we are.'

'That's about the short of it,' Wolf said.

'We have something you want, the valuable item as you call it, and we're prepared to give it to you,' Greg said.

'Well that's certainly very noble of you,' Rothchild said. 'Do you have the valuable item with you now?'

'Course not, you buffoon,' Wolf said. 'What kind of numpty would do that?'

'Do you know, I don't think I've ever been called a buffoon before! How very quaint!'

Evangeline shot a glance at Rothchild. Something was definitely up.

'So, how do you propose we proceed?' Evangeline said.

'Tomorrow morning,' Greg said. 'As the last of the traders leave the market. We'll meet you on the Blood Wastes and that's where we'll trade. No other deals, no other options.'

'Yeah, and bring as much money as you can carry, 'cause this little valuable item we've got is going to cost you,' Wolf said.

'The Blood Wastes! Of course!' Rothchild said. 'How very primal. Out in the open, lots of people making their way home. Smart move, Mr Hoffenbach, smart move!'

'We're just trying to make sure that both parties are treated fairly,' Greg said.

Rothchild stood and moved over to the window. He turned his back to the room and peered out into the darkness.

'Fairness is a concept favoured by those who work within the confines of a small mind.

Fairness is for the masses.' He turned to face the room; his gracious, bumbling host persona well and truly discarded. 'You two have no idea. You wander into situations hoping for the best, looking to make a quick penny without the slightest thought for the bigger picture. Of course we'll do business with you, but on our terms, not yours. You may not have the red stone with you now, you clearly aren't complete morons, but did you think you could waltz into here, make your demands and leave? Good grief, no! I think what we'll do is hold on to you two so that instead of trading with — how did your elderly friend put it? — ah, yes, as much money as we can carry, we'll use you two as our equity. How does that sound?'

'Sounds like a lot of words and not much action,' Wolf said.

'How's this for action?'

Right on cue, eight mercenaries burst through the door and surrounded the table.

Now Evangeline understood.

***

As soon as Ralph touched the spear in Augustus Malvern's hand, four of his personal security jumped on him. He now lay at the bottom of a pile of very heavy men.

'Right, that's him dealt with. Who are you?' Augustus Malvern asked Eve.

'I'm embarrassed to say I'm with him.' Eve gestured towards Ralph who was trying to breathe.

'I'm sorry sweetie, but I've no idea who you are. It's unfortunate you're caught up in this sorry excuse for a human being's predicament, it really is. Here's what I'll do.'

Augustus Malvern moved back towards the outer gate and swung it open.

'You be on your way, leave me to deal with farmer boy here and we'll hear nothing more of it.'

'You've no idea how much I'd like to do that, Mr Malvern, really you haven't, but I'm afraid I'll have to pass. You see, farmer boy is kind of my responsibility.'

Augustus Malvern leaned closer to Eve.

'Look missy, if you two have a thing going on, I'd suggest you find someone else, 'cause when I've finished with him, his dangly bits aren't going to be any use other than to skip with.'

'Mr Malvern,' Eve said. 'There's no way on the Gods' green earth that we've got a thing going on; I'd rather eat my own ear. No, I can't leave him because I'm the one lucky enough to make sure he leaves here in one piece.'

'You? You? I mean they said there'd be two of you... but you?! Come off it! Run along now, cupcake, and let the big boys play.' Augustus Malvern turned his back on Eve and started to walk over to Ralph.

It was one cupcake too many for Eve. All of her years of training flew out of the window along with playing it cool and aiming to negotiate a deal in a civilised manner.

'Listen to me, you jumped up pimp,' she said, stepping closer to Augustus Malvern. 'You call me sweetie, missy or cupcake one more time and I'm going to take that spear, turn it sideways and shove it so far up your arse it'll stick out your ears so you can hang your misogynistic euphemisms on each end.'

'Whoa there!' Augustus said, stepping back and laughing. 'This one's a bit feisty. Time of the month, is it love?'

Having known Eve long enough, Ralph felt a little sorry for Mr Malvern. But only a little.

Chapter 22
It's All in the Timing

King Siguld made his way quickly through the lower reaches of the palace. He moved through the many rooms, corridors and passageways with a practised ease. As a boy – before he became a boy-king – the palace had been his playground. He'd spent countless hours exploring, determined to discover every last inch of the building which would one day become his.

Finally, he opened the door to one of the many lower-level pantries and eased past the casks of ale and wine which filled the tiny room. Once at the back of the pantry, he relied on his memory of the room to locate the half-door, tucked away in the darkest corner. He forced it open, picked up the already lit candle on the shelf just inside, closed the door behind him and ventured forth into what he knew to be one of the many secret rooms hidden deep into the very hill the city of Calver clung to.

A set of steps had been crudely carved into the bare earth which, after only a short while changed to slick rock.

The King had only ever been down these stairs once before, when, as a boy, his curiosity had got the better of him. He therefore knew what to expect which was little more than a cold, wet and very dark room. He had no idea why it was here nor what it had been used for in the past but as far as he knew it was the safest place in the entire Kingdom as it was both entirely secret and had only one way in and out.

'Sneaking around in the dark like some common smuggler,' Perenholm said as he emerged from the shadows. 'Hardly behaviour befitting of a king.'

'It still bothers me that you knew where this place was,' King Siguld said, placing the candle on a stony ledge which had been dug into the wall.

'If it makes you feel any better, it took me bloody ages to find it. Although once I had, it gave me great pleasure suggesting we meet here on account of how pissed off you'd be that I'd found it.'

In this instance, Perenholm appeared much taller than he had at any of their previous meetings. Maybe it was because the ceiling was so low. King Siguld had long since stopped puzzling over Perenholm; he was just glad he had him.

'It must be pretty important if you wanted to meet down here,' King Siguld said as he rested on the ledge next to his candle.

'About as serious as it gets,' Perenholm said. 'It's all about to come to a head. Well, lots of heads actually. Things have gotten messy and probably will get messier both figuratively as well as literally.'

'How much time have we got?'

'It'll all be over by tomorrow morning. Soon as the market empties. Of course, once it's over – depending on who comes out on top – it could just be the beginning of our problems.'

'Right,' said King Siguld, snatching up his candle. 'Let's get a move on. We've a long night ahead.'

'Just remember, I'm on overtime after six,' Perenholm said as he followed his old friend back up the stairs.

***

Bud was starting to worry. Well, maybe not worry, but he was certainly becoming more and more concerned with each passing minute. He was at the meeting point – underneath the eaves of F. Chesterton & Daughters – and as yet there'd been no sign of either Wolf and Greg or Eve and Ralph. Part of the plan made allowances for one of the two pairs to be late, possibly even not to return at all, but both pairs not getting back might make things just a little tricky.

Not impossible, just harder. But Bud hadn't come this far to let a few minor issues stop him. He was so close to being free. He sank further back into the shadows, took a breath and started working on a contingency plan.

For the contingency plan.

***

Wolf spat out a tooth. It didn't make a sound as it hit the floor of Room 181 at the First Inn because it landed in a pool of Greg's blood.

'That's it?' Wolf said, shaking his head. 'That's the best you've got?' He turned his head to face Greg who was slumped in the chair next to his. Both were tied to their chairs.

'Chin up Greg, my boy. I told you this lot were a bunch of saggy bollocks. They just don't make 'em like they used to.'

Greg mumbled and shook his head. One of his eyes was now swollen shut and his jaw felt like it had been hit with a hammer.

'Please let me hit him again,' the largest of the mercenaries said.

'No. I think that'll be enough for now,' Rothchild said. 'We just need them to look like they've taken a good beating. It tends to promote sympathy in their loved ones. Gets the response we're looking for all the quicker.'

'Go on, Scar-boy, let him have another pop,' Wolf said, grinning and showing blood-stained teeth. 'He might get it right this time.'

'Enough!' Evangeline said. 'If you don't mind, we've got business to attend to and I, for one, have grown very bored, very quickly. Get the sacks on them and let's go.'

Greg started to lift his head, felt he was making progress, but then everything went dark.

Bud knew they were coming before he saw or heard them. It was a skill he'd developed during the years he'd spent trying to survive on the backstreets of Calver. He readied himself and stepped out of the shadows.

Immediately he knew. It had all gone wrong.

Greg stumbled as he was shoved hard in the back. He tripped over something and fell on his side. There was a metallic grating sound and then what sounded like a very heavy door slammed shut. Locks clicked and footsteps faded.

'Right then,' Wolf said from somewhere over to Greg's left. 'Let's have a butcher's at where we are, shall we?'

Greg heard a rustle and then rough hands lifted the sack covering his head.

'How you feeling?' Wolf asked.

'How do I look?'

'Like you've had your face ironed.'

'That's pretty much how I feel.'

'Yeah, a good slapping'll do that to you. Of course, by my age, and after the amount of beating my ugly mug's taken, they don't tend to hurt that much anymore. Must be something to do with damaged nerve endings or something.'

'At least we know what we're dealing with now. Bud was right.'

'We've got them rattled, that's for sure. As soon as we walked into that room I knew they meant business. I recognised scar-boy. He's one of the King's men. Rothfield or something.'

'You don't think the King had something to do with this, do you?' Greg didn't want to believe that the King could be involved. Not him as well.

'I don't think so,' Wolf replied. 'From what I've heard, King Siguld is as straight as they come. Which means that the people who've got us must have some big plans if one of the King's men is heading things up.'

'What about the woman?'

'Well now,' Wolf said. A sly grin spread over his blood-caked lips. 'That's where things get really interesting. I know exactly who she is.'

***

'So what you're saying is; you messed up,' Bud said. They were moving down the King's Pass, towards the Square and for once, Bud hadn't directed his comment towards Ralph.

'Yes,' Eve said, her gazed fixed straight ahead, her jaw clamped shut.

'You knew how important your job was, and yet...' Bud let the unsaid hang in the night air.

Eve slowly turned to face Ralph, who, to his credit had said absolutely nothing since they'd left Augustus Malvern's house.

'Well,' Ralph said and then stopped. 'You see,' he tried, but still couldn't quite get there.

'It's just that,' Bud said, 'of the two pairings, yours was supposed to be the easier of the meetings. Get in, say what needed to be said and then get out. On account of the fact that we needed your part to go smoothly as we'd need all the leverage we could get when dealing with Greg and Wolf's people.'

'It really was,' Ralph said and once again stopped. Truth was, he just didn't know what to say. And he was now really, really scared of Eve. That and a few other strange emotions.

'Fine,' Bud said as they crossed the square, weaving in between the carts loaded with market stalls ready to leave in a few hours. Bud brought them to a stop next to a double-wide cart, loaded with piles of belongings as well as unsold, leftover goods.

'Fine?' said Ralph.

'Way I see it,' Bud said, 'we haven't really got any other choice than for it to be fine, have we? Let's just hope that the rest of the plan works. Given that Greg and Wolf aren't back, it's pretty safe to assume that they've been taken.'

'Which is still part of the plan, right?' Ralph said. 'I mean, they'll still be okay, even after our... mishap?'

'Let's hope so,' Bud said, looking at Eve, who still continued to stare straight ahead, jaw set.

***

'And you're sure we shouldn't say anything about knowing who she is?' Greg said.

'Not just yet,' Wolf said.

'Well, if you think it'd be better to wait...'

294

'Oh, absolutely!' Wolf said, standing up. The various pops and cracks his body made as he stretched echoed around the small room.

'Information like that needs to be held onto until the perfect moment. Or as near as damn it.'

Greg too stood up. He reached up and gingerly touched his eye. Or where he thought his eye should be. Most of the left side of his face was swollen and numb.

'How's the war-wounds, champ?' Wolf said, reaching down to touch his toes, sending yet more pops and cracks around the room.

'I don't think I'll win any beauty contests anytime soon.'

'If it's any consolation, you weren't that pretty beforehand.'

'How do you do it?' Greg said, trying to stretch out his back.

'Do what?'

'A job which means there's a very good chance you'll end the day in pain, if not dead.'

'Well,' Wolf said. 'I wasn't much good at anything else and I seemed to have a talent for hurting people without getting too hurt myself. Not that I haven't been on the receiving end of my fair share of beatings. It's just that, well, in a weird kind of way, you get used to the pain. It's just pain in the end. The pain goes away. Eventually. And then the fighting side makes you feel, well, alive. You know?'

Greg rubbed his hand down the side of his face again. 'Not in the slightest,' he said.

'Yeah, well, it does alright for me,' Wolf said. 'Or should I say, it did alright for me. If I get through this little escapade in one piece, I reckon now might be a good time to start thinking about that tea shop of mine.'

Not for the first time, Greg's thought were drawn to home. Of Mollie. Of the farm. *All I want is a new plough.*

'You okay, pal?' Wolf asked.

Greg looked around at the dank room. 'Never better,' he said.

'Don't worry, chap, it'll soon be morning and that's when the real fun starts.'

Greg rubbed his face. 'Can't wait.'

***

'It's a bit bloody cold,' Ralph said, hopping from foot to foot.

'That's because you keep letting your hot air out of your mouth,' Eve said, peering around the corner of the building they'd been stood behind since first light.

Bud said nothing. In fact the only thing either of them had heard him say was: "It's time", when he woke them just before the sun came up.

They'd spent the night in what seemed to be an abandoned building three streets back from the market place in the backstreets. It had seemed abandoned to Ralph, although Bud had a key that fit the rusted lock and Ralph was sure he'd heard people talking during the night; but then he was so tired, it could've easily been a dream.

Ever since Bud had woken them, they'd been stood in the shadows of a building on the edge of the market place with Bud occasionally disappearing off somewhere. To begin with, each time he returned Ralph had asked him where he'd been or what he'd seen or if there was any sign of Greg and Wolf but after the first few times when Bud simply ignored him, he gave up asking.

But waiting was hard. And waiting for what you hoped was your brother in goodness only knew what state was even harder. So Ralph did whatever he could to take his mind off the unpleasant thoughts which were trying to push themselves into his mind.

And what he could do was annoy Eve.

'Actually, if you think about it, Miss Manslayer, I'm probably warming myself up through the use of my lips and tongue and facial muscles as I talk.'

Before Eve could reply, Bud spoke for only the second time that morning.

'They're coming.'

***

As soon as the sun came up, Greg and Wolf had been moved. Greg knew that it was at first light because he'd found sleep hard to come by. He'd been kept awake by a combination of the pain in his face, Wolf's horrendous snoring and thoughts of home. It hadn't been the most

297

pleasant of nights yet he still jumped when the door in front of him was wrenched open by one of the mercenaries.

'Wakey-wakey, sleeping beauties!' he growled and threw in two sacks. 'Put them over yer heads.'

'I could,' Wolf said, shaking himself awake. 'Or, you could come in here and make me.'

As the mercenary took a step into the small room, Greg sat up and put one of the sacks over his head.

'There's no need for any trouble,' he said from under the sack. 'Is there? Let's just get this over and done with.'

'You should take a leaf out of your lover's book, old Wolf. Remember, you ain't what you once were. A reputation's one thing but the reality is a bit disappointing, to be honest.'

'Fair enough, fair enough,' Wolf said.

Greg heard Wolf slide the sack over his head and move over to where Greg was.

'But know this, dangly-sack. Words are easy. Backing them up... not so much.'

'Whatever, old man,' the mercenary said as he led them out of the small room.

***

Greg and Wolf were led down a series of seemingly identical passageways, their echoing footfalls the only way they had of measuring their progress.

Every now and then the large mercenary would grab hold of Greg's shoulder and shove him to the left or right when they came to a corner. Pretty soon, Greg had no idea which direction they were headed.

Throughout the journey, Wolf said nothing. In fact, the only way Greg knew he was there was through the sound of his shuffling footsteps.

The mercenary, however, made his presence known. He hadn't stopped insulting Wolf since Wolf had placed the sack over his head. It was as if doing so confirmed what the mercenary thought, or at least hoped, to be true.

'You see, grey Wolf,' he said, once again giving Greg a rough shove in the back. 'I've heard all about you. We all have. It's like an unwritten law or something. If you're a mercenary, at some point someone's going to bore you half to death with stories of the mighty mercenary Wolf. For example, how vicious you were. Or how you fought in this battle or that battle and how, after said battle, the mere mention of your name would strike fear into the hearts of the other side. "Funny thing is," they'd say whilst I'd sit there trying to keep my eyes open, "the more Wolf becomes known the less people see of him." Then it'd all go quiet as if you were some mythical legend from the old stories. Almost ghost-like. What a load of crap!'

Despite himself, Greg was hanging on every word. He knew Wolf was a pretty good mercenary, otherwise Eve wouldn't have taken him and Ralph to meet him, but he had no idea he had this level of a reputation.

'And then, just when the mere mention of your name seemed to strike fear into any man's heart, you disappeared. Poof! Gone! Which of course made you even more of a big deal. Some said you'd died in a battle somewhere, others said you'd gone West to find the beasts of old to conquer. Want to know what I think?'

Silence from Wolf.

'I'll take that as a yes. I think your reputation got too big for you to live up to. You couldn't handle it. No one could. So, you did the only thing you could. You hid. You stopped fighting and you hid. Then, when things had cooled down a bit, you came back. Too old to fight but still trading off the old stories. That's probably how this poor sap got stuck with you.'

Still Wolf said nothing.

'Yeah, that's what I thought, old man. Nothing but smoke and mirrors. Such a bleedin' let down.' And with that, he gave Wolf a hard shove in the back. Or at least that's what Greg assumed based on the noise Wolf made. After having been shoved down endless corridors for what seemed like an age, the noise had become quite familiar. Shove, grunt, stumble. Then shuffling on.

Although this shove, grunt and stumble wasn't followed by shuffling on, but by a strange gurgle sound and then an odd wet-sucking type of noise.

The sack covering Greg's head was suddenly yanked off. He watched as Wolf wiped his hands on it before he threw it on the slumped mercenary.

'He liked a bit of a talk, didn't he!? Talk about flappin' your gums. Jeez!' Wolf said and with that he headed off down what appeared to be yet another dark passageway.

Greg took a look back at the mercenary lying in a heap on the floor.

'What did you do to him?' he said hurrying to catch up with Wolf.

'Didn't do anything. He must've slipped and banged his head or something. Probably paying more attention to talking than walking. Lucky for us, eh?'

'And all that stuff he said?'

'Well,' Wolf said, stopping to turn to Greg. 'They say the empty can rattles the loudest, and that fella was doing a lot of rattling. Know what I mean? Come on. We've got some people to find.'

With that, Wolf turned on his heels and strode off.

Greg followed, trying to remove from his mind the sight of the dead mercenary slumped on the floor, one eyeball hanging down onto his cheek.

***

They hadn't walked far before they came to a door. 'Right, then,' Wolf said. 'Better go in and face the music.'

Before Greg had a chance to answer, Wolf kicked the door open.

'Knock-knock, schemers, over-throwers and general undesirables,' he said and strode into the room.

Greg followed in his wake. It was as if someone had taken Room 181 at The First Inn, squashed it a bit, taken out some of the more expensive items and then dumped the rest behind the door Greg had just walked through.

The table, the chairs and even the very same two people were there. Rothchild stood with his back to the room looking out of the window as he had done previously. Although this window was covered in grime and soot which meant that Rothchild was actually standing looking at his own reflection.

Evangeline stood by a door which she promptly left through as they entered.

'I see you managed to find your own way here,' Rothchild said, still facing the window.

Wolf sat down at the table and leant back on his chair.

'Well, it's not as if old dangly-sack you sent to fetch us was doing much of a good job. Took him ages. Too busy talking.'

'How very droll,' Rothchild said, finally turning to face Greg and Wolf.

'Right then,' Wolf said, putting his feet up onto the table, 'shall we get this all underway?'

'You know,' Rothchild said, walking round the table, 'you really are a curious sort, Mr Wolf. You see, I asked around about you. Not that I hadn't heard most of it already myself. But once my mercenary friends filled me in on who you were it wasn't hard to add in the extra details.'

'You want to be careful, pal,' Wolf said. 'You start listening to gossip, you could hear all manner of half-truths and not-quite-lies.'

'Indeed.' Rothchild studied Wolf as if seeing him for the first time. Wolf, for his part, kept his eyes locked on the man with the scar. Whatever it was Rothchild saw in Wolf's eyes seemed to help him make some sort of decision, as in the next moment he turned, pounded on the door Evangeline had just left through and then stood back.

Wolf turned to Greg. 'This'll be the part where the room fills up with big scary men again. Next, old scar-chops over there will decide whether to take one, or both of us, to meet our friends. I'm guessing he'll plump for both, more insurance if things go tits up, but he may just decide to kill me and take you instead. That about sum things up, fella?'

Before Rothchild could answer, the room did indeed fill with rather large mercenaries.

***

Greg and Wolf were escorted out of the building. It turned out that it was three streets back from the King's Pass, deep enough in the backstreets to remain hidden but not too far for a quick exit which is what they were making now.

Rothchild pulled the hood on his cloak up and led them away down the King's Pass, escorted by four large men.

'Worried people will recognise you, Rothchild?' Wolf shouted.

Rothchild whirled around. 'Actually, no. For one, hardly anybody knows what I look like. I rarely leave the palace and when I do I'm careful. And after we trade you two sorry excuses for human beings for that blasted red stone, then plenty of people will know exactly who I am. Until then, kindly refrain from bellowing my name across the King's Pass because whilst most don't know what I look like, they most definitely know the name Rothchild.'

Wolf turned to Evangeline who had also raised the hood on her brown cloak. 'Is he always this prickly, Mrs Malvern?'

It was Evangeline's turn to turn on Wolf.

'Listen, you horrible little creature. I know exactly what you're doing, banding our names about as if that's going to change anything. So you know who I am. It doesn't change a thing. We've come a long way to reach this point and I'll not let some has-been thug piss all over my strawberries. You came to us when you had the chance to escape so I'm assuming you want to be here. Maybe you and your little friends even have some cunning little plan all figured out but either way, you're here. So either shut up and play the part, or I'll have one of these gentlemen stab you in the kidneys and leave you to slowly bleed to death.'

With that she spun away from Wolf and marched after Rothchild.

'I think you might have annoyed them a bit,' Greg said, moving forward with the shove in the back he received from one of the large men.

Wolf grinned, 'Yeah. That'll do nicely, pal.'

***

Shadows are funny things. Sometimes you see things that aren't there; tricks of the light maybe. But then sometimes you don't see the things that are actually there. That can happen for any number of reasons. Probably, the reason you wouldn't see the slighter darker bit of shadow tucked away in a pool of semi-darkness next to the door which Greg, Wolf and his accompanying party emerged from moments ago, was because it was a tricky shadow to pin down. And even if you did happen to pin down this shadow (which is an almost impossible challenge in itself), if you happened to glance in another direction, you'd be hard pushed to describe said shadow.

Tall? Maybe. Crooked? Possibly. Or was it short with kind of fuzzy edges? See? Hard to pin down. But then, of course, that was one of Perenholm's many talents.

Chapter 23
The Bit Where It All Kicks Off

739 was actually feeling pretty good. Unbelievable, but true. Things were starting to look up.

He'd been a spy for long enough to know that things were never good for long but he felt this good patch coming was long overdue.

After the debacle at The Halfway Barrel, which both him and 437 had only just managed to walk away from (231 hadn't been as fortunate – may the Gods savour his very punctured soul) and the fall-out from his meeting with Perenholm, he felt things had to change. Well, either they'd change or he would. He'd actually been considering getting out of the spy game. 437 had nearly fallen over when he'd told him. Of course, he nearly fell over in a very silent and unnoticeable way, but nearly fallen over he had.

'But you're the gov'nor,' 437 had said, silently rising back up from his nearly fallen-over state. 'You're the reason a load of us got into the spy game. What would happen if you left?'

'Things would inevitably carry on,' 739 had said as he scaled the side of the building they'd been watching for the last three hours. He waited until he felt 437's presence at his side on the roof before he carried on. 'Besides, you're more than ready to step up and take the lead. You're bloody good.'

'Thanks boss, but all the same, I think you've got a few more years left in you yet. Things'll pick up. They always do. What is it you're always telling us?'

'Never confuse your hanky pocket with your chloroform pocket?'

'Ha bleedin' ha,' 437 said. 'Come on boss, let's get this over and done with. It'll make you feel better, you just see.'

'Suppose so,' 739 said and followed 437 down onto the back garden of Augustus Malvern's house.

***

And it had made 739 feel better. For lots of different reasons.

Mainly because the series of events he witnessed, and later on played a hand in, helped him to start to feel good. Dare he say it, he was starting to feel... optimistic.

First, he'd seen the arrival of the farmer, Ralph, and the mercenary Eve Manslayer.

Next, he'd watched with an ever-widening grin as the mercenary gave Augustus Malvern and four of his personal security one of the most brutal good-hidings he'd had the pleasure of watching. And the icing on the cake was being able to saunter over to a prostrate Mr Malvern after the mercenary had left and deliver his message.

He was pretty sure Mr Malvern had got the message because, although seemingly unconscious, his left eyelid started twitching rapidly as did a rather large vein in his neck.

And now, the next morning, he was doing what he did best, what he loved to do. He was being a spy.

'Anything new, boss?' 437 said.

'Not yet. But it's coming. I can feel it.'

'Feel it?' 113 said. As 231's replacement, he wasn't a bad choice; certainly there were plenty of volunteers to join the boss' crew, it was just that he was a bit too logical. Being a spy demanded an element of creativity. 113 wouldn't know creativity if it jumped out in front of him and did a little dance. 'How do you feel that something's coming, sir?'

'Good question,' 739 said, hauling the end of what appeared to be a normal market wagon getting ready to leave Calver. 'A really good spy needs to develop a sixth sense, — yes I know 113, before you say it, we've only got five senses — but a really good spy develops a sense of intuition. And what's a really good spy, 437?'

'One who's alive, boss.'

'So, how do you know something's coming?' 113 asked.

'Because, young man, the square suddenly has a lot more King's Guards in it. See?'

113 looked around. 739 was right. It seemed as if the number of King's Guards in the square had doubled.

'What do you think about that, 113?' 739 asked.

'Seems a little illogical to me, sir. There doesn't need to be that many of them here. In fact, they should be at the gatehouse ready to let people out onto the Blood Wastes.'

'This is true,' 739 said. 'It's as if they're flies and someone's about to take a huge dump.'

'You can't ever leave, boss,' 437 said. 'I'd miss your poetic ways too much.'

***

The King was in his ante-room, using his spyglass to gaze down on Lower Calver. He was, indeed, looking down on his (mostly) loyal subjects. As if to combat any notions of grandeur, the room itself was sparsely furnished. No royal finery, no pomp and most certainly no circumstance. A single, slightly small wooden table, a battered and moth-eaten cushioned chair, a map of the Kingdom, his spyglass and books piled from floor to ceiling.

Of course, this was the King's favourite room in the entire palace. He'd even named it his ante-room as a private little joke. As in, it was anti-anything regal.

The door creaked open but King Siguld did not turn his attention from the market place. Only two people had a key to this room. He was one of them.

Perenholm flopped down into the chair. 'Picture the almighty King, gazing upon all within his command. O mighty King, what dost thou see-est?'

'I could have you hung, drawn and quartered, you know.'

'On what charge, fearless leader?'

'Being an arse.'

'That you could, that you could. But I think you'd kind of miss me.'

'Like I'd miss a dose of the lice.'

'You've never had lice in your entire pampered life.'

'This is true. Is everything going as you thought it might?'

'Sort of. Some elements are a little unpredictable but in the main, it should be fun to watch.'

The King turned from his spyglass and walked over to the map pinned to the wall.

'Are the spies in place?'

'That they are. 739's on the job so, all being well...'

'What about those men who were in The Halfway Barrel?'

Perenholm didn't need to ask for further clarification. Ever since he'd informed King Siguld that a small group of King's Guards were working for Augustus Malvern, he'd referred to them as *those men*.

'They have been dealt with, Siguld. It'll be a long time before they're allowed back from their extended posting on the south side the Great Hill.'

'Good. Make sure their families receive some sort of compensation. They shouldn't have to suffer for those men's weakness of character.'

'Already taken care of. Flowers, money and a nice fat pie.'

'A pie?'

'Yeah. Who doesn't like to receive a pie? Plus, a pie helps when your fella's going to be away for a long time. As my dear old nan used to say: there's not much that can't be put right with a nice meat pie.'

'And you still think it's all going to happen within the next couple of hours?'

'I do. They've moved the farmer and the mercenary. The farmer's brother, the mercenary and the fixer are all hidden on the edge of the square.'

King Siguld turned from the map, walked past Perenholm and towards the door. Perenholm leapt up to follow him. 'Do you think we've got everything under control?' he asked his old friend.

'Good Gods, no,' Perenholm said. 'But at least we'll have people there once it all kicks off. Best you can hope for really. Look on the bright side, if we get the outcome we want, all carries on as normal.'

'And if we don't?'

'Find a really fast horse.'

***

'Here we go,' Bud said, moving out of the shadows.'

'Wait! What are you doing?' Ralph asked. 'We've just spent bloody ages freezing to death waiting for them and now you're walking out in broad daylight. Call me a fool, but it kind of makes a mockery of the whole hiding in the shadows thing.'

'We *were* hiding,' Bud said. 'And now we're not. Because they're here. The last thing we needed was them seeing us first.'

'Bud's right,' Eve said. 'They spot us first and they could try and grab us. Hardly much of a bargaining tool if they've got us all.'

'But, won't they just try and grab us now?' Ralph said.

'They might try,' Bud said. 'But they'd be daft to do it now.'

'Why?'

'Because there's at least three spies over there disguised as market traders and doing a pretty good job of it, actually.'

'Three spies aren't going to stop them,' Ralph said.

'You're right,' Bud said. 'Thankfully, Marvin's prediction was spot on. Look.'

Bud pointed to the edge of the square. What looked like an entire regiment of King's Guards had moved into place, effectively creating a cordon trapping them, the spies and Greg's group inside.

'For starters, I can't believe that mole-man was right.'

'I can,' Eve said. 'There's not much that escapes the King's attention. He'll know enough to be ready, that's for sure.'

'Okay, fair enough,' Ralph said. 'But what I definitely can't buy is that Rothchild and Evangeline would walk into such an obvious trap.'

'The promise of power and the possibility of untold wealth does that to some people. It makes them both greedy and stupid.'

'I'm still not buying it,' Ralph said.

'Whether you buy it or not, we need to head towards the gatehouse as if we're heading off to do the deal on the Blood Wastes. We have to act like we haven't seen them and then act surprised when they stop us as if we're shocked they've foiled our plan.'

'Think that'll work?'

'Probably. Rothchild's too full of his own self-importance. Whilst he's cunning and clever, he's not smart. Not practical, real world smart. He's never had to get his hands dirty in this way before. There's cunning and clever when you're sat on the top of the hill and then there's on-the-fly, down-and-dirty smart. Besides, he'd never contemplate that we could out-smart him. Now, let's go.'

***

They knew they were in trouble when they tried to leave the square and walk to the gatehouse. How much trouble they were in would only become clear a little later. As Bud, Eve and Ralph reached the edge of the square and thus the edge of the market, they came face to face with a wall of King's Guards. Bud tried to side step but the King's Guards didn't move.

'S'cuse us, chaps,' Ralph said trying to inch through a gap between two King's Guards. One of the King's Guards grabbed him by the shoulder and shoved him back towards Bud and Eve.

'Well that's rich!' Ralph said. 'Here I am, a simple farmer, with my friend and our very simple sister, trying to make my way home after a wonderful and law-abiding visit to the market and I'm treated like a hoodlum no less!'

The King's Guards remained stony-faced.

Bud stepped forward. 'Listen, man. We just need to pass through, is all. C'mon.'

For the first time, one of the King's Guards spoke. 'We've got orders. No one leaves.'

'Why would the King give orders to keep everyone in the market place?' Ralph said.

'He wouldn't,' Eve said, taking a step back, drawing her sword.

'Then who the hell did?'

'Ah. That would be me,' Rothchild said.

***

'Well now,' 739 said. 'That's a turn up for the books.' Which was a seemingly calm way of

314

expressing just how quickly things had gone south.

'I think we may struggle a bit to see this one through,' said 437.

'I have no idea what's going on,' said 113.

'You will,' said 739. 'Just watch. And be ready.'

'Ready for what?' 113 said.

'At this rate,' 437 said, 'just about bloody anything.'

***

As soon as Bud tried to run he was hit very hard in the gut by one of the mercenaries not currently guarding Greg or Wolf. Bud crumpled to the floor, gasping for air.

'I don't think there's any need for any of that!' Ralph said. 'You'll never get what you want behaving in that manner! As a matter of fact, I'm seriously reconsidering our previous generous offer!'

Rothchild merely snorted. 'I'm afraid you don't have much of a say in anything anymore, muck-spreader.'

'Right!' Ralph said, grabbing a hold of Greg. 'The deal's off! You can take your trade off and stick it where the sun won't shine!'

Greg put a hand on Ralph's shoulder.

'It's okay. It's over.'

'But, they've insulted our good family name. Us Hoffenbachs won't stand for it.'

'Ralph,' Greg said, looking into his brother's eyes. 'You can drop it. It's not going to work, whatever you're trying to do. We lost. We thought we'd covered all the bases with our little plan but we didn't consider that Rothchild might use the King's Guard to stop us. We should've done, but we didn't. No amount of scheming, misdirection or clever word-play is going to change that.'

'But—'

'It's done.'

'Right,' said Rothchild. 'Now that's over and done with, can we move on?'

'So, you own all of these King's Guards?' Eve said.

'I wouldn't go so far as to say I own them. As far as they're concerned, they received an order from the King – through me of course – to stop anyone and everyone from leaving the market until I said so. I think you'll find the genius of my plan lies in its simplicity.'

Rothchild turned to speak to the King's Guards who'd grabbed Ralph.

'Good job, boys. I'll make sure the King's aware of your efforts. Especially after that other treacherous bunch let him down so. You've helped restore a bit of pride in the army. Spread the word, would you? We've got who we need. Everyone can go about their business as usual.'

'Right you are, sir,' said the guard and he signalled to the men around him who started to fall back.

'Thought you said people didn't know what you looked like?' Wolf said.

'That I did. But this was such a sensitive matter. I hand delivered the message from the King myself.'

'Except it wasn't from the King. Was it?' Wolf said. 'Wonder what he'd think of you if he found out?'

'Ha! By the time Siguld the Watcher figures out what's going on and then weighs up all the consequences, balancing the pros and the cons, I'll have bought every mercenary and every free man willing to fight for money. Not to mention those King's Guards who aren't averse to switching their allegiance. No, it'll be too late for dear Siguld. I'll have an army ready to storm his precious palace. He'll still be wondering what happened as I stick his head on a spike.'

'Oh, I don't know about that,' said the King.

***

'Told you to be ready for just about anything,' 437 said.

'Oh, come on,' 739 said. 'Even you couldn't have predicted that!'

'This latest turn of events would fall under the aforementioned statement of "be ready for just about bloody anything", would it not?'

'Yeah, but that's stretching it just a bit too far, isn't it?'

'Erm,' said 113, trying his hardest not to sound like he didn't have a clue what was going on.

'There has been yet another turn up for the books,' said 739.

'Really?' said 113.

'Oh, yes,' said 437. 'In fact, it would almost appear that if things continue in this vein, there may even be more turn ups than books.'

'Blimey!' was all 113 could manage.

'Blimey indeed,' 739 said. He was, in fact, enjoying himself immensely. This was starting to feel like the good old days. 'Now get ready and make sure you're upwind, because the shit's about to hit the fan.'

***

'Oh shit,' Rothchild said.

'Hello, Rothchild,' said King Siguld. 'How's things?'

His usual robes left back at the palace, the King wore the brown robes of an official.

'Well bugger me!' said Wolf. 'It's the King. Alright, Your Majesty? On a side note, it must be horrible to be you right about now, Scar-boy!'

'The King?' Ralph said. Then he performed what could only be described as the world's first bow-urtsey.

'You must be Ralph and this, if I'm not mistaken, is your brother Gregory. Good to meet you.'

'Your Royal Wonderfulness,' Ralph said still holding the bottom part of his bow-urtsey.

'Stand up Ralph, lad,' Wolf said. 'You look like you need a pee.'

'Your Majesty,' Rothchild said. 'What brings you to the market and dressed in such an unroyal manner? Are you well protected, sir? I only say this because I worry, what with you dressed as a commoner, you may be mistaken for a simple trader and things can get pretty rough down here.'

The King chuckled. 'Same old Rothchild; always trying to think two steps ahead. Gears whirring, always with an eye on the exits. It's probably time for a few home truths, my most trusted of advisors. You see, the problem with trying to remain two steps ahead is that you tend to miss what's right under your nose.'

The King placed his first two fingers on both hands in his mouth and blew a shrill whistle. Immediately, the King's Guards who had moved away at Rothchild's command, moved back into place. The guard who'd shoved Ralph smiled at the King. It was a strangely familiar smile, yet one which would be instantly forgotten once you turned away from him. As would his face.

'You dozy pillock!' Wolf said, doubling over with laughter. 'All the while you thought you were pulling the strings, masterminding some sort of fancy coup when, all along, your boss had your number good and proper. These King's Guards weren't here to stop us leaving. They were here to stop you leaving!'

The colour had drained from Rothchild's face.

'How long have you known?' he asked the King, his voice almost a whisper.

'We've had our suspicions for a while now but only recently have we managed to collect concrete evidence. Our thanks go to Mr Rosebud. Since rumours of Mr Hoffenbach's famous red stone started to circulate, you've gotten sloppy.'

'Would you believe me if I said I wish I'd never heard of that blasted stone?' Rothchild said. He turned to Greg. 'I just hope it's worth all this trouble.'

'Oh, it is,' said the King. 'When a certain hay salesman started brandishing it around, one of the jewellers he showed it to happened to know an old friend of mine. It pleases me greatly to tell you Rothchild that the stone you very nearly possessed is one of a set of three. These very special stones were once thought lost. How it ended up in Mr Hoffenbach's field, I don't know, but I do know it's worth more than this Kingdom twice over.'

Rothchild sagged.

And then sagged some more.

And then, he wasn't sagging at all. He exploded upright, flicking his right hand up, as if back-handing a fly. It was the last-ditch effort of a desperate man and it was a poor one at that.

The knife Rothchild threw missed the King completely. It sailed past the King and landed in Ralph's chest who immediately collapsed to the floor.

After that, everything got a bit chaotic.

Greg moved first. He launched himself at Rothchild. Evangeline, who had been gradually edging away from Rothchild, disappeared into the crowd behind. Eve ran after her. Bud grabbed Ralph and started to drag him away as people around the group started to realise what had happened. Some moved forward to see what was going on, whilst others jostled to get away. The King was ushered to safety behind a line of King's Guards whilst more still moved in to restore order.

It took four King's Guards to prize Greg off Rothchild. He immediately spun away towards where Bud was hunched over Ralph.

'Hey buddy,' he said, trying not to let his eyes wander to the knife sticking out of his brother's chest. 'You'll do anything for a spot of attention, won't you?'

Ralph smiled a bloodstained smile. 'It hurts, Greg. It really hurts.'

Greg looked at Bud. 'We need to leave now. He needs help,' he said.

That was when madness descended upon them.

***

In truth, it didn't necessarily descend on them as hurtle towards them. A strange cacophony of noise drew everyone's attention towards the King's Pass. It sounded like a combination of rolling thunder, wailing banshees and something entirely unpleasant.

Everyone stopped and turned towards the approaching noise.

'If I didn't know any better,' Wolf said, 'I'd say that sounds like one cluster-buggery of trouble heading our way.'

The crowds trickling down the King's Pass started to surge forward, almost as one. Something behind them was clearly worth getting out of the way of. As the crowd surged forwards, the noise got louder. Then people started flying.

Some upwards, some outwards and some to either side, but they were indeed flying. It appeared the act of flying wasn't entirely deliberate given the shocked looks upon the faces of those shooting through the air. Shocked looks which soon vanished when they hit things, like the ground or a building. Then they stopped flying and they stopped looking shocked and started being crumpled and started looking quite dead.

'What in the blue hell is doing that?' Wolf said to no one in particular.

'I'm not sure,' Greg said, 'but whatever it is, it's throwing anything and everything in its path, out of its way.'

'Oh no,' Bud said. If any of the people stood with him had been able to look at his face they would've seen a look of complete horror lodged there.

'We need to move,' he said, already scanning around to find a way out.

'You're going nowhere,' one of the large mercenaries said, grabbing a hold of Bud's shirt.

'You don't understand,' Bud said. 'It's really important that we're not here now. Me, you and anyone else who wants to live. We need to leave right now!' With that, Bud yanked his shirt free of the large man's grasp, tearing it in the process.

'Would you look at that!' Wolf said as something metallic whistled through the air, shortly followed by three neatly severed heads.

Before anyone had a chance to say anymore, the remainder of the crowd moving down the King's Pass erupted into full-blown panic and started to run.

Some – those at the front – managed to break into a sprint and stumble towards freedom. Those further back were either trampled on or slammed into the buildings lining the edges of the King's Pass.

Meanwhile, the rumbling thunder noise got louder, as did the wailing. In the market place, people started to surge towards the gatehouse, hoping to escape before whatever was coming down the King's Pass could reach them. People pushed and shoved, elbowed and jostled and then, the source of the noise and panic burst free like a nightmare released.

'What in the seven hells is that!?' Greg said.

'He calls it the War Machine,' Bud said as he dragged a stationary and dumb-founded Greg and Ralph off towards the side of the market place.

'That bastard looks like it could start and end wars all on its own,' Wolf said in part admiration as he moved in the direction of Bud, Ralph and Greg. Greg struggled to comprehend what it was his eyes were telling him he was currently seeing.

Hurtling down the King's Pass, launching people in all directions was a huge wooden armoured cart. At least that's the best Greg could do to describe it because it was about the size of a large cart and it had wheels like a cart but where all the other cart-like parts should be, on the War Machine they weren't. It looked like a very unpleasant wooden box on wheels. One which had things sticking out of it that could clearly hurt, maim and catapult people. And it was moving of its own accord.

The War Machine came to a screeching halt on the edge of the square. A wooden hatch flipped open and from within its bowels emerged a blood-stained face. A blood-stained face with a broken nose, most of the front teeth missing and one eye swollen shut. Even with the damage, there was no mistaking the maniacal glare of Augustus Malvern's one good eye.

'Where is sheee?' he bellowed.

An official-looking man wearing spectacles and an expensive-looking smock with far less sense than someone in his position should have, approached the War Machine.

'Now look here,' he said. 'I'm not sure what— aheeeeeee!'

'Well bugger me!' Wolf said as the flames shot out of the side hole of the War Machine and engulfed the man who whirled around and then collapsed screaming.

Augustus Malvern looked down at the man on fire as if he were nothing more than a minor inconvenience. He returned his single-eyed gaze back to the crowds trying to get out of Calver as quickly as they could.

'Where are you, my Evangeline?' he wailed.

***

'Now, me, I wasn't sure he'd heard you, boss,' 437 said.

'Yeah, I wasn't entirely sure, given that he'd just had his face pummelled by that mercenary girl and was lying flat out,' 739 said.

'What did you say to Mr Malvern?' 113 said.

'Well, son, sometimes being a spy means planting a seed and hoping it may bear fruit in the future. Not just any seed, mind. But the seed of a specific plant that, under the right conditions will grow into exactly the kind of plant you want to grow. Now this seed was — and try to remember this — the best kind of seed as it was equal parts truth and lie. You see? Creativity at work.'

'The truth part was that old Mr M's wife had been stealing from him and was working alongside the King's boy, Rothchild,' said 437.

'And the lie?' said 113.

'That the two are engaging in a spot of horizontal tango,' said 739.

'Oh. That'd probably do it,' said 113.

'That's not all,' said 437.

'No?'

'No,' said 739. 'I finished off the lie sandwich with another slice of truth. Namely to remind him that he'd just had the snot kicked out of him by a girl.'

'Talk about kicking a man when he's down,' 437 said.

'Yeah, I did that too. Well, you've got to, haven't you?'

***

'EVANGELINE!' Augustus Malvern wailed again. He cast his single-eyed gaze across the market place, his head twitching from side to side. 'EVANGELINE!'

'I wonder if Eve's managed to catch her. I'd love to see the reunion,' Wolf said.

'In case you've forgotten, we need to get out of here!' Greg said, grabbing Ralph under the arm.

Augustus Malvern's gaze settled on Greg and Ralph. 'You!' he growled, pointing. 'You bastards!'

The War Machine roared to life, belching smoke from the furnace at the back and began lurching across the square – giant metal-rimmed wheels scraping across the cobblestones. Greg and Bud tried to drag Ralph out of the way but the sheer volume of people around them meant that progress was slow. Too slow.

Augustus Malvern brought the War Machine to a thundering halt in front of Greg, Ralph, Bud and Wolf.

***

'Do we need to do anything?' 113 asked.

'Like what?' 437 said.

'I dunno. Maybe help?'

'Oh no, son,' 739 said. 'That'd be interfering. We definitely do not interfere.'

'Unless we're being paid to,' 437 said.

'Oh yes, of course. Goes without saying, that does.'

'Why doesn't anyone do anything? The square's heaving with King's Guards and they're standing there, doing nothing.'

'Like what?' 437 said. 'Knock on the door and ask if Mr Malvern's home?'

'What you've got here is your classic un-winnable situation.'

'Un-winnable situation?'

'Un-winnable situation. You see, the King's Guards have never encountered something like Mr Malvern's contraption. No one has. Throw into the mix that the last time any of them saw any real action was before you were born, well, let's just say they might be a little rusty. So they're not going to get too close. No one is. Who knows what that thing's capable of.'

But the logical thinker in 113 wasn't giving up just yet. 'They could get the archers to fire a round of flaming arrows at it,' he said.

'With this many people around? What if the thing exploded? What if they missed and hit a law-abiding market stall owner?' said 437.

'Exactly,' said 739. 'They can't attack it and they can't burn it. Which pretty much exhausts the military's list of available tactics they have to employ.'

'You might have gathered that the boss isn't the biggest fan of our fine King's Guards.'

'It's not that I don't think they have a place. It's just that that place is in a long-forgotten past.'

'So we're going to just sit here and do nothing?' 113 said.

'Oh good grief, no,' 739 said. 'We're going to move back a bit. You never know what that thing's going to do.'

***

Even though he only had one good working eye, the hate and pure fury with which Augustus Malvern fixed his gaze upon Greg and Ralph was strong enough to wither stone.

Then he smiled. Or tried to.

It looked part grimace, part sneer and, through his missing teeth he hissed at Greg, Ralph and Bud, 'Welcome to hell. Now you shall die!'

He reached down into the War Machine and pulled a series of levers. As he did, parts of the monstrous contraption started to open. Openings appeared in four separate places on the front, revealing long tubes which inched their way outwards. More sections of the War Machine on both sides slid away and from those emerged strange crossbow-like mechanisms, the cords already pulled taut – each one holding a sling containing a variety of nuts and bolts.

'We could always make a run for it,' Bud said.

'I can't leave Ralph,' Greg said.

'Besides,' Wolf said, who had remained at their side. 'I don't think we'd get far before something hit us in the back and then very quickly made its way out our fronts.'

Chapter 24
Things That Go Pertung

'Oi! Cupcake! How's the face? I think you might be looking for this!'

From within the crowd – which had been backing away from where Greg, Ralph, Bud and Wolf were gathered – a woman emerged. Although not adorned in her customary blue, it was clear that Mrs Malvern had indeed been found. Eve shoved her forwards and she stumbled to her knees in front of a slumped Ralph.

'I've got a knife in me,' he said, 'but I'd still say I'm less screwed than you.'

Evangeline turned to face her husband.

'Augy. I need you to listen to me. And I need you to listen to me very carefully. That piece of scum Rothchild made me do it. He threatened me. He told me that if I didn't take your money, he'd have you killed. He said he could have you killed in the blink of an eye. I couldn't let him do that to you. I just couldn't. It's true, I swear!'

Augustus Malvern looked down at his wife. Where once fury had burned in his one good eye, now there was nothing but a black void.

'Oh, Evangeline,' he said as a single tear coursed down his cheek. 'What a load of shit.'

More tears flowed down his cheeks and he gave a racking sob. 'That's it!' he shouted. 'I'm going to kill you all.'

He threw his head back and laughed. He was still laughing as he pulled yet more unseen levers causing more doors to drop open on the War Machine.

Then it started to rumble and shake. A sound like distant thunder emanated from within. Augustus Malvern stopped laughing.

'Now we're all going to die!' he shouted.

'I think the crazy sod's lost it completely. He's on his way to the first hell and he intends to take as many with him as possible.'

Strangely, the first thought to enter Greg's head was: *I just wanted a new plough.*

The War Machine rumbled and shook as people tried to get as far away from it as possible but simply ended up falling over each other. Greg, Bud, Wolf and Ralph braced themselves.

'I have to say,' Ralph said in between coughs, 'if you'd have told me three days ago that I was about to die at the hands of a crime lord and his exploding War Machine, I don't think I'd have—'

Ralph was cut short by a sudden, shrill whistle. It quickly rose in pitch until it became almost unbearable. Aboard the War Machine, Augustus Malvern looked concerned.

'What's that noise? It's not coming from me,' he said, although, of course, no one could hear him.

As suddenly as it had begun, the whistling ceased.

'That's better,' Augustus Malvern said. 'Now, let's get on with the dyi—'

There was an almighty PERTUNG! and where once Augustus Malvern and his War Machine were, they were not. The crowd followed the War Machine's progress as it shot through the air, high over the gatehouse and out towards the Blood Wastes. They all seemed to hold their breath as they listened carefully. Finally, they could hear a faint thud and then a not-so-faint explosion.

'Well, it would appear that works,' said Marvin, his head poking out of a storm drain which had, until very recently, been covered by the War Machine. Marvin picked up a matchbox-sized implement from the cobbles. 'Might need to adjust the power output slightly,' he said, climbing out of the drain. 'Sorry I'm late. Couldn't find my shoes.'

***

Fortunately for Greg, Ralph, Bud, Wolf and Eve, they were within leaping (or in Ralph's case, dragging) distance from the storm drain Marvin had just climbed out of. It was fortunate because after a brief moment of stillness and inactivity, everyone in the square tried to do something all at once. Most people tried to leave. They'd seen just about enough activity to last them a while and, quite wisely, thought they'd be on their way before anything else could happen.

There was a surge towards the gatehouse like a wave destined for a beach. In the ensuing crush, Rothchild made a break for the nearest entrance to the backstreets. He was closely pursued by the three spies. Evangeline had, apparently, very quickly moved through the four stages of grief and was now at stage five: run away and hide as she followed Rothchild.

Although the King tried to remain in the square, he was ushered to safety by a large group of King's Guards. After the week they'd had, the last thing they needed was to stand and watch as their boss got trampled to death.

And so, once again, Greg and Ralph found themselves under the streets of Calver.

'Oh dear,' Marvin said, holding his lamp over towards where Ralph was propped up against a wall. In fact, he didn't need his lamp as the passage way was once again clearly lit. Greg could tell it was a route Marvin used often because not only was it well lit but every so often he could see a pile of seemingly random junk.

'Ralph,' Marvin said. 'You seem to have a knife in you.'

'Thanks. Captain. Obvious,' Ralph said, struggling for breath.

'Is there anything you can do?' Greg said. Right now he would take any kind of help.

'There's always something to be done,' said Marvin with a smile as he bent over Ralph. 'Even if that something is to put him out of his misery.'

'Steady on!' Ralph managed.

The others gathered around as Marvin inspected Ralph.

'Well, I think we've got a classic good news, bad news situation here,' Marvin said, standing up.

'What's the good news?' Greg said.

'See the knife sticking out of Ralph?'

'Yes.'

'It's really nice. Just look at that handle. Once it's out of him and cleaned up, it'll look lovely.'

'That's the good news?'

'Yes.'

'So what's the bad news?'

'That Ralph'll be fine. Looks like the knife missed anything important. Not that his heart's big enough to hit anyway.'

'Sod. Off. Mole. Man,' Ralph wheezed.

'Okay,' Marvin said, ignoring Ralph. 'Here we go.'

Before anyone could ask if Marvin was medically trained for this kind of venture, Marvin reached down and yanked the knife out of Ralph's chest. Immediately, blood began to pour down Ralph's front.

'Huh,' said Marvin.

'Is that a good huh, or a bad huh?' said Greg. 'Because I'm pretty sure Ralph's blood would be better on the inside of him.'

Marvin reached inside the knapsack he was carrying and came out with a jar of something very brown. He bent down once more and smeared a dollop onto Ralph's wound.

'Ow! That stings!'

'That's a good thing,' Marvin said. 'Means it's working.'

'What is it?' Greg said.

'Oh, it's probably best you don't know. I know how squeamish Ralph gets.'

'Hey!' Ralph said. 'I'm starting to feel better already!'

Marvin smiled and put the jar back in his knapsack. Ralph slowly and shakily got to his feet.

'There's no reason to hang around now,' Bud said. 'We've still got work to do.'

'You still want to carry out what's left of the plan?' Greg said.

'I don't think any of us will be left in peace unless we do,' Bud said. 'Think about it. There's still a bunch of mercenaries who think we've got a very valuable red stone.'

'Not to mention the King,' Eve said.

'And Rothchild and Evangeline. Wherever those two might be,' Wolf said.

'That seems to be settled then,' said Marvin. 'Right! Follow me.' And he strode off down the passageway.

'Your period of mourning can officially end,' Ralph said as he walked past Eve on unsteady legs. 'I have survived. I won't mind if you wish to do your rejoicing in private.'

'You know,' Eve said as she stomped past Ralph, 'I think I preferred you when you thought you were going to die. You were so much quieter.'

***

'So, exactly how do you plan to draw this to a close?' Ralph said.

They'd made their way through the various passageways under Calver, first following Marvin through the use of his wall-mounted lanterns and then, once they were no more, following the bobbing lantern he held. After only a short walk, they'd all emerged in his underground workshop. Once again, they'd managed to clear just enough space to sit around one of his tables.

'I think we can finish this with a similar plan to our first one,' Bud said.

'Given the success of that plan,' Ralph said. 'I think I'll pass.'

'It sort of worked,' said Marvin.

'Yeah,' said Ralph. 'The getting captured and drawing everyone out into the open bit went reasonably well. The rest of it, culminating – might I add – with me being very nearly made dead; that bit could've gone better.'

'Look on the bright side,' Marvin said. 'Augustus Malvern's gone.'

'Yeah, like you planned that,' Ralph said.

'Not exactly. Admittedly, I had to improvise a bit. Once I came up and saw where he was heading, it was lucky I was close enough to the workshop to be able to dash back and grab the whirly-gig.'

'Who has one of those things just lying around? What on earth did you design it for, anyway?'

'Flipping pancakes.'

'Bloody hell!' Ralph said.

'If we could return to the matter in hand,' Bud said. 'Namely, our survival.'

***

So the group spoke and they planned and they argued. Each person had their say and sometime, late in the afternoon, they reached their decision which – as they saw it – was the only one they really had. Well, nearly everyone saw it that way.

'Ralph, it's four to one.'

'Doesn't matter. All that shows is that four people can be wrong all at the same time.'

'But you've yet to come up with a better idea.'

'That doesn't mean I won't.'

'Tell you what,' Bud said, pulling on his thick cloak. 'Whilst you help Ralph understand why he's being a fool, I'm going to set our plan in motion. Wolf, Eve, you ready?'

'Let's go,' Wolf said, setting off after Bud, who'd strolled off down one of the passageways that ran from Marvin's workshop.

Eve glanced back at Ralph, shook her head and then followed the other two. Greg sat down next to his brother for yet another chat.

***

Bud, Eve and Wolf returned a couple of hours later. It was testament to Bud's knowledge of the backstreets and the people who called them home, that he'd managed to find what they were looking for so quickly.

Once again, they all gathered around the table with the least amount of Marvin's stuff on it.

'They're holed up in a pretty secure place deep into the backstreets.'

Bud then proceeded to tell them how he'd found Rothchild, Evangeline and a group of at least six mercenaries in what appeared to be an abandoned butcher's.

'Must've been a prearranged location,' Wolf said. 'Somewhere they could hide out if things went south.'

Something bothered Greg.

'Why are there still some mercenaries with him?'

'Probably because Rothchild and Evangeline are still paying them,' Eve said. 'For most mercenaries, they go where the money is. I'm still only here because of the cut you'll give me once this is over and you sell the red stone.'

'That and the fact you're powerless to pull away from my sheer animal magnetism,' Ralph said.

'So,' Greg said before the intent in Eve's eyes became realised. 'How do we carry out the rest of the plan? We need to get into where they're hiding.'

'I don't think that'll be a problem,' Wolf said. 'Look around you. You've got a genius inventor, a guy with more knowledge of the backstreets and its people than anyone else in the Kingdom, an old mercenary with one or two battles under his belt and the lass who handed Augustus Malvern's backside to him on a plate. Between us, we'll get this done.'

'Erm, what about me?' Ralph said.

'You're the guy who could quite easily get us all killed,' Eve said. 'Which is why, as we discussed earlier, you're the decoy. Unless you've finally come up with a better plan?'

'Not exactly,' said Ralph. 'But I'm working on it.'

'You can carry on working on it whilst you're being the decoy. Let's go,' Bud said.

***

The six of them made their way through the backstreets. Firstly underground and then above ground. With Bud to guide them, their progress was quick. Even Ralph managed to move reasonably quickly and somewhat quietly. Probably because Bud was moving between streets, passageways and even buildings with a practised ease.

At one point he tapped an odd rhythm on a front door, let himself in and proceeded to march through a family's front room. The family – parents and three children – all nodded to Bud as they passed through.

'Excuse us,' Greg said feeling incredibly embarrassed at the intrusion.

'S'alright pal,' the father said. 'Nothing to excuse. You weren't even here.' He nodded to Bud who nodded back and placed a small bag of something on the arm of the mismatched chair the father was sat in.

This happened on a couple more occasions and once in the type of public house Greg and Ralph would never have set foot in a week ago.

'Blimey,' Ralph said as they made their way out of the back door. 'That's the kind of place you go in for a laugh and come out in stitches.' He hurried to keep close to the others.

'Quiet now,' Bud said. 'We're nearly here.'

He stopped them on the edge of a crossroads, although one only wide enough for foot traffic. The buildings on each corner of the crossroads had been built so that as they got higher, they jutted out further and further. This meant that very little of the fast-fading light was able to penetrate through.

'In here,' Bud said leading through the front door of one of the buildings.

The ground floor was a small space, nothing more than a single room. There were no furnishings at all aside from a long-forgotten empty fireplace in the far wall. Bud led them upstairs and into an almost identical room.

Almost identical because it was slightly bigger than the room beneath and, stood in the room by the tiny, grime-stained windows was what appeared to be someone's grandma. She was half as tall as anyone else in the room and most of her was covered in a shawl. She didn't turn away from the windows.

'Hello dears,' she said in exactly the kind of voice Greg expected her to have.

'Everyone,' Bud said. 'This is Auntie Flo. Say hello.'

'Hello, Auntie Flo,' they all chimed in unison.

'Now then,' Auntie Flo said, still looking out of the window. 'There's very little activity within. I've got girls stationed on every point of the compass and four runners relaying reports to me every half an hour. Seems they're staying put for now.'

She turned to face them, a big smile on her face. 'Now that's out of the way, would anyone care for a mint humbug?'

***

The mint humbugs were exceptional. It had seemed rude to Greg to refuse one when Auntie Flo produced a handful from her shawl and he was glad he hadn't.

'These are great!' Ralph said.

'Well aren't you kind for saying so,' Auntie Flo said. 'Made them myself. Old family recipe.

I often think there's not much can't be put right in this world by taking a moment to sit down and enjoy a nice boiled sweet. Want another?'

'Yes please!' Ralph said, sounding all of twelve years old.

Greg noticed that Auntie Flo had that effect on people. They'd all – even Bud – relaxed a little as they sat around her on the floor.

'Auntie Flo is a bit of a legend here in the backstreets,' Bud said.

'Oh, I wouldn't go that far,' she said, giving Bud a playful swat on the shoulder.

'She takes in girls who might otherwise end up in a different line of employment and gives them a chance to try and make something of the crappy hand they've been dealt.'

'I just try and do right by them. That's all,' Auntie Flo said, standing up and brushing down her dress. 'And right now, me and my girls'll be off. Hope all goes well for you, Rosebud.' Auntie Flo stood on her tiptoes and Bud bent down to kiss her on the cheek. She turned to leave but then stopped suddenly.

'Look at me!' she said, chuckling. She turned back to face them. 'I'd forget my own head if it wasn't screwed on! I got you a few things. Thought they might help.'

From beneath her shawl, she produced a large cloth bag which she handed to Wolf.

'You seem like the kind of gentleman who'd be able to sort these out,' she smiled and scurried off down the stairs.

'What a nice old lady,' Ralph said. 'I hope she's alright, it's getting dark.'

'Oh, I think she'll be fine,' Bud said.

'Yeah, there's more than meets the eye with that one,' Wolf said, showing the others the contents of Auntie Flo's bag.

'Those are most certainly not mint humbugs.' Greg said, peering into the bag at the array of weapons it contained.

**

As soon as the sun set, they moved into position. Ralph, Wolf and Marvin hid in the shadows close to the front of the abandoned butcher's. Greg, Bud and Eve skirted the side of the building and settled in the enveloping darkness by the large rear door.

Greg tried to slow his heart rate by imagining what the old butcher's must have been like in its heyday.

That didn't really work as the thought of dead meat and carcasses being hauled off of carts and through the door he was staring at only served to increase his unease.

'I hope this works,' he whispered.

'Me too.' Eve said.

'How will we know exactly when to move?' Greg said.

'Don't worry,' Bud said. 'Ralph's involved. We'll know exactly when it's time.'

**

Ralph edged out of the shadows. His heart was beating so fast he was having trouble breathing. Right now, he'd give anything, absolutely anything, to be back on the boring, mundane farm, continuing a dull and soulless existence.

Yet he could see no other alternative. He had to do this.

Not just for himself, but for Greg too. And, for the first time in his life, there were others depending on him. This whole thing needed to end tonight.

If it went well, then maybe, just maybe, he and Greg could get on with the rest of their lives. Bud too. And maybe, just maybe, after they'd paid Eve, he'd ask her if she fancied heading to the pub for a drink or two. Surely it was worth a shot. A long shot, against a heavy wind but, worth a shot anyway.

Unfortunately, Ralph was still thinking about asking Eve out for a drink when the front door of the abandoned butcher's was yanked open and he came face to face with a large mercenary.

Chapter 25
Let's Have a Butcher's

The mercenary, who'd been on his way out to have a pee, blinked and furrowed his brow. He wasn't the sharpest knife in the kitchen drawer but he knew enough to know that when things didn't quite add up, you were supposed to furrow your brow. Coming face to face with Ralph in such an unsuspecting fashion caused him to pause and thus crease his large forehead.

Ralph, to his credit, recognised the situation for what it was: his one and only chance.

However, Ralph had never hit a man in his life. He didn't know how to throw a punch, let alone one which might floor a confused but still large mercenary.

The punch he threw could only be described as full of effort but somewhat lacking in other areas. Such as accuracy and technique.

It started from down behind – as if he were reaching back to pick something up from the floor – wind-milled high in the air and stopped when it clonked the large mercenary on the top of the head. Having never thrown a punch before, Ralph wasn't sure what one was supposed to sound like when it connected but he was pretty sure it wasn't supposed to clonk.

The large mercenary furrowed his brow yet further. His eyes moved upwards as a trickle of dark blood ran down from his hair, made its way across the aforementioned furrows in his brow and then plip-plopped onto the floor from the end of his nose.

His eyes continued to roll up and then back into his head and with a shudder he collapsed at Ralph's feet.

Ralph looked at the mercenary at his feet. He looked at the brass knuckles he was wearing, selected for him by Wolf from Auntie Flo's bag. Then he looked around, back in the direction of Wolf and Marvin.

'Did you see that?' he whispered.

'That I did, lad,' Wolf whispered back. 'Not sure how you accomplished the end result with one of the ugliest punches I've ever seen thrown but nonetheless, the end result does speak for itself.'

'I properly knocked him out!' Ralph said, only just managing to keep to a whisper.

'You did,' Wolf said.

'Now, would you mind properly carrying on with the plan?' Marvin hissed.

'Right. Yes. Of course,' Ralph said, stepping over the mercenary. He still wasn't sure how he'd done what he'd done but he liked the feeling after it.

'I just knocked a man out,' he muttered to himself as he approached the open doorway. 'With one punch. And not just any man, but a mercenary.'

He took a look back at the mercenary, more to convince himself that it'd actually happened than anything else, then crossed over the threshold and into the building.

***

Round the back of the building, Greg was having a hard time waiting. He knew the kind of trouble Ralph could get himself into – even in the most seemingly conflict free of places – so walking into a building full of mercenaries could clearly lead to disaster.

'It's been too long,' he said.

'Relax,' Bud said. 'Trust the plan.'

For the first time, Greg's nerve started to falter.

'You said that with the last plan,' he said.

'Which would've worked if Eve hadn't attacked Mr Malvern,' Bud said.

'I've already apologised for that,' Eve said. 'It's one of the reasons I'm still here. That and the money.'

'Yeah well, things would've gone according to plan. Just like they will tonight. They have to.'

Greg noted the slight tinge of desperation in Bud's voice. 'You really think Mr Malvern would've confronted Rothchild?'

'Don't think it. *Know* it,' Bud said. 'If he hadn't been beaten within an inch of his life he'd have been thinking a lot clearer. He certainly wouldn't have driven the War Machine into a packed market screaming for his wife, that's for sure. He'd have been there, somewhere in the shadows with a small army of his own. And when he saw us hand the red stone over to Rothchild and his wife, that's when he'd have lost it. Right where we needed him to. Not at home where he could climb inside a death trap, but a few feet from Rothchild and Evangeline and the mercenaries. There was a very good chance they'd wipe each other out and when you throw in the King's Guards, then if anyone had survived, they would've been arrested on the spot. Was it the best plan the Kingdom's ever seen? Gods, no. I didn't account for Rothchild being stupid enough to try and use the King's Guards to prevent us from leaving Calver. I still can't believe he thought he'd get away with that. But, that oversight aside, it was the best we could come up with given how quickly everything kept changing. Just like this plan. It's not ideal but neither's the alternative.'

And that was when they heard Ralph scream.

Greg burst from his hiding place.

***

'What yer screaming for? I only grabbed yer arm!'

'I know, but you've got a very firm grip and you made me jump,' Ralph said.

He'd only made it a few feet inside the butcher's before the second mercenary on door duty had grabbed him whilst his eyes were still adjusting to the dark. Ralph screamed again.

'What yer doing?' the mercenary said. 'I'm still just holding your arm!'

'Yes, but I'm really rather distressed.'

'You're really rather stupid more like. The boss said you might turn up here. The lady boss didn't think you'd be so stupid but it turns out you're all kinds of stupid. I mean, who tries to sneak into a place and then screams at the first sign of bother?'

'I suppose you want to march me off to the bosses, don't you?'

'As a matter of fact, that's exactly what I've got to do.'

'Oh well. It's a fair cop. Would you mind at all if I screamed again, just to get it out of my system?'

'Don't see why not. Not as if anyone round these parts is gonna do anything.'

***

By the time he heard Ralph's second scream, Greg had crossed the yard and reached the huge rear doors. When Ralph screamed for the third time – a little over the top for Greg's liking but then that was Ralph for you – Greg had managed to wedge open a gap between the doors big enough to squeeze through.

He was in.

The mercenary escorted Ralph up three flights of very old, very creaky stairs. At the top of each flight of stairs stood a mercenary with some kind of weapon.

Upon reaching the final floor, there were two more mercenaries waiting by a small door at the end of a dimly lit corridor.

The mercenary escorting Ralph stopped in front of the two mercenaries.

'Pay up, lads,' he said.

'Farmer boy, you dozy git,' the mercenary stood to Ralph's right said. 'You cost us a coin each. We said even someone as dim as you would never come here.'

'Sorry chaps,' Ralph said as the two mercenaries paid up.

'Was that you screaming?' the mercenary to Ralph's left said.

'That it was,' Ralph said. 'Pretty embarrassing, really. More of a lover than a fighter to be honest.'

'Come on, lover boy,' said the mercenary who'd brought Ralph up. 'Time to face the music.'

He leant forward and knocked on the door three times. There was a slight pause, followed by muffled breathing which sounded to Ralph as if there was some kind of wild animal waiting behind the door.

Then the door swung open and Ralph realised he was nearly right.

'Hello, Short-and-Stumpy!' he said as Hargaard glowered up at him. 'Long time no see.

Speaking of seeing, I can see you're still as ugly as ever!'

Hargaard slammed the door shut behind Ralph and stood, fists clenched, shoulders heaving.

'Stand down, Hargaard,' Rothchild said.

He was stood with his back to an enormous empty fireplace in a room which was completely devoid of furniture. Evangeline stood off to his left. The only light in the room, three large candles on the mantelpiece, cast a flickering yellow glow over one half of her face. Gone was the powerful business woman on the verge of seizing power, replaced by someone who looked much older, and someone who looked as if they weren't quite sure why they were here but had nowhere else to go.

'Well, here we all are again,' Ralph said. 'Just like old times. You two do remember the old days when you thought you'd take over the world?'

'You know,' Rothchild said. 'I honestly have no idea how you're not dead. I don't just mean surviving a knife in the chest, but in more general terms. I would've thought that by now someone, somewhere would've killed you.'

'There's more to me than meets the eye, Rothchild, my man.'

'No. I don't think there is. I think you're a smoke and mirrors man. In the not too distant past you could've eked out a living travelling from village to village, peddling potions that didn't work and then disappearing into the night before anyone could throttle you.'

'Don't forget stealing all the girls' hearts and having a woman in every port,' Ralph winked at Evangeline who stared blankly back at him.

'What's the matter with the ex-Mrs Malvern?'

'I think the reality of the situation has hit her a little hard. Which, coincidently, is what I intend to let Hargaard do to you.'

'Now wait just an over-zealous minute, my good man. I've come to offer you a once in a lifetime deal.'

'Have you really? And you think you're in a position to do that, do you?'

'I think so. You see, the others who were with us have abandoned us. All got a bit much for them. King's Guard, exploding War Machines, you get the gist. Not exactly what they signed on for and all that. So it's just me and my brother. We want all of this unpleasantness to end so we can go back to our farm. The deal is: we give you the red stone and you leave us alone. You get what you want and we vanish, back to the middle of nowhere.'

'I can see the appeal of such an offer,' Rothchild said.

'If I may dispense with the smoke and mirrors for a bit,' Ralph said, 'it's all gotten a bit much for us both too. Me and Greg just wanted to make a quick buck so we could take it easy for the rest of our lives. Next thing we knew, we'd got a bunch of people trying to take the red stone from us, a bunch of other people who said they wanted to help us but were really just in it for themselves and more trouble than we could handle. We just want to go home.'

Rothchild considered Ralph for a long time.

'What's to stop me simply taking the red stone from you?'

'Oh, I don't have it!' Ralph said. 'That would be foolish! No, Greg's got the red stone and he's hidden far away from here. If we agree a deal, I go back to him, we leave the stone in a prearranged, safe location. Once we're clear of the lower gatehouse, you receive a message telling you where the stone is.'

'What's to stop me coming after you once I've got the stone?'

'Nothing's stopping you. But if you'd rather waste time hunting down a couple of farmers – who, in the end, gave you what you wanted – if you want to do that instead of overthrowing King Siguld, then be my guest.'

'And what's to stop you two double crossing me and leaving with the red stone?'

'You really are becoming paranoid! If that's what we were going to do, why in the God's names would I have come here tonight? We could've just done a runner. Look, we both know that if you really wanted to, you could find us and kill us. We have no more options. All we can do is give you the stone and hope you're too busy to bother with us.'

'And you say all I've got to do is agree and you'll head back to your brother, leave the stone and then run away?'

'That's about the short of it. No offence, Stumpy. Do we have a deal?'

Before Rothchild could reply, the door opened. Two mercenaries walked in and flung Greg onto the floor at Rothchild's feet. 'Suppose the deal's off now, isn't it?' Ralph said.

***

Rothchild held the red stone up to the nearest candle. As soon as the flickering light hit the surface of the stone it bounced off and sent an array of colours cascading around the room.

'So this is what all the fuss has been about,' Rothchild said.

'It's beautiful,' Evangeline said, speaking for the first time.

'It is,' Ralph said. Both he and Greg were sat on the floor in a corner, their backs to the wall, Hargaard stood on one side, the mercenary who'd found Greg trying to sneak up the stairs on the other.

'Do you think you'd consider letting us be on our way?' Ralph said.

'I think not,' Rothchild said. 'I was actually surprised by the logic of your plan and you're right, after getting my hands on the stone I would've been far too busy to bother with you. But then Gregory here turned up and, unbelievably, brought the red stone with him. I should kill you both now, just to rid the world of

354

your incessant stupidity. What were you thinking?'

'Remember I told you we were out of options?' Ralph said.

'Well, we really were,' Greg said. 'We're farmers. We don't know anyone. It was a mixture of blind luck and good fortune that we stumbled across this place. We got lost in the backstreets after the commotion with Mr Malvern in the market place. Our so-called friends ditched us and we were looking for a way to get home when Ralph spotted a mercenary walk in here. We quickly cobbled together a plan and Ralph decided he would be the one who went in. I couldn't go far, for one I had no idea where I was and two, I didn't like the idea of leaving Ralph so we decided I'd hide outside. But when I heard him scream, I had to try and help.'

'How in the Gods' names have you two managed to survive this long? I'm embarrassed for you, I truly am. Evangeline and I will leave now. I'll leave Hargaard and a couple of mercenaries to do what they want with you. Their only instruction will be to make sure your bodies have lots of painful looking holes in them. Can you do that for me Hargaard?'

Hargaard got up and turned to face Ralph and Greg and smiled. As Evangeline and Rothchild made their way to the door Greg had not so long ago been thrown through,

Hargaard took three short strides back from Greg and Ralph.

His smile widened and he began to shuffle his feet.

'What's he doing?' Ralph said, a hint of panic creeping into his voice.

'If I didn't know any better,' Greg said. 'I'd say he's giving himself a run up.'

The Hoffenbach brothers looked at the smiling, swaying dwarf and back at each other. Then, in unison, and as loud as they could, they shouted the one word which, they hoped, could save them.

'MARVIN!'

***

Bud was impressed. When he'd first set eyes on Greg and Ralph, he'd written them off as a couple of clueless farmers. He'd been wrong. Sure, Ralph had his moments, but the two brothers had kept everyone inside the old butcher's occupied long enough for everyone outside to get into position. When he heard them shout Marvin's name, he knew it was time.

***

Everyone in the room froze. The smile on Hargaard's face shifted into a look of puzzlement. Rothchild turned, his hand still on the door knob.

'Marvin?' he said. 'What the hell's a Marvin?'

Before Greg or Ralph could answer, something rattled in the chimney. At first, it sounded like a bird had somehow managed to get trapped and was bashing around in the darkness. Except this bird – or whatever it was – seemed to be metallic and was clattering its way down the chimney. With a couple more clanks whatever was in the chimney fell out and into the empty fireplace. In the relative darkness, no one could quite see what it was.

For a moment the room was quiet again. Then the thing in the fireplace started to whistle. Low at first, but gradually increasing in pitch. The mercenary next to Greg walked over to the fireplace and picked up what looked like a lump of coal with tiny, fluttering wings. He held it up to the candlelight and turned it over to reveal a wind-up key whizzing around in the back.

As suddenly as it had begun the whistling stopped. Greg and Ralph covered their eyes.

The thing in the mercenary's hand gave off a small pop and split open. Instantly, the room was filled with a blinding light. The mercenary holding the object screamed as his eyes melted. Hargaard tried to shield his eyes but he was too late. He collapsed on the floor, writhing in silent agony. Rothchild managed to drag Evangeline in front of him and buried his face into her back as she too screamed.

Then with a short whistle and a pop the blinding light disappeared. Downstairs, the front door exploded inwards.

Wolf stood up, picking bits of door off his clothes. All in all, entering the old butcher's had gone about as well as it could've considering the mercenary left guarding the front door now had lots of it sticking into him. Wolf had hit the door at full speed and hadn't stopped. The effect was that the door was ripped from its hinges as he rode it, shoulder first into the mercenary behind it. Wolf had carried on, legs pumping until he and it – not to mention the mercenary the other side – hit the far wall. That was when the door had split into lots of pieces, most of which punctured the mercenary.

Wolf dusted himself down, saw Bud hurtle up the stairs, checked for any serious injuries, then he made his way to the stairs.

***

Greg and Ralph stood up and surveyed the scene before them.

'I can't believe that actually worked,' Ralph said.

'I heard that.' came an echo down the chimney.

'Sorry Marvin,' Greg shouted up. 'You should see it down here. Your device worked brilliantly!'

'The Blinderball was a little brighter than I thought,' shouted Marvin. 'Did it melt anyone's eyes this time?'

'This time!' Ralph shouted. 'You never told us it'd melted eyeballs in the past!'

'You'd only have fretted,' Marvin said.

Greg looked down at the mercenary who'd been holding the Blinderball and felt his stomach roll.

'Eyeballs were indeed melted,' he said.

'Oh dear,' Marvin said, although he said it in a way that suggested he was only mildly disappointed.

'Right,' said Ralph. 'We've got work to do.' And then screamed for real this time as Hargaard grabbed his ankle.

***

Ralph's scream very nearly put Eve off.

She was crouched on a roof ledge, just across from a window on the second floor of the butcher's. As Wolf crashed through the front door, Bud snuck in through the back door which Greg had wedged open a crack with the key to Room 181. He'd then made his way up the stairs as Wolf was picking himself up off the floor.

As he neared the top, he lit the candle he was holding. It wasn't a normal candle but one specifically designed for what Bud needed.

The two mercenaries stationed on the second floor were under strict instructions not to move from their positions no matter what. The last thing Rothchild wanted was mercenaries thinking for themselves and charging off downstairs leaving fewer bodies between himself and any possible means of escape. They were also under strict instructions to kill anyone who came up the stairs unless they were accompanied by a mercenary.

So, as Bud reached the landing they drew their weapons. The larger of the two, an immense man of over seven feet, pulled an axe from his belt. The other, unsheathed a broadsword.

'Hey fellas,' Bud said, grinning as he strolled towards them. 'Would one of you hold this for me?' He threw the candle in their direction. The mercenary carrying the axe shot out his left arm and grabbed the candle.

'How come it didn't go out?' he said.

Outside, Eve steadied herself. She raised the spear – which until recently had been lots of parts of a spear in Auntie Flo's bag – and looked for the light. The window across from her was like all the others in the butcher's, covered with grime. She'd just made out the flicker of the candle as Bud had emerged onto the second floor. She'd heard Bud's muffled voice and tracked the glow of the candle as Bud threw it. Then she heard the muffled words from the mercenary.

Now was the time. She took a breath, let it out and was just about to throw when Ralph screamed as upstairs Hargaard grabbed his ankle.

'Pillock!' she hissed and threw the spear.

It crashed through the window but the moment's hesitation had cost her.

Inside, Bud had already dropped to the floor when the glass shattered.

He watched as the spear hit the large mercenary holding the candle in the back of his leg. It carried on its path and the tip came through the other side of his leg.

The mercenary grunted as his leg gave way under him and he crashed to his knees. The plan was to kill him but at least he'd been reduced to average height. The other mercenary ran to the window the spear had come through, but Eve was already gone.

The large mercenary threw the candle to one side. It hit a wall, spluttered and finally went out.

'I might be on my knees,' he said, raising his axe, 'but there's no way in hell you're getting past me. Looks like I'll end up dying here and I intend to take you with me, so let's get this done.'

***

'Get him off! Get him off!' Ralph shouted as Hargaard tightened his grip on Ralph's ankle and started to pull himself closer.

His eyes were so red it looked as if every blood vessel in them had burst. Greg figured that there was no way he could see yet it didn't seem as if that was going to stop him.

Greg stomped on Hargaard's hand but it seemed to have little to no effect.

As he pulled himself closer, Hargaard opened his mouth.

'He's going to eat me!'

Greg launched himself into the air and brought both feet crashing down on Hargaard's wrist. He could feel the bones snap and finally Hargaard let go and rolled away.

Ralph slid back along the wall, trying to put as much distance between Hargaard and himself as possible.

'We need to find the others,' Greg said. It was as they turned towards the door that they realised Evangeline and Rothchild had gone.

***

'You know, I could just wait. That wound looks pretty bad. You're losing a lot of blood,' Bud said.

'That you could. But I don't think you've got the time. You need to get past me and quick too, if you're going to help your friends.'

The mercenary was, of course, right. The second mercenary had looked at the scene: one man on his knees with a spear in his thigh, screams coming from upstairs and he figured his orders to stay where he was could probably be ignored. Things had changed. So he ran off up the stairs.

Bud needed to get upstairs. But even with the mercenary on his knees he knew he didn't stand a chance. He was so large he nearly filled the landing. His axe was half the size of Bud and more importantly, Bud wasn't much of a fighter which is why he'd followed the career path he had – one which required quick thinking rather than quick fists.

'Hello Bud, how's it going?' Wolf said as he reached the top of the stairs. 'Why's that big lad praying to you?'

Bud honestly felt he'd never been so glad to see anyone in his life.

'I need to get upstairs,' he said.

'Well, let's get that sorted then, shall we?' Wolf said, easing past Bud. 'Now then, big lad. I can see you haven't got too long before that there spear in your leg starts causing you a problem or two so I'll get right to it. Name's Wolf Dangerpunch. Might be you've heard of me. Here's what I'm proposing: you let my friend go past. Then, when he's good and gone, me and you have an old fashioned scuffle. That way you either kill the infamous Grey Wolf or you die honourably in one-to-one combat with the aforementioned Grey Wolf.'

'What if I just kill him and then we have our scuffle?'

'Could do, could do. Only problem is, once you have a pop at my friend, I'm going to send one of these throwing knives into your face – something which, I might add I could do right now except I'm trying to be honourable. So. You let him past and I'll put everything down apart from my sword. Mercenary's honour.'

The large mercenary seemed to be mulling things over. Then he winced and rubbed his leg.

'Alright then,' he said and shifted to the side.

Bud didn't wait to see if it was a trap. He leapt past and headed for the stairs. The large mercenary shuffled back.

'Right then, Wolf Dangerpunch. Let's one of us die with honour.'

'If it's all the same to you,' Wolf said. 'I'd rather stay living dishonourably.' And he threw a knife which hit the mercenary between the eyes. The mercenary had time to look surprised before he crashed backwards.

Wolf stepped over him, stopping only to retrieve his knife.

'Mercenary's honour, my arse.'

***

Greg and Ralph stepped out onto the third-floor landing. It too was dimly lit – just one candle in a wall-holder halfway down. As far as they could see, there was no one else on this floor but it was hard to tell for sure.

They had no choice but to press on.

'Wait,' Ralph said. 'What's that?'

He was pointing to a dark area at the top of the stairs.

'I don't see anything,' Greg said.

'I do. It looks like a body.'

Carefully, they made their way towards it. Once he felt they were close enough, Greg tugged on Ralph's arm and motioned for him to stop. Then he signalled for Ralph to move over to one wall whilst he moved to the other.

Greg counted to three and, as quick as he could, rolled the body over towards him and onto its back. As he did, he quickly jumped back, fearing it was a trap.

He soon realised he needn't have worried.

Ralph stepped over.

'Looks like Rothchild's severing all his connections. Literally.'

Evangeline's pained, bloodshot eyes stared unseeing at the ceiling above her. Her head lolled back at an unnatural angle, revealing a deep gash in her neck which ran from just under one side of her jaw to the other. A thick bib of blood – which in the low light looked black – covered the front of her cloak.

'I wonder if it was all worth it,' Greg said.

'Clearly not,' Ralph said.

'Why would a woman like her get tangled up with a man like Rothchild? I guess things are much simpler when you're a farmer. I don't think I'll ever be able to understand the way some people think.'

'We certainly could stand here and discuss the trappings of power and the way in which greed lures some towards unthinkable acts, or we could deal with the mercenary and his broadsword coming up the stairs,' Ralph said.

***

Once again, Eve was waiting. This time, she was concealed just inside the front door to the butcher's in a dark corner behind the long-redundant meat counter. Her part of the plan was to remain here just in case anyone managed to get past everyone else, in which case, they were all dead and she was the last chance.

Eve did not like this part of the plan.

She hadn't been happy with it from the start and now, crouched in the shadows, she liked it even less. In fact, the more she thought about it, the idea of hiding and waiting, rather than doing something, anything, seemed pointless.

'Bugger this,' she whispered and set off towards the stairs.

***

The mercenary from the second floor with the broadsword didn't know what hit him. Mainly because nothing did.

Ralph, buoyed by his earlier success, slipped on his brass knuckles and launched another windmill-esque punch, aiming for a two for two score when it came to mercenaries.

Unfortunately, he'd not taken into consideration the fact that this mercenary was still coming up the stairs and was much lower down.

Also that this mercenary was ready. Ralph's swing sailed harmlessly in front of the mercenary. Its momentum carried Ralph forwards whereupon he stumbled, tripped over Evangeline and fell, face-first towards the mercenary.

***

Bud had just rounded the corner and set foot on the stairs when, as he looked up, he saw Ralph throw himself down them.

Towards the mercenary and his sword.

Bud had no time to think. No time to try and work out what the hell Ralph was doing.

He launched himself forwards and upwards, driving his shoulder into the back of the legs of the mercenary above him. Unable to keep his balance, the mercenary sagged to the right, the downward arc of his swinging sword missing Ralph by mere inches. Ralph continued on his path downwards, rolling past both the mercenary and then Bud, only stopping when he hit the second floor, landing in a crumpled heap.

***

Greg watched, frozen to the spot as Bud saved his brother's life. And then, time seemed to slow. Greg watched as Ralph continued down the stairs. He didn't see him land in a heap on the second floor because his attention was drawn to the mercenary who was already moving.

Although the broadsword had missed Ralph, the mercenary was using its momentum to turn and swing it back above his head so he was now facing down the stairs.

Facing Bud who lay prone beneath him.

Like his brother moments before – only this time intentionally – Greg threw himself down the stairs.

***

Call it instinct, call it something picked up after many years of fighting, call it whatever you want, but when the voice in his head told him to wait, Wolf waited. Listening to that quiet little voice, the voice which only spoke but rarely, had served him well. So he held back from following Bud straight up the stairs. Which was why he was able to hear what he could best describe as a grinding sound coming from the other side of the wall he was crouching against.

The grinding sound started above him, passed by and carried on downwards. Then Ralph came crashing down the stairs, followed a moment later by a ball of people containing Greg, Bud and the mercenary minus his broadsword. They clattered into Ralph, who was starting to stand up and the four of them hit the far wall with a thud.

The mercenary was the first to stand but instantly collapsed screaming as his broken ankle completely gave way. As he landed, Wolf heard one of his arms break too.

Bud was up next and, although he seemed pretty wobbly, he didn't look too hurt.

'You lot look like you've got this under control,' Wolf said, tossing Bud one of his throwing knives. 'If he tries to get up, stick the pointy end in him. Preferably more than once.'

'Where are you going?' Bud said, leaning against the wall to stop himself falling over.

'There's a little voice in my head that says noisy walls need investigating. Holler if you need me.' And he ran towards the stairs he'd recently climbed.

Eve had just started up the stairs when there was an almighty crash from above as if someone had thrown themselves down a flight of stairs. Her first reaction was to dash up, after all great big thuds tend to mean there's a problem but just as she was about to, she heard an odd noise. It was coming from the wall next to her. She paused and put her ear to the wall. It sounded as if something was scraping on the other side of the wall. She headed back down.

***

Eve waited behind the counter once more. She could barely hear the noise now as she was in one corner of the room and the wall next to the stairs was in the other. She let her eyes adjust to the perpetual gloom as the noise disappeared completely. Then, with a soft whoosh, a hole opened in the far wall.

Part of the wall slid upwards and part slid downwards, only by a couple of feet, but enough to see that the place where the wall once was, was now darker. Eve watched as someone climbed out of the wall, looked both left and right then strode quickly towards where the front door once was. Eve vaulted the counter, landed without making a sound and took two strides towards Rothchild.

'Leaving so soon?' she said as she slammed his head into the wall.

Rothchild wobbled but, to his credit, didn't fall down.

Eve sensed movement to her right, and spun towards the open doorway.

'Oh, that must've hurt like the dickens,' 739 said as he moved into the room, hands held up. 'Relax, Manslayer,' he said as 437 and 113 followed in behind, their hands also raised. 'We're not here to fight. We just need the red stone and we'll be on our way. Purely business, you understand.'

Eve tried to watch all three spies but they spread out so that, in effect she was cornered. They slowly lowered their hands and, before Eve could do anything, the hands they brought back up contained knives.

'Thought you said you weren't here to fight,' Eve said as she readied herself. This wasn't going to be easy.

'We're not here to fight, per se,' said 437, 'but if we have to, well, you know. It is, as I stated a moment ago, purely business. Our job is to relieve whoever has the red stone of it. If, in doing so, we have to have an altercation with you, then so be it. Personally, I'd really rather not. I've seen your work and I'm a fan. So, if you could step aside so we may relieve Mr Rothchild of said stone, then we'll be on our way.'

'You know I can't do that,' Eve said, setting herself.

'Well then, I'm afraid you leave us no choice. Which is a shame, really.'

The three spies slowly advanced as one, leaving Eve with only a few options. She'd probably kill one, two maybe but the third would get her.

'Evening all. Mind if I join in?' Wolf said as he slid in alongside Eve.

'That does change things somewhat,' said 739.

'Thought it might,' said Wolf.

'For a while anyway,' 437 said. 'That is until...'

'Until what?' Eve said, glancing towards the doorway.

A group of King's Guards entered the butcher's and formed a line behind the spies, swords drawn.

'This really is shifting back and forth, isn't it?' said 739. 'Can't we just have the stone and be on our way? You know, on any other day, we'd probably be able to share a pint together, it's just, well, you know...'

'Yeah, purely business,' Eve said. 'And, trust me, on any other day, we'd be happy to hand over the stone, it's just that—'

'The stone is ours,' Greg said as he wobbled off the bottom stair and lurched along the wall Rothchild was still leaning on.

'*All* of ours,' Ralph said as he was helped down the stairs, one arm slung around Bud's shoulder.

'You see, fellas,' Bud said, 'we've kind of been through a lot to get to this point and just handing over the stone would mean it was all for nothing.'

Greg, Ralph and Bud came and stood alongside Eve and Wolf, their weapons held, albeit shakily, at the ready.

'You really are making this bloody difficult,' 739 said, shaking his head. 'You're all stubborn sods and, in an odd way, I kind of admire you for it. You also present us with a difficult moral dilemma. You see, whilst we have a job to do, we don't normally make a habit of killing normal folk. The two mercenaries, my conscience can deal with, they're armed and dangerous, but you three,' he said, pointing his knife at Greg, Ralph and Bud, 'well, you've got to have a code to live by, haven't you? And you've got to be able to sleep at night. And I know for sure these King's Guards can't attack you unless provoked. Is there any chance one of you three could have a pop at us first so we could retaliate?'

'We just want to keep the stone and to be able to walk away from this whole mess,' Greg said.

'Balls,' said 739. 'It would appear we have ourselves a bit of a tense situation.'

'Maybe I could just leave you the stone and be on my way?' Rothchild said.

'Shut up, dickhead,' Wolf said and smacked him on the forehead with the hilt of his sword. Rothchild slumped to the floor.

For a while, no one spoke. The two rows of people stood, tensed and ready, neither wanting to move first.

Then, almost unnoticed – which was a feat unto itself – one more person slipped into the room.

'Might be that I can help sort this little predicament out,' said Perenholm.

'Oh good,' 739 said. 'The boss is here. Now, maybe we can get somewhere.'

'Oh, I'm hardly the boss,' Perenholm said, leaning back and resting his elbows on the counter behind him. 'He is.'

As if things hadn't gone from odd to very strange over the course of the last few days for Greg, they now got even odder as for the second time in less than a day, the King walked in. He removed the hood covering his head and stood next to Perenholm. 'I think we can all put our weapons down, don't you?' the King said.

Chapter 26
An Ending, of Sorts

It was all a bit surreal.

Greg did his best to explain to the King, from start to finish, exactly how two farmers, two mercenaries and a finder for a notorious criminal came to be held at knife point by a group of spies and six King's Guards in an abandoned butcher's in the backstreets of Calver.

He was too tired and too hurt to bother trying to hide anything anymore. So he told the King everything; from finding the red stone in his field right up to now.

'So you see,' he said, 'I just want a new plough. And to go home to my wife and probably sleep for a long time.'

He hoped it would be enough. He hoped he hadn't left anything out which he should've mentioned. Once he'd finished, a wave of relief washed over him.

King Siguld hadn't spoken since Greg had begun his tale. He didn't speak now. He simply turned to Perenholm and smiled. 'Oh, you soft bugger,' Perenholm said, shaking his head and smiling too. 'You're supposed to elicit fear, not dole out sympathy.'

'Erm, what's going on?' Ralph said.

'Ask the soft sod next to me,' Perenholm said, nodding towards the King.

'It would appear to me,' the King said, 'that you five have done us all a favour.'

'Really?' Greg said.

'Really,' the King replied. 'You've exposed a plot to overthrow me, got rid of a notorious criminal and given our spies here the first bit of decent action they've seen for a while.'

'That is true, your Majesty. Quite enjoyed it, to be honest with you, sir,' 739 said.

'So I see no reason why we should take this matter any further than this room,' the King said.

'Does still leave us with the problem of the red stone,' Perenholm said.

Rothchild stumbled to his feet. 'I have it right here!' he said, fumbling in his pocket. 'I managed to procure it for you, your Majesty, at great personal cost. I can only throw myself upon your gracious mercy and hope that in some small way that the stone I now offer to you might, contribute towards my restitution. Here is the stone!' And he held it aloft.

'That's not the stone, you berk!' Wolf said. 'We've all got one of those.'

On cue, Bud, Ralph, Wolf and Eve all produced an identical red stone and held it out.

'Oh yeah,' Greg said. 'There was something I should've mentioned. Part of the plan was that we got Marvin to make copies of the original red stone. That way, if all else failed we could hand over a fake red stone and buy ourselves a bit of time.'

'Or just chuck them all up in the air at the same time and leave you lot to fight over which one was the real one,' Ralph said. 'The one you're holding, Rothchild, is as worthless as the ones we've got.'

Rothchild sunk back down and threw the stone across the floor. Then he started to cry.

'What a clever idea, making copies,' the King said. 'But what, might I ask, is a Marvin?'

Marvin, who'd found it much easier getting onto the roof, had had a little difficulty getting off the roof. It had taken him so long, in fact, that he'd only just clambered to the floor as Perenholm entered the butcher's. Marvin watched from the alley next to the butcher's as a man in a hooded cloak slipped through the shadows and in through the front door, followed a moment later by another man in a similar hooded cloak who he had no idea was the King.

Back inside, Ralph was trying to explain what a Marvin was without much success.

'So, he lives underground,' 739 said.

'Bit weird, isn't it?' Ralph said.

'And he makes things?' 437 said.

'Sort of,' Ralph said. 'Although some of the stuff he's got down there, well, it'd give you nightmares.'

'And that's where you left the red stone?' 739 said.

'Yeah, it's a pretty safe place. Not like anyone's going to stumble across it.'

'When do we get to meet this Marvin?' 437 said. 'He seems interesting.'

'He should be here by now,' Ralph said. 'Marvin!' he shouted.

Right on cue, Marvin leapt into the room, performed a neat little forward roll and allowed a small leather-bound ball to drop out of his trouser leg. Unseen, he deftly kicked it towards the King.

'Sorry I took so long,' he said, still in a crouch. 'Bit of bother getting down from the roof. Better late than never though. Right, quick follow me!'

'Follow you?' Ralph said, completely bemused.

'Yes. And be quick about it!' Marvin said, heading towards the door.

'What in the hells are you doing?' Ralph said.

'What am I doing? I'm rescuing you!'

'From what?'

Marvin pointed in the general direction of the spies, King's Guards, Perenholm and the

King. 'From them. Now hurry!' he said, motioning them towards him.

'Marvin, you fruit-loop, we don't need rescuing. It's all over,' Ralph said. 'And besides, that's the King.'

'Ah,' said Marvin. 'Oh dear.'

At which point the leather ball exploded.

Chapter 27
We Plough the Land and Don't Quite Suffer as Much as We Once Did

As the morning light searched across the tops of the surrounding trees, a crisp shaft of radiance settled upon the tips of the recently ploughed land. It was on these wondrous December mornings, full of promise for the year to come, that Gregory Hoffenbach felt the most alive. He was a farmer, doing what farmers do: turning his land. Although they don't usually do it this late in the year and on half-frozen ground.

But then, Greg had a brand new plough; not to mention a couple of oxen who, along with a few other additions to the farm, would make life a lot easier.

Greg made a turn at the end of the field and brought the oxen to a stop, their breath billowing out clouds in the cold morning air.

'Have you finished farting about?' Ralph said. He was sat hunched beneath a thick cloak on a fallen tree by the edge of the field. 'Only, it's bloody freezing and you look like a right pillock ploughing in December, especially with that daft grin plastered across your face.'

'Can't a farmer enjoy his new plough?' Greg said.

'You see, that's why I'll never quite understand you, o brother of mine. Who in their right mind would enjoy ploughing?'

'It's not just about the plough, Ralph.'

'For the Gods' sake, don't try and get all philosophical on me.'

'It's not that. I guess I'm just happy things worked out the way they did.'

And, in truth, things had worked out quite well for Greg. It turned out that the explosion in the butcher's orchestrated by Marvin was nothing more than a smoke bomb, designed to help them escape.

When the smoke finally cleared, no real harm had been done, although it took a lot of persuading to stop the King's Guard from lynching Marvin.

After they'd cleared the air – both literally and figuratively – things moved quite quickly. It was decided that the spies and the King's Guards would accompany Marvin back to where he'd hidden the red stone in his workshop. He was adamant that they be blindfolded but that presented more problems when two King's Guards inadvertently crashed into one of his shelves and set off a domino effect culminating in cascading oddities raining down on everyone.

After that, Marvin was so distressed that he didn't care who saw what. He handed over the stone and ordered everyone out whilst he began sorting his things back into piles.

Greg, Ralph, Bud, Wolf and Eve had been escorted to a room somewhere in the palace. After waiting for a few minutes they were joined by the King.

'Looks like that red stone of yours is the real deal,' the King said. 'Are you sure there aren't any more out in your field?'

'Positive,' Greg said. 'My family's been ploughing that field for generations. This is the first time we've ever found anything like the red stone.'

'It might be that I need to send a search party out to your farm, just to make sure.'

'Be my guest,' Greg said. 'I doubt you'll find anything and even if you do, I want nothing to do with it. I think me and Ralph have had our fair share of excitement.'

'Indeed,' the King said. He clapped his hands and two palace guards came in carrying a small chest. They set it down on a table next to the King, bowed and left.

'As a token of my appreciation and in recompense for the red stone, please accept these.' He opened the chest and took out a bag of coins for each of them. 'There should be enough in there for you to feel you've been treated fairly.'

'I'll say!' Wolf said, looking into his bag.

'If there's anything else you need, you just need to ask. Although, I'm quite tricky to get hold of, so you'd probably better ask now.'

And, of course, no one could think of anything. Except Ralph.

'I still can't believe you asked for a Knighthood,' Greg said, wiping his hands on a rag and walking away from the plough.

'You've got to have a go, haven't you?' Ralph said. 'Sir Ralph of Hoffenbach. I reckon it would've sounded rather noble. Shame he turned me down.'

'Come on, Sir Ralph. Let's go. Don't forget Eve said she might stop by again tonight.'

'Think she might not punch me this time?' Ralph said.

'It's possible,' Greg said. 'So long as you can keep your mouth shut.'

'Still think she wants me?' Ralph said.

'Of course she does. You head back. Tell Mollie I'll be in soon; might just give the new plough another whirl.'

'Sad git,' Ralph said and shook his head.

Greg watched as Ralph walked back towards the farm. He walked back over to the plough, grabbed the reigns and kicked a pile of dirt over the blue stone he'd just dug up.

Then he moved on.

Tim Beeden is someone who likes to make things up. Things like stories, ideas and friends. He's lived a varied life, has had thirteen different jobs, likes piña coladas and getting caught in the rain. He loves to travel and is utterly convinced he's part Viking (much to his wife's continual annoyance. Although he was once on holiday in Denmark where the locals often spoke to him in Danish which pretty much confirmed it as far as he's concerned).

He's married with one child. His wife is nothing like him (thank goodness) but his son is (thank goodness).

Greed is his first novel in a planned series of eleven books but he's pretty new to this so isn't aware of how ridiculous an ambition that is.

He genuinely hopes you enjoy reading Greed and that if you love it you tell your friends. If you read it and hate it, he wants you to tell your enemies so they have to suffer too. His website is **www.sevendeadlyandfour.com** and he'd love for you to stop by and say hello.